MACKENNA'S GOLD

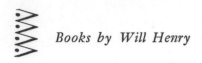 *Books by Will Henry*

NO SURVIVORS

TO FOLLOW A FLAG

THE FOURTH HORSEMAN

DEATH OF A LEGEND

WHO RIDES WITH WYATT

THE NORTH STAR

RECKONING AT YANKEE FLAT

THE SEVEN MEN AT MIMBRES SPRINGS

FROM WHERE THE SUN NOW STANDS

JOURNEY TO SHILOH

SAN JUAN HILL

MACKENNA'S GOLD

Mackenna's GOLD

ᴧᴧᴧᴧᴧᴧᴧᴧᴧᴧᴧᴧᴧᴧᴧᴧ

Will Henry

Random House
New York

m.H.

395

C

This One
FOR *Brother Bob*

Contents

Author's Note

There are many versions of the Lost Adams Diggings legend, both verbal and published. However, I have chosen to follow the facts as set forth in *Apache Gold and Yaqui Silver*, by J. Frank Dobie, a collection of legends of the Southwest, published by Little, Brown & Co., Copyright, 1928, 1931, 1938, 1939, by J. Frank Dobie. A grateful acknowledgment therefore is made to Mr. Dobie, to Little, Brown & Co., and to Bantam Books, for permission to base this purely fictional story on Mr. Dobie's version of the old legend.

WILL HENRY

MACKENNA'S GOLD

I

The Last Apache

"ARE you greedy for gold, Mackenna?" asked the ancient warrior. "Are you the same as all white men I have known? Would you sell your life, or your honor, or the honor of your woman for the yellow metal?"

The white man did not understand how the old Apache knew his name, since he knew nothing of the old Apache. He had no idea of what tribe he might be, from what *rancheria* he had wandered out into this remote wilderness, or where he had been bound when Mackenna had picked him up in the desert that blazing noontime. But he did know the old fellow to be very near death, and his kindly blue eyes darkened with concern at the same moment they narrowed slightly over the odd remark about gold.

"What do you mean?" he countered. "We were not speaking of the yellow metal." He made his reply in Spanish, as the old man had stated his question, and the Indian nodded as though pleased to hear the tongue.

"That is so," he said, "but I wished to do something

for you, even as you have done for me. You know my people; we don't leave a debt unpaid."

"*Madre!*" smiled the white man softly. "I ought to know your people. I have avoided them successfully for eleven years. Isn't that knowing them?"

"Aye," said the old man, "it is what I mean. Do you also know Cañon del Oro, Mackenna? The place we Apaches call Sno-ta-hay?"

"Do you mean the old tale of the Lost Canyon of Gold?"

"Yes, the one the white man found in Chief Nana's time."

"That would be Adams; you're talking about the Lost Adams Diggings. Don't waste your strength, old man. I am a prospector, not a ghost chaser. Fool's gold is not what I seek."

"But you do know the story?"

"Is there a white man in Arizona who does not? Or, indeed, is there one in all of the West who does not know of Adams and his lost canyon of free gold?"

"Gently, gently," said the old Apache. "I merely seek to be sure that you know of the place."

"To know of that place is nothing, old one," said Mackenna, not unwarmly. "There are a hundred 'canyons of gold' in this land. Such tales of lost treasure are commoner than sandfleas."

"True, true . . ."

The old man sighed, trailing off the words, his rheumy eyes staring out over the heat waves and the sun glare.

"I love this land," he said. "It makes my heart sad to leave it."

Mackenna nodded. He himself was a man of but young middle years, yet he had seen much of life.

"Nobody wants to go when the time comes," he answered his companion. "Nobody is that old or tired."

"True," said the old man, "true."

The white man got up and moved out of the shade of the deep rock cleft guarding the issuance of the spring from the necklace of yellow mountains enclosing the scar desert a hundred miles and more around. Thoughtfully, he moved one of the old man's legs out of the sun. Dipping his own neckcloth in the spring, he bathed the ancient Indian's face, squeezing the cloth to let the cooling drops run down inside the old man's shirt, upon his chest.

"Good," the latter said, "that is very good. I wonder why it is that you, a white man, would trouble yourself to this amount for an Apache?"

Mackenna smiled again and shrugged.

"I was never one to look for reasons," he replied.

The old man nodded.

"You are surpassing wise for one so young," he said. "How did that happen?"

"Experience," said Mackenna, bathing the wrinkled face again. "Can you drink some more now?"

"Yes, a little, thank you . . ."

He took several halting swallows of the spring water and then could take no more and spilled the last of it down his front. He smiled, shaking his head apologetically.

"An old fool, an old fool," he said softly.

"Old, perhaps," agreed Mackenna, "but no fool."

"*Gracias*," murmured the old man and was still.

The younger man, too, held his thoughts. It was too hot to talk. Moreover, this was not a good place for a white man to be, with or without talk. Mackenna wondered where Pelón might be at this moment, what poor devil the Chihuahua renegade might be trailing right at this particular time. The thought of Pelón was a natural one.

It had been only this same month that the Apache half-breed had let the word travel up from his hideout in the Mexican Sierra that he was coming north again, and that, in particular, he had business in this very Burnt Horn Basin and would consider its scorched earth *prohibiendo* for whites during his visit. When he had heard this news Mackenna had puzzled over what it would be that such a devil as Pelón would risk his neck in Arizona to achieve. Both the Army and the U.S. Marshal's department had put him on their "wanted dead" lists long ago, and he had not been heard of north of the border since '94, when he had been rumored to have accompanied Apache Kid on the latter's last raid.

Mackenna shook his head. He ought not to be sitting here at the only fresh water in fifty miles, with Pelón López on the loose. He would not have been, either, except for stopping to ease the departure of this ancient warrior by the spring. It was the kind of thing which had to be done—a man couldn't leave the old wretch out there in the sun—but at the same time it was a dangerous and foolhardy thing to do, and Mackenna was neither a reckless nor a foolhardy man. Of course, there weren't any more Indian wars going on in the Territory. The Apaches were all finished in Arizona as an organized force. But the lone wolves of their scattered bands, such as Pelón, were in reality worse than ever. If the settled folk in those parts had less to fear from the Indians presently, the prospectors and drifters had more. Glen Mackenna shook his head again and knew that here at Yaqui Spring in the Burnt Horn Desert this July of 1897 he was in immediate, real peril.

"Old man," he said uneasily, "you haven't told me your name. I think that you should, as I may meet some of your people who will want to know of you."

Now it was the old one's head which moved from side to side. "You may meet them," he answered, "but my people will not care where I am. When one is old and without teeth and can no longer work or hunt, no one will care about him other than some white man like yourself. That is the one thing which I have never comprehended about your people. They do not turn out their old ones. It's a strange weakness for a people so bloody in all other things, don't you think?"

"Yes," agreed Mackenna, "I would say that you are right."

The silence came again, and now the fierceness of the sun was lessening. But the old man was no longer seeing so clearly the parched and baking land that he loved.

"It is evening soon," he said, "and my name is Enh. Do you know what it means, Mackenna? Prairie Dog."

"Well, Enh," said Mackenna, "yes, it is evening. The sun is nearly gone over the yellow mountains. Soon it will be less trying for you. The night air will revive your strength. We can travel on. I know where the best way lies to Gila City. We can be there by dawn if our luck is good. How does that sound to you, Prairie Dog?"

There was a pause and then the old man said, "You know how that sounds to me. It sounds as though you had not had enough water for two or three days; it sounds crazy and you know that this is so."

"All right," said Mackenna, "I can see that you're not afraid."

"No, not a bit. I have lived a long time and many is the meeting I have had with death. But I want to do this thing for you which I have in my mind, and I want to do it now, before the last light goes. *Por favor,* raise me up, my son, and give to me a small, pointed stick that I may draw something in the sand for you."

Mackenna did not move.

"You are the one that is crazy, old man," he muttered. "Why would I want you to draw in the sand for me? Save your energy. Rest. I won't leave you."

"No, I want to draw you this picture, do you hear? I want you to copy it down in your mind, too. I ask this of you; I want you to remember this picture and when I am gone I want you to go and see the place with your own eyes. Do you promise?"

"I don't want the picture, old man. It is more than ample that I have your gratitude. I was happy to bring you here to shade and water. It was no great service."

"It was a very great service," said the other. "Bring me the stick and raise me up, as I have bid you."

Mackenna saw that the dying Indian patriarch truly did have it in his fading mind to do this thing for him; to sketch out on the sand some sort of pagan nonsense as a token of his indebtedness, and so he got the stick and gave it to the old man and raised him up so that he could draw with it.

The latter gathered strength for the effort, achieving some final clarity of both mind and eye. He worked quickly but in no sense carelessly. It was not at all as though he were on the edge of the last twilight of his life, but only talking with a trusted comrade over the supper fire from which both would ride away after the moon rose. Mackenna was astonished at the scope and clarity of the map which now began to appear on the smooth red sand by the spring. All in a few seconds the old Apache created the mountains, the passes, the mesas, trails, waterholes, all of it. It lay there on its grainy canvas like a bright painting, and Mackenna said quickly—with some awe even— "Why, I know that country; it is to the north and west of old Fort Wingate, over there in New Mexico. I see Chacra

Mesa. I see Chaco Canyon. Is that Devil's Pass? Yes, I see
that it is. And the Kin Yai ruin. The Chuska Mountains.
It is astounding!"

The old man was pleased. He made a motion of
urgency, however, and his voice faltered.

"Good, I hoped you would know it. Now, please,
brush it all out. First, though, do you see this point which
I place the stick upon? Here, beyond the three points of
Chacra Mesa, the Chuskas and Chaco Canyon?"

"Yes, surely. You have drawn two sugarloaf peaks.
They would appear somewhat far to the north."

"Yes, *los dos piloncillos*. Very important, my son. Do
you tell me that from this map you will be able to find
those twin peaks? Aye? Do I hear you say yes?"

"Yes," nodded Mackenna, "I can find them."

"You must be absolutely sure of that," his companion
insisted. "These peaks are eight days' ride into New Mexico—that is, it is eight days' ride by this first map I have
drawn for you, to that place where you will first see the
peaks. Then, after that, it will be another five days' ride to
the canyon itself. Be very certain, now, that you have this
part of it firmly in your memory. Do not destroy this map
of the trail to the Sugarloaves until you are positive you
can follow it."

"I can follow it," said Mackenna. "Go on."

"All right; steady me this one more time, my son. I
am going to draw you another map. This is the final one.
It shows the detail of those last five days after you have
seen the Sugarloaves. Also, it furnishes directions *into* the
secret entrance of the canyon of Sno-ta-hay, and the very
location of the gold that the white man, Adams, lost his
mind and his memory over. Are you ready now, Mackenna?"

The prospector nodded. He smoothed the sand, removing the stick lines of the Sugarloaf Trail map.

"I'm ready," he said.

The old man worked very carefully this time, talking as he drew. Mackenna knew the legend of the Lost Adams Diggings as well as any man, red or white. He was, therefore, impressed with the manner in which the old man's second sketch illustrated the accepted fable. It would be impossible, granting that any such fairy-tale bonanza existed at all, for a man of Glen Mackenna's experience *not* to locate it from the old Apache's final drawing. If there was a shred of fact in the thousand-and-one stories of the haunted canyon and its enormous treasure, the second chart now being drawn was beyond all price. Yet the bearded, blue-eyed desert wanderer did not leap to familiarize himself with its detail, nor, indeed, did his gold hunter's heart speed measurably in its steady beating.

Mackenna had seen a hundred such maps. He had followed more than one of them to its bitter, always-same ending. He knew them, and the men who drew them.

But the drawer of this map was very old and deserved to have his dignity protected and his art rewarded. So the white prospector marveled aloud at the manner in which these red children of the desert could carry each line of a landscape in their mind's eye for endless years, and he told the old man that the work was lovely. He said that he appreciated seeing it and that one day he would go to that country and visit the canyon as the old man wished. This would help him to rest for the moment with assurance in his breast, saving himself against the cool of night coming on. What Mackenna did not marvel at—and which was far more unusual than the old Indian's art—was his own ability to recognize at once the location which was being re-created. Yet he was that kind, Glen Mackenna was; he didn't think eternally of Glen Mackenna but thought much more often of the other fellow and of his concerns and fears and hopes. The old man saw this.

"Now," he said, putting down the sand stick, "at last it is done. Do not forget to brush it out when you have transferred it safely to your memory. You know that others in this land also look for the gold. It is said among my people that Pelón López is on the march up from Sonora. You know he has relatives in my band. A dangerous and bad man. He must not learn of the secret way, Mackenna. The same is to be said of some other Apaches. You know how the Indian people have changed of late. These weakling Apaches have been taught by the white man to love the yellow metal and to die for it. They are bad Indians and would betray even their own kind, if they but knew the secret way to Cañon del Oro. I charge you to protect this place when I am gone, Mackenna. I give you the trust because you are a good man, not greedy but one who respects the land and its meaning for us old ones. Do you hear me, *hijo?* Will you guard the secret?"

"Yes, all right," agreed Mackenna. "I hear you, old one. It will be as you say. Rest now. Lie easy."

"No," said the old warrior. "Please to study the map while I watch you. I wish to see that you commit its lines to your memory. I will go over it with you."

It was very hot there in the rocks by Yaqui Spring. Even with the sun gone behind the yellow mountains, it was difficult to breathe with comfort. Mackenna's nerves were exhausted with the rest of him. He wanted, in that moment, only for the old man to go ahead and die.

"In a little while," he said to him. "Surely we don't need to go over it just yet. It will wait. Can't you see that I am tired, too? I also wish to rest, you know."

Enh, the old Apache Prairie Dog, nodded obediently.

But by the way in which he turned aside his head, Mackenna knew that he had injured his pride.

"Here," he said, "don't turn away from me like that.
I am still your friend. See. Watch me. I am going to study
the map now, as you directed me. All right?"

"Ah," sighed the old man, nodding gratefully, "that
is a good young friend. I am glad that you recognize the
need to do this thing. Maps are made to be followed, remember that. Don't just put its picture into your mind and
then forget all about it. Do you know what I am asking of
you, Mackenna?"

The bearded prospector nodded.

"Yes, indeed I do know, *anciano*," he said. "But I shall
be entirely honest with you, too. I don't really know if I
shall follow this map or not, once I have traced its lines in
my memory. You understand, of course, about such facts
of life?"

He thought, watching the old Indian, that he saw the
hint of an ironic smile flick across the weathered features.
He was certain that the old man bobbed his head in assent,
and spoke with unusual vigor.

"But of course I understand, my son. It is you who do
not understand."

"What?" said Mackenna irritably. "What is that you
say?"

The Apache stared up at him.

"Am I very old, Mackenna?" he asked.

"Yes, very old. Why?"

"Do I lie to you, or you to me, when we both say that
we know I am dying?"

"No, we don't lie; we know what is to be."

"Well, then, why should I lie to you about the
Canyon of Gold? An old man is dying. A young man, even
of another skin color, befriends the old man. The old man

wishes to pay for his passage made gentle by the young man. Would he lie to his last friend on earth?"

Mackenna flushed guiltily.

"Of course not," he said. "Forgive me."

"You believe me about the gold, then?"

Mackenna shook his head. "No, old one," he said. "I won't lie to you when you do not lie to me. There are a thousand such tales of the lost Canyon of Gold."

This time Mackenna knew that he saw the fleeting smile, and he leaned forward with proper respect to catch the slowing words.

"Yes, Mackenna my friend, that is quite true—more even than a thousand such tales, eh? *But only one such canyon.* Ahah! At last, I see that you hold your breath and wait for me. I can tell that you have come closer to me. I can hear you listening. So listen to this: the map I have drawn you was drawn for my father by his father and given unto our family for safekeeping, and only to our family, by the original Apache people."

"Wait now," said Mackenna softly. "I understood all these years that it was the family of Chief Nana who had this secret."

"True," said the old man. "I am Nana's own brother."

"*Madre!*" breathed Mackenna. "Do you mean it?"

But the ancient Apache Enh, the wrinkled and lost old Prairie Dog of Chief Nana's band, had spoken his valedictory of Indian gratitude. When Mackenna called to him, using his name, and shaking him by the thin shoulder, he did not reply. The glazed dark eyes were looking out once more over the barren land they loved, and this time they would look over it forever.

"Go with God," murmured Mackenna, and closed the old man's lids.

Easing the wasted form back upon the ragged blanket

by the spring, he stood up slowly. Three choices confronted him. He could cover the old Indian with loose rocks where he lay. He could carry him farther into the cleft of the spring's origin, back into the naked yellow ring of the Yaqui hills, and there provide him with more decent burial. He could merely allow him to rest where he was, uncovered, for his people to find and dispose of when next they passed that way.

It was while he still stood there studying the matter that he heard behind him the trickling slide of small stones down the flank of the ridge which cupped the spring and put it apart from the open desert beyond it. Deliberately then, and with great care, Mackenna came about to face the sound. He was in time to see the half-dozen members of the renegade band slink to a crouching, bent-kneed halt, rifles in hand and waiting.

He could guess that they had spied him at the spring from afar, and had circled in off the desert to determine what it was that a lone white man did in this forbidden land. What he could not imagine was what had stayed their guns before he turned around at their immediate approach. Neither could he understand what they were waiting for now. But that it was *something*, he was utterly certain. It could be felt, as death could be felt, in that lengthening silence.

Beyond him, the renegades stood motionlessly alert, like red and half-red desert wolves. Their wide lips were drawn partly back over white strong teeth. Their slant eyes burned hungrily in the gathering twilight.

After a long, long time of it, Mackenna nodded carefully and said to their leader, "Hello, Pelón. It is good to see you again. Why is it that you didn't shoot me in the back when you had the chance? Why don't you shoot me in the belly right now? Can it be that you, too, have grown old?"

2

A Mestizo *of the* Monte

PELÓN SMILED, and Mackenna would rather he had not.

"Well," said the outlaw Apache breed, "no, I would not say that I had also grown old. But, of course, I am older than the last time, eh? You, too, Mackenna?"

"Why not?" shrugged the prospector. "Only good wine improves with age. Why didn't you shoot me?"

"I had a reason."

Mackenna nodded, stalling for time to study the situation, and what he should, or could, do about it.

Francisco López, called Pelón, had been known to him for eleven years. He was a half-Mexican, half-Apache *mestizo* of the Monte, that long, desolately beautiful spine of mountains running down into Mexico from the U.S. Southwest. His heart held a double charge of dislike for the whites, inherited from both sides of his pedigree. He had made a living off his hate. It was his whole aim. He was dedicated to it. From this, Mackenna could assume that those who elected to be his comrades in the venture would share his faith in it. The one swift look which he now allowed himself in the direction of Pelón's comrades confirmed the natural suspicion. Two of the five appeared to be Mexicans; three, Apaches. All were brigands of the professional type, dressed for their calling in soft Sonora leggins, leather cartridge bandoleers, faded cotton shirts, and either big cartwheel sombreros or bright-colored Indian headbands. Each carried a rifle and two revolvers.

"I suspect," said Mackenna finally, "that you did have a reason. I suspect, as well, that I know what it was—indeed, what it still is."

He let the suggestion stand. In the manner of any conversation being conducted in so gracious a language as Spanish, Pelón courteously observed the pause. During it, both he and Glen Mackenna weighed one another anew, reviewing old estimates and remembrances.

Mackenna, Pelón found, had the same red beard and friendly, clear blue eyes as before. He had, too, the same easy soft look and mannerisms which Pelón knew to be a bad guide to reality. If Mackenna had added a pound of weight, Pelón could not see where it might be. He was still lean and trim in the hips, wide and well-muscled in the shoulders. Withal, at thirty, the gold-hunting white man was much the same quiet-spoken mining engineer he had been at twenty. His Eastern background and education had been sun-hardened and dehydrated in the ensuing decade but Pelón could still understand the vast difference between himself and the thoughtful six-footer who now waited for him to make his move.

For his part, Glen Mackenna saw a man of forty, wide all the way up and down. From his flat, turned-in feet to his huge fleshy head, he was evil-looking in an eerie, special way that the white prospector had never forgotten. Pelón, as his nickname would indicate, was that rarity among his parent races, a baldheaded man. His enormous skull, with

its heavily corded neck, wrinkles of thick flesh and jug-
handle ears, gave him the appearance of a dark, squat
gargoyle carved from the native desert rock. His coarse
features, the nose both broken and bottle-cut, the mouth
disfigured by knife scars which drew the thick lips upward
in a perpetual, meaningless grin, and the massive progna-
thous jaw, combined to give an impression of abysmal brutality which, unlike Mackenna's disarming mildness, was a
certain indicator of the man beneath.

In his origins, as well, Pelón López was the antithesis
of Glen Mackenna. He had neither church nor secular
education. Illiterate, profane, insensate, he gave the effect
of utter ignorance seeking constantly a lower level than
its natal pit of nothingness. Yet there remained that about
the notorious outlaw, some peculiar hint of better things,
some faint congenital spark of sanity and sanguinity, which
was completely belied by his history. It was this scant
glimmer of suspected decency which Mackenna hoped
presently to exploit.

"Well," he said, smiling blandly, "we have stared too
much for good manners, eh, Pelón? Let us say that neither
man has changed greatly, and that both of us are the same
as we were before. We are thus returned to my first question: Why did you not shoot me? As for that, why don't
you do it right now? *Madre!* I think you *have* changed!"

"Never," said the other. "When the time comes, I
will accommodate you. You have my word for it. Meanwhile there is the matter of the body of that old dead
Apache lying there."

The reference to Enh froze Mackenna's smile. Of a
sudden he knew Pelón's presence at Yaqui Spring was no
accident of the trail. His calm glance tensed.

"What matter is that?" he asked.

The bandit stared at him. "You know what matter I

mean," he said. "We're here for the same reason you are
—trailing that damned skinny old Indian. Don't make me
angry. You know his family held the secret to Sno-ta-hay."

Mackenna nodded, forcing an indifferent shrug. "As
for that," he said, "what family in this cursed land does
not? My family, your family, the families of your men,
we all have the secret. You can buy the secret to Sno-ta-hay
in any cantina in Sonora, or any saloon in Arizona."

Pelón returned the indifferent nod, cocking his rifle
as he did so.

"Patience," he said, "is a virtue I was whelped without. I will count to three, possibly four, and then shoot
you."

Mackenna knew that he would do it. And, if not him,
then his five hungry-looking wolfmates, who now also put
their Winchesters on the cock and moved forward. But
the white prospector was still not sure of his ground.
Neither was he well-armed for an argument. His own
weapon, a vintage Civil War Spencer, was with his saddle-
bags thirty feet away. His only other armament was the
mesquite branch he had broken off to use as an eraser for
old Enh's sand maps. The thought of defending himself
with this thorny wand brought a wry smile to his lips and,
belatedly, a hazardous notion of escape to his desperate
mind.

"All right," he said, easing two steps forward and in
front of the sand map—the second, vital one—which he
had not had time to scrub out. "It is true that I was after
the old man. But I was too late, as you can see. I found
him there on his blanket dead of age and thirst and the
great heat of today."

"It isn't even a good lie," said Pelón, "but I must
remind myself to be cautious. To shoot you before I was
assured you had not gotten the secret from old Enh, that

would be a terrible blunder for a man of my professional reputation."

"You are too clever for me, Pelón. Yes, I did come upon the old rascal before he breathed his last. We talked a little, that is all."

"Yes, about what?"

"Oh, you know how it is with the old ones when their time comes. He was going back into his good years."

"What did he say when you asked him about the mine?"

"You mean Sno-ta-hay, the Canyon of Gold?"

"Do not ask me that one more time, Mackenna."

"But of course, Pelón. One seeks only to be sure. When I asked the old man about the mine he behaved as though the heat was in his brain and he could not understand me. I am certain that he could, but there was no way to be—well, you know how it is with such an ancient one."

"I know," said Pelón, lifting his scarred upper lip, "how it was with *this* ancient one; how it was, was that he was the only brother of Nana, and he carried the secret of the Lost Adams Mine with him out into the desert this past week. So much I learned from friends in the band of Nana. They told me the old man had gone out to die, and that no doubt the secret of the mine in Sno-ta-hay would die with him."

"I cannot change any of this," said Mackenna. "Why do you tell it to me?"

"Because, as I said, we are here on the same business, and I can use you in that business."

"This means what?"

"Well, I will tell you how Apaches keep a secret. Do you know that no one save Nana knew that old Enh held the secret with him until one month ago? Yes, that is a fact. Isn't that a disgrace? Such treatment of one's own people! Those Indians are crazy."

"Some of them," agreed Mackenna. "Just as some white men."

Pelón's face twisted. "But not you and not me, eh, *amigo?*" he said. "We know what we need to know."

"Sometimes," said Mackenna.

"Well, this time," said the outlaw leader, "we do."

"Is that so?" announced Mackenna. "In what way?"

"This way," said the squat breed. "I know that in some way you, too, found out about Enh's part in the secret, and that you came out looking for him the same as I, hoping to find him before he died and to twist the story of the lost canyon from him."

Mackenna set himself. "Very well, let us agree that we are both here looking for the Lost Adams gold," he said. "Let us also agree that old Enh had the secret and that we both hoped to pry it out of him, one way or another. Having come so far, let us then ask ourselves this question: if the American, Mackenna, got the old man to tell him where the mine was, how will the Mexican, Francisco López, know this fact?"

"I could kill you," growled the outlaw.

"That is a way to gain knowledge?" asked Mackenna in surprise. "I never heard a dead man give very good directions, did you?"

"Of course not. That's why you are alive this minute. I am still trying to decide if the old man told you anything."

"Well," said Mackenna, "let me put your curiosity at rest. He did better than that. He drew me a picture of the way to the canyon. He put it in this sand right here at my feet."

"Another bad lie," sneered Pelón. "You are not skill-ful, Mackenna. A child could see that you lie."

Mackenna hunched his shoulders and made a light gesture with his left hand to indicate the ground behind him. At the same time he stepped aside.

"In that case," he said, "and since it is so simple, per-haps even Pelón could see the evidence of my claim. This late light is poor but I believe you will still be able to recognize this work on the sand as that of old Enh, and also as that of the map to Cañon del Oro and all of the Lost Adams gold."

In the moment's stillness which followed, Pelón and his fellows exchanged startled glances, while Mackenna said a small, swift prayer and tightened his grip on the mesquite branch.

"*Por Dios!*" rumbled Pelón. "Is it possible?" And, with the question, he led the delayed rush of his outlaw band toward Mackenna and the map on the sand beside Yaqui Spring. The bearded prospector let them slide to a stop, glittering-eyed with greed and avarice. He permitted them just the correct fraction of time necessary for the impression but not the detail of Enh's map to strike their minds. Then he drew the ragged mesquite brush in a whipping, zigzag smear through the center of the sand map, obliterating it before the agonized glances of Pelón López and his five desperate men.

3 〰

The Packmates of Pelón

MACKENNA, who was something of a philosopher, decided that, but for the circumstances, the night would have been enchanting. There was a three-quarter moon of a color challenging ripe pumpkin. The desert, after what had been an atrociously hot day, had cooled delightfully. The air, if not sharp and keen as it was at the greater altitudes which Mackenna preferred, held a certain balm not to be found higher up, either. And so the captive gold hunter drew in deeply of the aromas about him—of the lavender blooms of desert willow, the yellow blossoms of palo verde, the acrid perfume of piñon and juniper—and wondered if this were to be his last night on earth.

A little beyond him, but within earshot, his hosts were discussing the same question. Some interesting small differences of professional opinion were developing. One of the two Mexican outlaws, a fellow who had turned out to be an engaging Irish half-breed, was insisting, with a great deal of wit and charm, that Mackenna should be put to death at once. His comrade, a businesslike Sonoran, was disagreeing via sound commercial arguments. Of the three

Indians, the first two were U.S. Apaches. They were thus properly deferring to Pelón as visiting headman of the expedition. But the third Indian was a Mexican Yaqui, not an Apache, and he was an entirely original thinker. A dark-skinned, powerful specimen, with grotesquely long arms and short, ape-bent legs, he was not so much the eloquent charmer or practical bandit-merchant as the direct action-ary who made his points by animal power applied un-diluted. His company nickname, not unexpectedly, was Mono, meaning Monkey, and when Monkey was hungry he ate and when he was weary he slept and when he caught a lone white man out on the desert he killed him—slowly, of course—and that was that.

Presently he was explaining this to his fellows. "I would begin," he said, "by making some little knife cuts in the calf of the leg. Then, there is a place on the bottoms of the feet, and another in the pits of the thighs, where judicious carving will bring an ultimate of hurt without bleeding your pig too quickly. With these small things accomplished, I would—"

"*Por Dios*," shouted Pelón, "you have the mind of a meat seller! What the devil is wrong with you, Monkey? We are not up here to dress out a carcass!"

"Yes," put in the first Apache, a slimly handsome Chiricahua who was a grandson of Cochise. "Let's not forget what we're after. Isn't that what you say, Hachita?"

He addressed the question to his Mimbreño Apache companion. The latter's name meant Little Hatchet. His mind went with the "little" part of the description but his gross body did not. He was the grandnephew of the old killer, Mangas Coloradas, and was a throwback to his famed great-uncle who had stood six and one-half feet tall, with a massively ugly face. He was a throwback in appearance only, however, for where old Mangas had been the most implacable white-hater of all the Apache, Hachita was kind-hearted and gentle. Thus the untrue grandnephew of the savage old man bobbed his huge head and rumbled in reply to his friend's inquiry, "Aye, that is what I say, Besh. You speak for me. I don't know what it is you have in your mind, but it is all right. It goes for me."

Besh was an Apache word meaning knife. Hearing it applied to the slender Chiricahua, Mackenna was not reassured. Two Apaches named Hatchet and Knife scarcely added to the credit side of the ledger. But Mackenna was eleven years wise to these red desert wolves, and he kept his tongue where it should be kept at all times in dealing with those of the Apache blood. At the same time, he opened his ears and eyes wider still. But the precaution paid not. What he continued to hear were forecasts of worsening weather for wandering white fools in the Burnt Horn Basin.

Laguna Cahill, the Mexican half-breed whose Irish side provided the sparkle to his good-humored discussions of homicide, held tenaciously to the need for judicious murder of the white man.

The purebred Mexican, Venustiano Sánchez, a defected sergeant of Federales, and a man who saw things with an old soldier's clear hard eye for profit, remained horrified by the mere suggestion of destroying the key to a treasure such as the Lost Adams Diggings. Indignation was the weakest word for his feelings. Killing money? Murdering wealth? *Ay, Chihuahua!*

"As God is my witness," he raged to Pelón, "what is this talk of killing? Are we all gone mad? Wake up, Pelón! It is I, Venustiano Sánchez, speaking. The subject is the buried fortune in Cañon del Oro—one hundred thousand American dollars in raw gold, already mined and stored away, with God Himself knowing how many more millions right at the grass-roots and in the stream's sand and gravel at no greater depth than a spade's length! *Vuese-ñoría!* Don't listen to these doltish clowns. We came for the gold! That gringo pig over there in the rocks has got the map in his mind from old Enh's sand drawing, and all that we need to do is force it out of him. *Por Dios*, Pelón, deny these lunatics and donkeys! Say *something* to them!"

Mackenna, for all his wisdom and his knowledge of desert diplomacy, could not forego the opportunity.

"Yes, Pelón," he pleaded in Spanish, "say *something* to them. My Scotch ancestors will be spinning in their burial plots. That's a lot of money to lose for the want of a little common sense. I don't think you can sell my scalp for anything like that amount—I mean Adam's one hundred thousand dollars, naturally. Not to mention the gold Adams and his party left in the grass-roots, as Sánchez says. Think about it, Pelón. What am I worth dead?"

Laguna Cahill, the only one of them other than Sánchez who could understand and apply such economic theorems, smiled speculatively. The smile was like that of a gray shark, showing the underteeth only. Mackenna was attracted by it but not happily.

"Well," estimated Laguna, "we could flay you and offer the hide in Oaxaca for drumheads. I think your skin would bring three pesos. Maybe five. It's better than nothing."

"Bah," grumbled Sánchez, the mercenary sergeant, "why must you insist on saying 'nothing'? This man is worth a million dollars in *yanqui* currency, at the very least. Be reasonable, Laguna. You may not care for money, as such, but think of what it will purchase in terms of wine and wenches. Yes, and *mozos* to serve each in the best style, eh? Ah, I thought so! You see, all it requires is a bit of thought."

"Perhaps," conceded the Mexican breed. "After all,

it is a difficult thing to argue against hard drink and soft flesh."

"Unless," grunted Hachita, "you include good food. If you do that, then the other things become as nothing. I can get pulque or mescal anywhere. Women come to me like flies to a ripe carcass. But good things to eat? Ah, now there you are talking about something!"

Laguna shrugged. "I can agree with you in part," he admitted. "Your carcass is indeed ripe. There's a breeze springing up right now and it comes to me from your direction. Would you mind moving to the other side of the fire, away from the wind? *Por favor, amigo.* You will spoil my appetite."

Pelón now knew that it was time to speak. In a moment the giant Apache would realize he had been insulted, and from that point anything might ensue.

"Hachita is right," he put in quickly. "Here in the desert nothing is so difficult to obtain as a good meal. But we don't need to blacken the idea of weak women and strong drink in their place, either. All things are good if taken in excess. Especially *gold*, eh, *compadres?*"

He directed the end question to all of them, and with an evil laugh which seemed to prove the common language of their fraternity, for all responded in kind and Venustiano Sánchez spread his hands in haste to dry the cement of agreement before it might be loosened by another suggestion of throat-slitting from Laguna Cahill.

"*Segura que sí.*" He smiled. "Everything is understood. We hold this white dog captive and decide in which ways it is best to persuade him to share with his new friends the secret of Cañon del Oro. Is this not true, comrades?"

"Of course, it's true," said Laguna, with his shark's grin. "Was it ever in doubt?"

Francisco López, called Pelón, eyed him with a coldness which reached even to Mackenna thirty feet away in the rocks.

"No," answered the bandit leader, "I don't think that it ever was."

With the slow words, he brought out from under his serape his right hand which, somehow, had managed to slide, unseen, beneath the soiled garment. In the hand was a cocked Colt's revolver of very large caliber. During the little stillness which followed, Pelón delicately lowered the big curved hammer and smiled mirthlessly at his faithful men.

"Now," he said, "let us get on with it. We've talked the moon up over the hills and we still haven't had our supper. I think better on a full stomach. Also, the others will be wondering where we are. Come on, let's go."

Mackenna again felt compelled to intercede at the risk of physical hurt. "The *others?*" he said to Pelón. "Am I to understand that these five are not the total of your party?"

"You're to understand whatever you wish," said Pelón. "But, yes, I said 'the others.' They are with the horses waiting for us up in the rocks." He pointed into the yellow stumps of the Yaquis still showing light against the evening sky. "Did you think we traveled on foot up into this land? Hah! It's you that grow old, Mackenna."

"It may be that I do, Pelón. But it does not sound like you to be moving in the enemy's land with so large a party. Isn't that taking chances better not risked?"

"Oh," said the bandit leader, shrugging in dismissal, "we didn't bring these 'comrades' with us; we came by them up here."

He followed the remark with another of his barking laughs, which was joined in by all his fellows, save the grotesque Monkey.

"Speaking of those ones up there in the rocks," growled the powerful Yaqui, "makes me ache in the loins. Come on; let's go fast."

Mackenna caught the odd flavor of this remark but did not pin it down at once. Pelón graciously filled in the puzzle for him, replying to the Yaqui with a shrug.

"Don't worry, Monkey," he said, grinning. "You won't go hungry. I'm not a selfish man, and I know the obligations of the *jefe*. Come, do not look so dismal. Have I not promised that you will not go unfed? You may have my meal if you wish. I don't think I could digest her, anyway."

"*Her?*" said Mackenna, his voice small with dawning truth. "Did you speak of *her?*"

"But of course," replied Pelón. "Listen, *amigo*, we Apaches don't believe in doing women's work. Cooking the supper, tending the horses, do you think that is work for men? We don't. Come on; wait till you see my little morsel!"

With the words, he hauled Mackenna to his feet and struck him a clap on the back which nearly separated his shoulder blades. The white prospector recoiled both from the blow and the idea which had preceded it.

"Women?" he said weakly. "Here in an enemy desert? You've brought your women with you?"

"Hell, no!" bellowed Pelón. "Not *our* women, just somebody else's. I told you we picked them up along the way."

"My God, Pelón," groaned Mackenna, "you can't mean it. No man needs a woman that bad!"

"That depends on the man," grinned Pelón.

"And the *woman;* always the *woman!*" muttered Monkey, thick lips twisting. "Hurry up, Pelón, or I leave alone!"

"Sure," said the baldheaded renegade, "here we go. I will come last, and each of you knows why. I will keep Mackenna with me, so that all will go well on the trail. Besh, you show the way. Sánchez, stay by me."

The bandits began falling into trail line, save for the giant Mimbreño youth, Hachita. Pelón saw him hesitating and bawled angrily at him to know what it was that disturbed his obedience to the orders.

"It's this poor old man," mumbled Hachita, pointing down to the huddled body of Enh. "I don't think it's right to leave him all alone. It's not a kind thing to do. The coyotes will get at him."

"My God," exploded Pelón, "what is this? Worrying about a toothless old fool dead of age and disuse at a waterhole in the desert? I thought you were an Apache!"

Hachita stared at him. He moved over and picked up the still form of Enh, cradling it in his arms as though it were that of a sick child. Turning to Pelón, he said in his slow voice, "So is this little old one an Apache; I will carry him to his people."

"What? We may not see his band for a month!"

"Nevertheless, I will carry him."

"*Santísima María,*" cried Pelón, "I have surrounded myself with imbeciles! What is a man to do?"

"Go get a drink," said Laguna Cahill.

"Find a woman," rumbled Mono the Monkey.

"Get some good hot food inside of him," said Hachita, finding his place in line, with old Enh resting against his broad chest, "and *then* get a drink and have a woman."

Mackenna looked at the sweating Pelón. The crow's-feet crinkled swiftly at the corners of his innocent blue eyes. "For myself, *Jefe,*" he said humbly, "I could think of no single other thing, unless it would be a troop of American cavalry, to add to your present blessings."

Pelón struck him in the face with brutal, unexpected violence. Mackenna went down, head whirling. Pelón kicked him heavily in the ribs, and he scrambled up, blood dripping from the torn corners of his mouth.

"Remember yourself," nodded the bandit chief. "Save your jokes. I am a man who likes to make his own laughs."

"*Dispenseme*," mumbled Mackenna, spitting out the hot salty blood, with some shards of split tooth. "It was a poor jest, scarcely worth such a noble reminder."

"Go ahead," said Pelón to Besh, the Chiricahua, "lead the way." He drew his right-hand Colt and added, without seeming rancor but with complete convincingness, "I believe that I will shoot the next man who says one word that I don't ask of him. The talking is done with."

No one of them seemed disposed to deny the ruling. Certainly Glen Mackenna did not. He set out obediently with the others, at a steady dogtrot, up the narrow and brightly moonlit trail through the ancient Yaqui hills.

What might lie ahead for his companions, he could not begin to imagine. What lay ahead for himself, he did not dare to think about. For the moment, only one thing was to be regarded as absolutely certain: in such a company of human animals as that with whom he now loped through the desert night, death was no farther away than the nearest member of the pack.

4 ⋛⋛

Into the Yellow Yaquis

THEY HAD not far to go. After the wolflike Apache habit, the men of Pelón's band had traveled during the day on foot, their women taking another but approximately parallel path with the horses. This was no extraordinary method, but merely one reserved for the land of the enemy, where any people contacted would be against them and would raise the hue and cry which would bring either the U.S. Marshal with a posse, or the U.S. Cavalry with a patrol. By moving on foot the intruders could keep out of sight, and could, if pressed to it, elude nearly any white pursuit which might be mounted. In the heart of the real desert, such as the Burnt Horn Basin, Apaches on foot were an easy match for white men on horses. It was only for the long journey up from and back to the Sonoran mountains that mounts were required. Meanwhile, in the immediate search going forward for the missing patriarch, Enh, ponies and women would have been only burdensome baggage.

Mackenna, knowing these ways of the Apache, wondered briefly how Pelón could entrust his saddle animals to women whom he had picked up en route. His curiosity enjoyed small opportunity to gnaw at him. The nature of the trail to the rendezvous was entirely too compelling. It might have been three miles, Mackenna thought—or five. It was impossible to gauge, going at night and with the frightful switchbacks demanded by the virtually "hanging" track. All he could be sure of was that the way gained altitude with every foot.

Of a sudden, however, he was surprised to see fireglow directly ahead. In the same moment an odor of roasting meat came to him. It had the subtle burnt and bloodraw mixture known only to the abject art of Apache cookery and, scenting it, he turned to Pelón.

"*Jefe*," he ventured, "either I've forgotten the fragrance of paradise, or that's broiled mule blessing the night wind."

Pelón, recovered from his bad temper, nodded agreeably.

"You're right, it's mule," he said. "Too bad you had to be a white man. In many ways you are of my mother's people. You don't talk much. You have a good nose. You trot strong. You don't carry any fat. You don't lie or cheat. You don't eat much. You don't waste anything."

"*Gracias*," said Mackenna, and did not press his luck.

In another moment, they had broken free of the rocks and were come into the little pine-guarded glade where the outlaw women waited with the horses.

At the sight of the place, Mackenna drew in his breath. "*Madre!*" he muttered. "It's a miracle!"

"No," said Pelón, grinning, "only a small Apache secret."

Whichever it was, Mackenna did not argue it. The idea was the same either way. Here, within no more than three miles of the only known water in fifty miles—known to the white man, that was—lay a tiny green jewel of a foothill mountain meadow, complete with bubbling live spring and stunted dark green pine trees.

It wasn't possible, of course; yet there it lay. The Apaches! thought Mackenna; what a strange and mysterious race of human beings. Where there was no water in fifty miles, they brought forth an artesian fountain, cold, pure, sparkling. Where there grew no grass closer than three pony rides, there they caused to spring up green feed in plenty for their tough small mustangs. Where there were no true pine trees within a hundred and more miles of sun-withered desert, there they made to spring forth from the naked rock dark, long-needled conifers with the fat cinnamon bark and uncontorted trunks of the true mountain pine. It wasn't a miracle, after all, it was a mirage; it had to be!

The initial bemusement obtained only for the time required by Mackenna to reach the fire and to fasten his startled gaze upon the Apache women. It was replaced, then, by another, far more sinister vision. This second vision, the bearded prospector prayed, would prove to be an hallucination induced by his fatigue and low spirit. But the hope was abruptly denied. When he had closed his eyes, shaken his head and reopened them, once more, the white girl was still there.

The Fourth Woman

MACKENNA SWAYED with weakness and felt ill. The old crone tending the fire and the cooking of the mule meat was plainly a full-blooded Apache. The plump squaw caring for the coffeepot and its precious contents was of another band, possibly Pima or Hopi. The third camp follower, a gaunt, hot-eyed creature of about thirty, was another straight-bred one, her Apache origin established by the fact of her nose having been cut off nearly flat to her face, the effective custom of her people in marking the adulterous wife. It was the fourth woman, the young one, the slender, light-skinned girl, who had startled Mackenna She was neither of Apache nor Pima nor Hopi nor any other Indian blood. Neither was she Mexican nor *mestizo* nor a half-blood of any mixing. She was as white as Glen Mackenna.

In the stunned silence of the meeting, Pelón López reached and touched Mackenna on the shoulder. "Well, *amigo*, what did I tell you?" He grinned. "Didn't I say your blue eyes would pop when you saw my little tidbit?"

The bearded prospector controlled himself, knowing

that any interested move on his part could do the girl harm. He must ignore her, must play off the sickening surprise of finding her here, and must do it just so, neither over- nor underacting his part in the dangerous charade.

He nodded, looking at Pelón.

"That is two times, now, that you have called her a bit of food," he said. "How is that?"

"Oh," answered the other, scarred grin widening, "that is because I haven't yet had time to partake of her. *Comprende?* Ha, ha, ha, ha!"

"Extremely amusing," agreed Mackenna. "Are you saying you took her only today?"

"Yes. This morning. We interrupted her people at their meal. You might say we joined them for breakfast. Ha, ha! Perhaps that's a second reason I call her my little tasty dish. Is it not funny, Mackenna?"

"Yes," said Glen Mackenna, "it is not."

Pelón stared at him suspiciously. It was not clear to the bandit chief what, precisely, his guest had meant.

While he stood there scowling blackly, a third party intruded on the impasse. It was Monkey, the squat Yaqui killer with the ache in his loins. His low growling broke suddenly into the stillness building between Mackenna and Pelón. Both of the latter shifted their gazes to the apelike redman. The others, also, swung their glances in his direction; all, for the moment, hesitating at the edge of the fire's light.

Monkey was not returning their looks. He was staring at the white girl. She had been hard-used by the Apache women in the absence of the men. Among other attentions, they had torn her shirtblouse to shreds by striking her with mesquite whips. The tattered garment hung from her thin shoulders in a manner to hide only in tantalizing part the sharp thrustings of her small, hard breasts, and it was the sight of these which now held the glittering obsidian-black eyes of Mono the Monkey.

Jarringly, then, Pelón laughed. "Gently now, Monkey," he said. "Remember to leave a little for the rest of us, eh? Ha, ha, ha!"

His companions nodded and grinned their agreement with this code of renegade ethics, and Monkey began moving in a crouch toward the terrified girl, actual slaver dripping from his loose-lipped mouth. It was bestial, primordial, pagan. Mackenna, watching it, could not accept the evidence of his own senses.

"My God!" he said, low-voiced and in English to Pelón, "you're not going to stand there and let him do it!"

The outlaw leader looked at him, gargoyle's face expressionless. He palmed his great, hairy hands in helpless resignation.

"But what can one do?" he asked the white prospector. "Did I not promise Monkey back at the spring that he could have my share of her? Do you want me to go back on my word? What kind of a man do you think I am?"

Mackenna didn't answer him with words. He interlaced the bony fingers of his hands and, swinging the knotted fists as one, backhandedly, he struck Pelón López a blow across the slope of his Neanderthal jaw which nearly tore his head from his shoulders. The half-breed was knocked staggeringly to his knees and in the instant before he, or any of his dumbfounded pack, could recover, Glen Mackenna had leaped silently toward the Yaqui ape-man.

6

Mono the Monkey

So INTENT upon the girl was Monkey that he did not see Mackenna rush at him. The girl did, of course, and could not help reacting in such a way as to alert the Yaqui. He whirled in the last instant, and just as Mackenna was raising his knotted hands to smash him as he had smashed Pelón. Monkey's speed was incredible. His hands shot out and pinioned those of his white adversary while they were yet upraised. With a grunting heave, Monkey literally threw Mackenna through the air, by the wrists. The prospector landed with a tooth-jarring wrench among the pine needles and small rocks beyond the fire. The shock of the fall dazed him and in the moment of his uncertainty Monkey was upon him.

Here the fight would have ended, for the Yaqui's hand instinctively closed upon one of the loose rocks with the clear intent of bashing in the skull of the white man beneath him. But for the second time within as many breaths, a hand upraised in anger was stayed. Pelón fired from the hip and without seeming aim. The rock, nonetheless, shattered in Monkey's grasp. The apeman gave a yowl of surprise, as the shock of the bullet hitting the granite chunk was transmitted to his hand. He was then upon his feet in the instant, his brutal face turned toward Pelón and the others. There was murder written upon the writhing dark features, but even for such an animal as Monkey, the ring of the pack awaiting his move was too much. He hesitated and was saved, the blood lust leaving him as suddenly as it had come. Pelón nodded and put away the smoking Colt. Flanking him, Besh, the tall, slender Chiricahua, lowered the poised steel of his knife. Hachita, on the other side, slowly replaced the huge trunk of his right arm, and the razor-bladed hatchet in its belt scabbard. Sánchez and Laguna Cahill, who had not moved, exchanged glances and straightened their crouched forms. Monkey, too, came up out of his fighting crouch and stood, slope-shouldered and sullen, before his chief and his fellow outlaws.

"Everything considered," said Pelón thoughtfully, "I should say that this is an evening of great luck for you, Monkey. Had you killed our key to Cañon del Oro, I should have pulled the trigger again. As it is, we are all well disposed toward one another, I am sure, and the key sits there on his hams, unharmed." He turned to the white girl, adding sharply in English, "What ails you? Won't you even give a helping hand to the man who offered you his life?"

The girl blushed and went quietly to Mackenna and gave him her hand. He took it and managed a rueful, bloodied grin, as he tottered up to his feet. Brushing the pine needles and sand and small sticks from his mouth, he made a gesture of apology.

"I don't see how you can believe me," he said, "but one way or another we'll still manage something. I have a constitutional objection to young ladies of refinement tenting on the plains with such rough companions."

The girl, he was pleased to see, greeted the lame sally with a tense grin of her own.

"It won't take me long to pack," she said.

Pelón López moved between them.

"I like a good laugh myself," he said to both. "See? Ha, ha, ha, ha!" He threw back his ugly head, barking like a rabid coyote. In the next second, he flashed his Colt from beneath his serape and struck Mackenna with its long barrel across the chest just at the collarbone. The pain of the blow was intense and Mackenna knew the bone had been either chipped or fractured. He set his teeth, however, and stood to it. Pelón eyed him and nodded.

"It's as I said before, you would have made a damned good Apache. Strange, too, with those innocent blue eyes and that calm, friendly face."

"Very strange," said Mackenna. "What next, *Jefe?*"

"Just do not talk with the girl, do you understand? And see that she does not talk to you."

"As you will," bowed the prospector, and told the girl in English what had been said. She nodded and returned to her former chore of scouting the glade for firewood. Mackenna could see, from this wise action, that she had already learned the first rule for survival as an Apache captive—silent obedience and effacement at all times. He gave her a little wave of approval and was promptly thrilled at the bright, quick smile she exchanged for the token. This, he began to suspect, was no ordinary woman. He was no good judge of such things, of course. To say that he was a woman hater, or that he was shy of women, would not be true. But the actual fact was that he didn't care for the female temperament, and felt that men and women thought with two distinctly alien intellects. Accordingly, he shunned all females and had not until this present moment any occasion to question his course.

Now, looking into the cool gray eyes of the brown-haired captive for the little time which Pelón allowed, he was taken with an overwhelming need to know this woman better. For the first time in his adult life he was positively certain what it was that he wanted. It was not gold he had been hunting all these years of his lone manhood. It was something infinitely more rare, exciting and essential, and something incalculably more lovely. It was, in a word, this waifish, undefeated Arizona girl, who was far too young to arouse in any decent, Christian-thinking man the thoughts which were presently firing Glen Mackenna's imagination. It was, in another word, love. And what Glen Mackenna had to do about it was to get this gray-eyed child of inspiration safely away from the wolfpack of Pelón López and return her, unviolated, to white civilization.

With the thought, the red-headed prospector nodded and drew in a deep breath. He had been right in the first place, back at Yaqui Spring. Despite a bruised jaw, bloodied mouth, split tooth and cracked clavicle, it was, indeed, a most enchanted evening.

7 ≷≷≷

The Gila City Agreement

"You see, Mackenna, that is the entire problem."
Pelón shrugged, helpless to stand against the fates. "You
must do as we ask—guide us to the gold—or we will kill
you. By the same token, you are a stubborn man not given
to softness. Therefore, we know that you well may permit
us to kill you. But remember, *amigo*, Pelón always prepares
for these little disappointments of life."

Mackenna shrugged in his turn. It was a fact that his
nerves were good. It was also a fact that the bandits might
do him in before he was ready to accede to their demand
that he lead them to the Lost Adams gold. Yet he was
curious to know what decisive card it was that Pelón
thought he held against him. He wondered if it might be
that the brigands were still thinking in terms of torture,
and he hoped that they were not. Certain of the toes on
his right foot had been treated by the Mescaleros at one
time in a matter of persuading him to stay away from an
area they regarded as sacred. He remembered the therapy
with astringent exactness, having no great urge whatever to

repeat the experience in defiance of a request which he must, in the end, submit to one way or another.

"Pelón," he said, finally, "it was always that you were a superb talker, but it would seem that age overtakes you these times. You are worse than an old squaw. Be brief; what is it you threaten me with?"

"The girl, of course. Do you think I didn't observe your foolish looks at her? What do you say? Let us now think of those sweet small breasts which our friend Monkey found so exciting. How do you think she would look with one of them cut off?"

Mackenna assumed they would do it. The girl meant nothing to them. She was not even regarded as a good blanket prospect in all likelihood. He could guess that, as old professionals, they had probably picked her up purely to use as a hostage, should pursuit form and draw too close. There could be no doubt they would use her meanwhile to secure his coöperation. There was also, however, the outer stirrup to that same saddle: he might use his position to secure her against them. Carefully, he put this picture to Pelón.

"Now," he said, "I can see that you have lost none of your old slyness. I feel better. All right, I will agree that the girl is important to me and that I would not wish to see harm come to her. Also, I would not wish to see any attention, at all, come to her from your campmates. Do I make my meaning clear?"

"Of course. Go on."

"Well, naturally, it is an arrangement," said Mackenna. "As you say, we have to admit each of us has certain strengths over the other."

"Yes, that's true. Let's have your terms."

Mackenna grinned. It was quite a wonderful expression, considering its components of tanned bronze skin, clean white teeth, attractive crow's-feet and warm blue eyes, and even Pelón López was affected by it. Not favorably, of course. But he was affected.

"I have warned you about your innocent ways!" he snapped. "See that you don't try me too far."

"I would never do that, Pelón. Are we not both men of honor?"

"I am," said Pelón, returning the grin. "As for you, I wouldn't trust you with anything more important than my sister's virtue, and as for that, you can judge the quality of the article for yourself. That's her, yonder, with the nose missing."

Mackenna looked over at the gaunt Apache squaw. The woman, having heard the reference to herself, grinned at the white man in a way which made Pelón's knife-scarred grimace seem softer than a mother's kiss at night. Mackenna shivered and looked away.

"You see," said Pelón, "already she gives you looks which promise great things. What do you say? The terms, *hombre*. I won't wait all night for you."

"That woman," said Mackenna, stalling, "is not your sister. She's the pure blood. Why do you lie to me?"

"Who lies to you, dear friend? Did I say sister? Ah, a small slip. Make it half-sister. We had the same mother. Isn't that so, woman?" he said to the squaw.

The creature bobbed her skull-like head, making at the same time an obscene gesture with her hands and hips toward Mackenna, then breaking into the same barking staccato laugh as her half-brother.

"Observe," said the latter, "you have made a conquest without lifting a finger. Wonderful! Should you care to further the matter after we are through here, her name is Hesh-ke. But you won't need it."

Mackenna was anything but reassured. The woman's

name was an Apache word meaning an unreasoning urge to kill. It might be translated broadly in English as "the murderess." It was not unusual for the Apache to bestow such musical appellations, however, and there was always the probability that Pelón had been only worrying him by the use of the singular title, so the white prospector maintained his poker face, nodding soberly.

"Many thanks," he said, "but I am a little too weary for a woman tonight. Hesh-ke will forgive me, as I know you will, Pelón. And now, for the terms, eh?"

Pelón and the others drew in, watching him. They were all on their haunches after the Indian fashion, in a half-ring a little back from the fire. Some picked the remnants of roast mule from their teeth, others belched or made wind or scratched themselves like dogs, but all were intent on what the captive had to say and none missed a word of what had gone, or was to follow.

"First," continued Mackenna, "it should be clear that some way must be found in which I can guarantee my safety and that of the girl. Agreed?"

"Agreed," said Pelón.

"Then," nodded Mackenna, "in exchange for this concession, it is my part of the bargain that I shall lead you to Cañon del Oro from my memory of the map which old Enh drew in the sand. Agreed?"

"Agreed."

"All right, then here is what I propose: it must be arranged that an equal number of my friends will go with us upon the journey. We won't count the women, naturally."

"Naturally," said Pelón. "Go on."

"There are six of you, or you may say yourself and five men. Therefore, there should be five white men to go with me. Agreed?"

This time a long stillness stretched itself around the fire. Pelón's men were watching Pelón now, and not the white prospector. The bandit was conscious of this, and cautious because of it. He thought hard.

"Well," he ventured at last, "how would you propose that these five friends of yours should be gathered?"

"You know Al Seiber, of course?" Mackenna asked.

"Yes, of course. A good man. Even the Apaches trust him. Tough, too. A true *hombre duro.* But go on."

"Seiber would be my main friend. I would leave it to him to choose the four others."

"And how do we find Seiber?"

"I know him to be in Gila City. We were to have met there tomorrow for a trip we had planned into Sonora. There's a new strike down there near Fronteras. Maybe you've heard of it?"

"Yes. There's no gold there. Go on."

"I suggest you send your most trusted man to find Seiber at a place I will state. He can tell Seiber what we have—about the map, I mean—and that I have arranged to guide you in, but that I felt there ought to be more men and supplies and that this is the reason we have sent in for him, Seiber, and the others. As for me not coming myself, that is a simple matter. Your man can tell Seiber that you do not trust me and that I am staying with you to show good faith. How do you say?"

Pelón studied the matter. He looked at his men. "*Muchachos,*" he asked, "how do you see it?"

For a moment, none of them replied. Then the Chiricahua, Besh, nodded.

"Hachita and I are with you, Pelón. We said that to begin with. If you say to send for Seiber, we do also."

"I am for it, as well," said Sánchez, the sergeant deserter of the Mexican federal army. "After all, it's a long way to Cañon del Oro."

By the way that he said it, Mackenna knew exactly what he meant, but it was no time to question such moral niceties. What he, Mackenna, needed now were votes.

"I say yes, too," said Laguna Cahill, his undershot shark's smile gleaming momentarily. "That is, providing I am the one sent to Gila City. *Ay, Chihuahua!* The girl at that cantina down by the river is—well, no matter, *amigos* —just give me a minute to get my horse saddled!"

"Hold on!" barked Pelón. "Nobody said you could go. I don't think that I would depend on you to fetch fresh water from that flowing spring over there." He turned from Laguna to the last member of the pack. "Monkey," he demanded, "how say you? Do we send for Seiber and those four more white men?"

He didn't say gringos or yanquis or americanos, as ordinarily such a question would have been styled. He put an accent on the whole phrase "four more white men." This immediately took Mackenna's attention. It did not miss Monkey's, either.

"Four more, you say?" growled the Yaqui. "Four more *yori* brought right to us here in the desert? That sounds good to me, but how will we know that more than four will not follow? Who is to guarantee that?"

"You, if you like," said Pelón quickly. "I will send Laguna, who is least certain to have trouble in that place, and you can go with him to make sure that he does what he is supposed to do. All right, *hombre?*"

"Sure, that's fine." Monkey's agreement was made with an alacrity which did not escape the sharp eyes of Besh. The young Chiricahua raised his hand.

"If this animal is to go, then one must go to watch

him, as well," he said. "If he started back from Gila City with forty *yori*, he would arrive here with none. You know that, Pelón."

Mackenna's knowledge of the Yaqui tongue was limited to a dozen words. One of them was "*yori*, white men." He nodded swiftly in support of Besh's claim.

"That's so, Pelón," he said. "A third man must go."

Pelón grinned delightedly. "*Amigo*," he said, "it is more 'so' than you have any idea. The only reason that this one"—he pointed to the scowling Yaqui—"came along with us was because of the opportunity to see if there were any white scalps yet to be taken in Arizona. He knows the Indian's time is soon done in this land, and he wants a little something to show his grandchildren. You know how these things are, Mackenna. Just sentiment. A thing of the heart. But what is a man to do? Can I deny my own *muchachos* such a small thing?"

"Apparently not," nodded Mackenna grimly. "So that is it, eh? Laguna, Monkey and one other go to Gila City tomorrow. Which other will it be? Besh?"

At the calling of his name, the slender Apache stood up. He looked at Mackenna steadily.

"Yes, Besh," he said, in his deep rich voice.

If this were a challenge to Pelón, or to any of the others, it was not taken up. The bandit leader shrugged and waved his assent at once. Certain other details of the trip to and from the settlement were arranged and agreed upon by all parties. The camp then quickly made down for the night, both Mackenna and the white girl being chained to separate pine trees with centuries-old Spanish leg irons, which the ancient Apache crone produced from the camp baggage. There was no talk and no chance even to exchange glances. In a matter of minutes after Pelón signaled the end of the council, the tiny meadow was dark. The only sounds were those of the sleepers stirring occasionally in their blankets and of the stake-roped Apache ponies feeding in the gray-black grama grass beyond the spring.

8

Cornmeal Mush and Mule

WHEN MACKENNA awoke next morning it was with a belated start. The camp, save for the old woman, was deserted. The latter was at the fire cooking a gruel which, from its morbid odor, was *pinole con carne*, corn-meal mush with mule. Mackenna winced both at the smell and the attendant thought that the old woman would undoubtedly insist on serving him some of the stuff. To avoid this matter, as well as to establish the whereabouts of the vanished band, he decided to employ a portion of his dubious irresistibility.

"Good morning, Mother," he began cordially. "The beauty of the day is dimmed only by your own enchanting grace. *Santísima!* What is that I smell? *Pinole?* How wonderful! A lovely morning, a gracious woman, and good hot food. *Ay de mí!* What more could there be?"

The old woman straightened. She looked at him with the certain speculative detachment of the sand viper estimating the range of the approaching deermouse. Eventually she nodded, returning his greeting.

"Well," she said, "for one thing there could be this gun butt laid alongside your head."

She picked up the battered Winchester lying propped on the rock behind her cooking place, and Mackenna held up both hands in quick supplication.

"Please, Mother, I meant no disrespect! You must know that. But hear the birds sing! Smell the pine needles! Listen to the springwater calling to the grass! See it sparkle as it kisses each round stone and spit of gravel in its dance across the meadow! Isn't it all beautiful?"

The crone peered at him. She came a few steps closer to his chaining tree, head cocked, filmy reptilian eyes glittering with suspicion and yet holding some light of curiosity, as well.

"That's Indian talk," she challenged in her raven's croak. "White men don't care about the birds and the water and the grass."

"This white man does, Mother. I love this land."

"No, that's a lie. You are hungry for the gold that is here. You care nothing for the land."

"But I do," Mackenna insisted. "I hunt gold only so that I may stay in the land. I do it to buy food and blankets and ammunition and sometimes a little whiskey."

"Your tongue is a white tongue," said the old lady.

"No," smiled Mackenna, sticking out the member in question. "See, it's red. Just like yours."

She came on again, peering harder.

"It's a white tongue," she repeated. "It has its root in the middle instead of at the back. It wags both ways at the same time."

Mackenna spread his hands, surrendering gracefully. "There is truth in what you say, Mother. My people have many times talked two ways with your people. But think about it; is that my fault? Did I ever deceive the Apache? I am Mackenna. You know me. Do I lie?"

The old woman began to grow angry. Like most of her race, she did not know what to do about a good white man. All her experience had been in the other direction. Yet she knew that this red-headed and red bearded gentle-voiced captive was a good white man. And she got madder and madder because it was true and because he had stayed her hand by reminding her of it.

"Curse you," she snapped, "that's not fair! Of course, you have a good reputation among the Apache. How else do you think it is that Pelón has let you live? But now you obligate me by making me admit that you don't lie or cheat with us. Damn! That's a sneaky thing to do!"

"Well, Mother," said Mackenna soberly, "I didn't want you to split your gun stock on such a lovely morning. I'm sorry, but what else could I do?"

Suddenly, in that perverse way of her dark-skinned, savage kind, the old crone grinned and gave in.

"*Ih*," she exclaimed, "why should I lie to you, either? I didn't want to split your skull any more than you wished to break my gun. I think it's that bright red beard and those happy blue eyes, Mackenna, but you do have a way about you that calls to a woman. Hah! I saw that smirk! You think I'm too old, eh? Watch yourself. I can always mend a cracked gun stock, you know."

"As well, I will wager," said Mackenna gallantly, "as you could break a strong man's heart. What makes you think I ever doubted you as a woman, Mother? A little seasoning only brings out the full flavor, eh, *muchacha?*"

"Hih, hih, hih!" The wrinkled squaw showed her few stumps of teeth in the giggling laugh, and patted him on the head like a good dog. "Aye, that's right, *hijo!*" she cried. "Come on now, and have some of this *pinole*. We'll talk a little. I can tell you a few things that Pelón wouldn't. Here, let me unlock that damned old Spanish trap you have on your leg there."

"Mother," said Mackenna, putting out the manacled limb, "were I ten years younger, and you twenty, it would be a great mistake to unfasten me."

"Pipe smoke!" snorted the old lady, but was very pleased all the same.

At the fire, there was no way out for Mackenna and he was forced to eat of the mush and mule and to do so, lest he lose his little advantage with the Apache hag, with the appropriate lip smackings and belches to indicate that the latter was not notable alone for her great beauty but was, inclusively, a marvelous cook.

When he had choked down the last mouthful which he could manage, he helped the old woman with the cleaning up about the camp. In this, he was somewhat handicapped by the four-foot pine log to which she had chained him, in the fashion of a drag on a bear trap. But his companion was properly impressed, nonetheless, to see a man working at the homely chores. In return for this rare sight, she was of a mind to inform Mackenna of a few things pertinent to his position and to the time of Apache day there in the tiny mountain oasis of Surprise Grass.

For his interested part, Mackenna let the old lady talk as she would. Here and there he put in a word or two to direct the line of her chatterings, but in the main she required no such promptings. After all, she was an Apache of the old blood. She had seen many a white man sitting where Glen Mackenna was sitting, and she knew what were the thoughts which filled the mind of the gringo awaiting the return of the tribe's men from the war trail. They were simple thoughts and they had to be, for this white man knew Indians and knew Apaches in particular. He would not be wasting the powers of his brain in fanciful hopes or vain imaginings of mercy. He would be thinking straight thoughts, like an Apache, about the only two things which counted when all was said and done.

He would be thinking thoughts of life. And he would be thinking thoughts of death. *Naturalmente*.

9 ⋛

The Secret of Sno-ta-hay

A GARRULOUS INDIAN, much less an Apache, is hard to find. After five minutes, Mackenna knew he had struck it rich in the old lady. Her story proved a combination of loneliness, age, female perversity and an apparently honest liking for the blue-eyed white man.

To begin with, she told him—first gladly filling her own pipe from Mackenna's pouch, while permitting him his first smoke in twelve hours—this expedition of Pelón's was in good part her own fault. She was the last surviving child of the sister of Nana and Enh. As a female, her mother had never been permitted the secret of Cañon del Oro, called Sno-ta-hay by the Apache, and, of course, neither had she in her time been to the canyon. Only the men went there, ever.

Now in the old days of her mother, this sort of thing might have been acceptable. Presently, the times were changing. She herself did not take kindly to any such outright discrimination against women.

The old squaw paused, studying her listener. Presently she nodded, seeming to have taken a decision. Her name, she went on, was Mal-y-pai. This was plainly taken from the Spanish *malpaís*, meaning badland. Looking upon her, Mackenna would understand that the name was well chosen. He would agree, too, that her people did not flinch to call a stone a stone, or a toad a toad.

In response to this forthright confession, the bearded prospector declared soberly that he himself was little enough blessed in form and feature. Any discerning woman such as Mal-y-pai could surely observe that he was more bone than bulk, more string than strong.

The old Apache's good impression was scarcely diminished by such charming graciousness. More and more, she could see that this red-headed one might truly be what he claimed. She could almost begin to believe that he would sit and listen to the birds, smell the water, watch the grass grow, and be kind to poor people. What a peculiar white man!

"All right, Mackenna," she agreed. "As a woman, I refuse to accept your statement that you are stringy and bony. But even if I did, since when has a goodly portion of bone been a handicap to a man, eh? What do you say to that, *hombre?*" She broke into her silly cackle and Mackenna, blushing, nodded. In another moment, she wiped the tears of enjoyment from her eyes and continued.

"Now, for many years I have cared for old Enh. You must know he was nearing ninety summers. Nana, you remember, was over seventy when he began his last campaign against the Army, and that was fifteen summers gone. Enh was a little younger than Nana, but not much.

"So, being that I had the work of cooking and watching out after the old devil, and inasmuch as I was rather of a mind that a woman was at least half as worthy as a man, it began to take root in my cautious female thoughts that I ought to know where all of that gold was hidden over there in Sno-ta-hay—even where the canyon itself was.

"Thus, I started carefully to talk a circle around old Enh about it. At first, he thought I was merely chattery. Then he saw that I meant it, and he grew quiet and nervous.

"You see, he felt that his time was near and he did not know, really, what to do about the secret. He was half of a mind to let it die with him and half of a mind that it would be a crime against our people if he were to do so. I could understand his trouble and did not press him over it. But then I realized, some weeks later, that he was failing for the last time. It came to me that if someone did not get this secret from him, it would actually be lost to our people. I prevailed upon him with this argument, convincing him that the conquest of the Apache by the white man did not lessen the woes of the Indian in this land, but only increased them. Our people might stand in need of the gold in Sno-ta-hay far more in the summers to come than they ever had in the days of Enh and Chief Nana and Victorio and Mangas Coloradas and Nachez and Goleta and Cochise, those great fighters of the high old days of our power in Arizona; yes, and over there in New Mexico, too."

She paused to fish a piece of mule from the congealing bed of the cornmeal in the black pot over the breakfast embers. Mouthing the tidbit, she cocked her birdlike black eyes at the white man.

"I will wager my old Winchester against your saddle," she said, "that you are wondering why I left Geronimo out of that naming of our great ones. Am I right?"

Mackenna admitted that the thought had occurred to him as naturally as it would had a white soldier omitted the name of General "Redbeard" Crook from a listing of the finer officers who had fought the Apache.

"Aha!" cried the crone. "Just as always with you white *idiotas!* You don't know the real Indians, at all."

"Well," said Mackenna, "there you may be right; but I know this of Geronimo: such as Mangas and Cochise would not have given him a good morning. Geronimo was just a treacherous dog. His people, those who went with him when he broke his word and fled from Crook after his surrender, were also treacherous dogs. Whatever the color of their skin would have been, they would not have been people that you and I would want in our *jacals*."

The old lady looked at him a long time. Finally she spat out a piece of the hide of the mule which had adhered to her morsel from the pot and was too much for her remaining tooth snaggles to deal with.

"I take it back about your tongue," she said. "You don't have a white tongue. To begin with, you have that strange little sound to your *yanqui* talk. That's different. One ought to have noted that in the start and been made to think by it. You are not really an *americano*, are you, Mackenna?"

"Yes, Mother, by adoption. I was born in a far country called Scotland, but my father and my mother brought me here when I was only a child, and I am an *americano* as much as any man who is born in this land of white skin. Of course, you know that your red people are the real Americans."

The old hag exposed her few fangs in what Mackenna guessed was a good-humored grin. "Yes," she said, "we have been saying this for some time; it is the *yanquis* who don't seem to understand the matter, not the Apaches."

"True, true, Mother. But I have interrupted your thoughts. You were telling of Sno-ta-hay."

Mal-y-pai nodded slyly. "*Something* of it," she corrected.

"But of course," said Mackenna. "Please to go on."

The peculiar thing about the secret of Sno-ta-hay, said the old lady, accepting his direction, was that all the people thought its location had died with Nana. The old chief had been taken suddenly some years before and was assumed not to have made preparation to pass along the key to the treasure. But the people ought to have known Nana better than that. Still, for all those years the secret lay hidden and, as far as any Apache—save one—knew, also gone forever. That one Apache was, of course, old Enh. All along he had held the secret in trust from Nana but it had been only the past month, when he himself knew he was going to die, that he had let it be known to the next inheritor that he had the location of the gold locked in his mind and his memory.

At this point, Mackenna told Mal-y-pai that he knew of this from Pelón, to which the old lady snapped that Pelón's knowing of it constituted her whole story, and that if Mackenna wasn't interested in hearing it he had merely to say so.

"What the hell do you think I am wasting my time on you for?" she demanded angrily. "Didn't I say I would tell you some things Pelón would not?"

It took Mackenna five minutes of small lies and Celtic blandishments to soothe her ruffled feathers, but finally she quit scolding and went on.

The sneaky old coyote, Enh, had been unable to find any man of the tribe whom he would trust with the secret of Sno-ta-hay. The thing was, actually, that he and his niece, Mal-y-pai, were the last of the "old ones" in the band, and none of its modern members had been to the canyon but had only heard of it. Some said—and Mal-y-pai believed it true—that no Apache had been in Sno-ta-hay since Nana's death. Another story held that the canyon's secret had originally been given to three bands, the Chiricahua of Cochise and the Mimbreño of Mangas Coloradas the Elder, as well as the band of old Nana. But if this were so, Mal-y-pai could not say. All she knew was that in her time no Apaches other than those of Nana's had visited the gold. It might truly be that the Chiricahuas and Mimbreños had originally shared the custodianship of the canyon with Nana, but of what point were any such speculations? If the other two bands had once known the way into Sno-ta-hay, they no longer did so, any more than did Nana's people. It was a matter which only Yosen, only God, might decide anyway. Old Mal-y-pai was only interested in what *she* knew.

And what she knew was that Enh, failing to discover the man with whom he could safely leave the secret, had broken Apache tradition in a moment of senile despondency and left the location of the gold with a woman! Yes! Mackenna had heard her correctly. A woman!

"I don't need to tell one with such sharp blue eyes as your own," she chided the prospector, "which woman that was, do I? Of course not. It was myself, old Mal-y-pai."

Mackenna spread his hands and moved his wide shoulders with that all-meaning hunch which he had acquired from the Larins and Indians of that parched land.

"Why not?" he asked her. "What better *olla* could he have chosen into which to pour such precious fluid?"

Unadorned as the flattery was, Mal-y-pai chose not to examine it, but went along with her story. Now it had come about, she said, that shortly after his confession of the secret to her, the old man disappeared. Naturally this caused some talk among the people. Just because they were of the new ways and no longer honored the old legends and histories, this did not mean that they were not greedy for gold. These modern Indians, damn them for their next

ten returns to earth, had been poisoned by the white man's
worship of the yellow metal. They had been shown what
it would buy in terms of whiskey and rich food and fast
horses and new guns and anything a man might wish to
soften his life and his head. And so they had come to think
of Sno-ta-hay as more of a place where they had a lot of
money waiting for them than as a sacred place which they
must defend from the white man and the Mexican because
it was holy and because it had belonged to the Apache
since time was counted.

But now, with Enh's disappearance, a terrible thing
was discovered. All of the people of the various bands who
had assumed that someone in their own tribes had also held
the secret, began asking about for their own particular
keeper of the trust. It was then they found out only Enh
had the secret.

"So, believe it," gestured the wrinkled crone, stabbing
a taloned forefinger at Mackenna, "there really was some
excitement going forward presently.

"There was enough, in fact," she continued, "to travel
along the Apache 'telegraph' all the way down into Sonora
and to reach the ugly ears of Pelón López.

Pelón, of course, had come up into Arizona on the
gallop, gathering his band along the way, including that
wretched betrayer of her people's trust, the withered and
traitorous old Gila monster named Mal-y-pai.

Mackenna's blue eyes opened a bit at this information,
and the ancient squaw removed her pipestem from between
the four yellowed stumps which held it in her mouth. Rolling her tongue, she spat noddingly into the fire and fumbled
beneath her skirt to bring forth a pouch which the white
man recognized as the "medicine bag" used to hold the
hoddentin, or "magic powder of sacred meaning" of the
Apache people. Taking a bit of this between thumb and

forefinger, the old lady sprinkled it into the fire. It made a moment's blue and yellow and green flame, like common salt, but formed also a puff of pure white smoke as large and thick as that given off in the discharge of an old black-powder trade musket. Mal-y-pai's dark lips moved sound-lessly and her pouched eyes turned briefly up toward the morning sun.

"That's for Yosen," she explained apologetically to Mackenna. "You never know when he might be listening. He's a snoopy old devil."

She sat a moment, thinking back.

"Well," she said, "you know what happened. Pelón, because his Apache mother had been a member of Nana's band, came directly to us when the story had reached him of old Enh's flight with the secret of Sno-ta-hay. Also, of course, he had this half-sister of his living with us. So no doubt he expected to get something important from her about Enh, where he might not have gotten much from the rest of us."

"That's the woman called Hesh-ke?" asked Mackenna. "The one without the nose?"

The crone threw back her bony head and cackled like a loon at sunset.

"Hesh-ke!" she snorted. "What is that? Some more of Pelón's nonsense? That she-dog's name is Sally. Yes, it's true, a *yanqui* name. That Apache mother of hers and Pelón's shared her blanket with every scrub animal which wandered into our *ranchería*. One of these brush-breeders was a white man. I won't mention his name; you might know his people: one of them has gone very high in the affairs of Arizona since that time. Well, regardless, this mother-bitch of Sally's, she thought to give her she-whelp some advantages with the Agency people and so claimed that this white scrub stud had fathered the child. You can see for yourself how white that one's sire must have been. Hah! I have the skin color of an old army saddle, and I am six shades lighter than she is! White father, indeed! *Dios mio!*"

Mackenna, sensing that the old crone was at last coming to the nub of it, said nothing, and she went on.

"You may imagine," she sighed, "that I am a woman of many virtues, but, alas, I deceive you. My weaknesses are more than my resolves, and the greatest among them is a certain inability to withstand the administration of *tulapai.*"

Tulapai was a corn-mash liquor manufactured by the Apache to a proof standard about twice that of frontier whiskey. Mackenna, having sampled it on more than one *ranchería* in his wanderings, understood Mal-y-pai's great sigh of regret. It was a liquid of many good uses. It would burn in a lamp. It would soften leather. It would cauterize wounds. It would bleach cloth. It would disinfect the *jacal* after smallpox or tuberculosis or glandular epizoöty. It would remove rust from an old gun. It would make a rubbing liniment to cure a lame horse, or a pouring medicine to burn out screwworms from the hide of a sick cow. But it was never, never to be taken internally. Not unless the intention was to cremate the stomach and cut a hole straight through the bowels.

"You have my sympathy, Mother," the bearded prospector nodded. "I have survived this experience myself."

"*Valiente!*" cried the old woman. "I knew you were a real man. How long were you sick with it?"

"The *tulapai?* Only a week or so. I took but a small cup each time. And, of course, this was some years ago."

"Aye," said the old lady, with another of her epochal exhalings of regret. "When we are young nothing is fatal, not even *tulapai.* But you must remember that I am no longer a girl, Mackenna. So it was that when Pelón arrived in our village he heard that Enh had transferred the secret to me and he recalled in this connection my well-known lack of strength. All that it cost him to wring from me what I knew of Sno-ta-hay was the price of one small jug of *tulapai*, and perhaps half an hour devoted to getting the cursed stuff out of the *olla* and into me. *Ay, María!*"

Mackenna was frowning now. "I don't understand, Mother," he said. "If Pelón got the secret out of you, why was he trailing old Enh? And why, *por Dios*, is he holding me?"

"Very simple," shrugged the old lady. "I got so drunk I forgot all about the canyon. I couldn't remember one damned thing about it, except that Enh had told me how to get there and had drawn me the same sand maps he drew for you. It was in my mind like a reflection in a looking glass. But that *tulapai* bleached my brain just like it does a feedsack for making a dress out of. *Ih!*"

"*Ih*, indeed," said Mackenna. "What else?"

"Oh, a few small things else. Not too many. Such as that Pelón brought me along in the hunt for Enh, thinking I might get my memory back. He knew better than to try and torture me. I am an Apache."

"Of course," said Mackenna.

"Then, there was the matter of Sally; Pelón needed someone to keep Monkey's mind on the business of the trip. That one has to have a woman every day. So Pelón brought along his half-sister from our *ranchería* and also that fat Pima girl, who was a sort of slave in a Mescalero camp we visited and for whom Pelón paid a good price—three belts of Winchester cartridges and a lame horse, as I remember. He does not steal from his mother's people, that Pelón. He is a good boy."

"A very good boy," nodded Mackenna. "I am in your

debt, Mother, for all this kind talk. As you know, a man grows desperate in his mind to know what his enemies are doing."

The old woman looked at him, snake's eyes glittering.

"But you don't really worry about your enemies, Mackenna. You don't fool this old crow. I saw you staring at that skinny girl last night. That's the one you're thinking of."

Mackenna did not know how to play the next approach, but decided to stay with the straight course.

"The morning that I can deceive you, Mother," he said, "has not yet seen its sun. I may as well confess; the slender girl interests me."

"Hah! Interested in her, you say? *Ay de mí!* If you were loose and her parents or her big brother were not around to watch over her, you would run her up the nearest blind canyon and put her in the grass as quick as that damned Monkey."

"My God, Mother," protested Mackenna, "that's a terrible thing to say!"

"Oh, sure," said the old lady. "You could lie there with her in the grama and weep about it all day long."

"I won't listen to such villainous talk," said Mackenna. "That poor girl doesn't deserve it. She's a good girl and you know that she is."

"I am overcome by your indignation," said Mal-y-pai. "Let us hope she's still a good girl when she gets back today."

This was what Mackenna had been waiting for; this was the crux of all the counterplay over the breakfast-fire ashes. Where was the girl? Where were all of them? What were they up to?

"Mother," he said bluntly, "where are the men? What

are they doing that requires Sally and the Pima woman and the white girl? Something is wrong. I feel it."

"You had better get a new feeler," croaked Mal-y-pai.

"Oh?"

"Certainly. There is nothing wrong. Pelón has gone out with Sánchez and Hachita to watch the trails until Besh and Monkey and Laguna get back from Gila City with those white men. All left together in the blackness of first dawn. As for the women, Pelón thought that he would rather have Sally where he could watch her. You see, she has decided that she likes your red beard and blue eyes. Moreover, she is weary with Monkey. *Ih!* Who wouldn't be! What an animal! Anyway, Sally has been watching you."

"Damn!" said Mackenna. "Don't talk like that!"

"So," said his companion, ignoring him utterly, "Pelón, who sees everything in this camp, took Sally with him in order that she wouldn't get at you today and perhaps be swayed to help you escape." She paused, eyeing the white man. "You know," she said, "that Sally is what you would call a female of the same precise wildness which inhabits Monkey as a male. Do you understand me?"

"Only too well," groaned Mackenna. "But the white girl, Mother, what about her? You know that she is the one about whom my heart wonders."

"What does your heart wonder about her?" asked the old woman leeringly. "Does it ask if those little breasts are as hot and hard as they look? Or has it noticed that for a slim one, her skirt stretches very tightly across the buttocks when she walks? Come now, Mackenna, I know all about men's hearts. They aren't located in the chest, like a woman's heart. They're down below the—well, never

mind; just don't insult me with any more talk of your
'high' feelings, *chico*. A man is a man."

Mackenna flushed but remained silent. He had the
rare touch for not saying anything when there was nothing
to say. The old crone, seeing his color change, showed
genuine surprise.

"*Valgame!*" she cried. "Could it be that you mean it?
You were embarrassed just now. My God, possibly you do
have the true feeling for her. Damn! That's not fair, Mackenna. You know that any woman is made foolish by the
sight of true love. You're taking advantage of me."

"Come, be foolish then," said the quick-witted prospector, recovering. "Tell me about the girl, Mother, *por
favor*. You can see that she has me by the heart, that I am
helpless. Will you let me suffer, then?"

Mal-y-pai stared at him, her seamed face showing no
hint of charity, no clue to any kindness whatever.

Then her ochred fangs were uncovered and what was
almost certainly a twinkle glinted far back in the beady,
birdlike orbs.

"Ah! Those blue eyes!" She sighed. "Small wonder
Pelón had to tie Sally to him with a staking rope last night
to keep her in her blankets. The slut. She knows a good
thing when she sees it."

10

A Troop of Cavalry Far Off

"WELL," began Mal-y-pai, "as for the white girl being taken with the men this morning, I don't know. My guess would be that she will not suffer. I think Pelón meant only to have her away from you; to let you fret and to get your concern fed to that point where you would make easier handling in the matter of the long trip to Sno-ta-hay. If she will return as virtuous as she set out, God alone can guarantee. But she will return. Pelón is a peculiar one, you know. He has a certain few rules by which he lives."

"Yes," said the white man brusquely. "I am familiar with some of them."

"No, I mean honor rules. Do not be funny with me."

"Please, Mother. Pelón López? Honor rules?"

"Mackenna, all men have some honor. In Pelón, it is deep-hidden, but it is there."

"We won't argue it, Mother."

"Good."

"Will you go on about the girl? Where did you get her?"

"Oh, yes. Well, it was yesterday morning, as Pelón

has told you. We were all at this white *rancho*, watering
our ponies and being given some nice warm food by the
good people there. Naturally they did not give us this kindness because they were good people, but because they were
frightened people. You know how that would be with such
as Pelón and Monkey and that giant Hachita seated to your
table. Well, when the food was eaten and the ponies had
drunk their fill, Besh, who had been left on the back trail
to watch for soldiers, came up on the gallop to say that a
troop of cavalry was coming far off. At this, Pelón, who
knows the outlaw business as you do that of the gold hunting, seized your slim girl, the daughter of that household,
and he said to her people: 'Too bad, my friends, but if the
soldiers come after us, then we must have something to
serve as our passport back across the border. We won't
hurt the girl if we can help it, and you have my word that
we will sell her back to you for a fair price when the
time comes. Now, don't make trouble, I beg of you. I
know what I am doing.'

"Well, you can imagine what the parents of such a
fine-looking but skinny and underfed young woman would
think. The father was very brave. He tried to reach his
rifle on its pegs above the kitchen door. Monkey killed
him with his bare hands, by beating his head into the frame
of that door. Of course, his wife screamed pretty loud at
this, and before Pelón could interfere, Monkey had also
killed her, striking her in the face with the iron poker from
the stove. He damn near drove it to her ears, from across
the bridge of her nose. You never saw such a mess."

Mackenna swallowed hard to keep down the mule and
cornmeal mush, which wanted mightily to come up.

"You know," said the old lady, "it was a strange thing,
then. This Besh said something to Hachita, and Hachita

took up Monkey in his great hands, as though Monkey were a day-old baby, and it was plain to all of us that the Yaqui was drawing his next-to-final wind. But Pelón was out with that *pistola* of his, which is forever ready beneath the serape, and he commanded to know what Besh had ordered his friend Hachita to do with Monkey. Besh answered frankly that he had told the big Mimbreño to bash the head of Monkey, as Monkey had bashed those of the white people. It seemed that Besh knew these people, and that they had been good to him at one time."

Mackenna frowned quickly.

"Do you mean that Besh knew this white girl, then, before yesterday?"

"I didn't say that. I said her parents. The girl was not living there at the time the parents befriended Besh."

"How do you know she's the daughter, then? Did this develop in the talk before the killing?"

"Yes. The girl was not their true daughter, but a niece, the daughter of the man's brother in the other part of the country." Old Mal-y-pai pointed eastward, and Mackenna nodded his understanding that "the other part of the country" meant anything beyond the Apache realm of Arizona, Mexico and New Mexico.

"Go on," he said quietly.

"There's little more to tell. We went on. We rode fast and got away from the soldiers. The girl, naturally, went with us. We also got a nice Mexican woman while at the same *rancho*. She was the servant there. Pelón decided to add her to Monkey's supply of women. But at the second camp from there, when it was her turn to receive the Yaqui, she killed herself with a knife drawn over her wrists and when Monkey went to get her he found only the blood under the blanket. That was a brave woman, but not smart.

Lupe, the fat Pima, she is smart. She had a knife, too, but
would rather take Monkey's blade than her own. Hih, hih,
hih! That's a devil's choice, eh, Mackenna?"

"Yes," agreed the bearded prospector.

"Well, I've told you all of it, *hombre*, except about
Besh and Hachita and Laguna and Sánchez. I can be quick
about them. The last two came up from Sonora with Pelón.
The other two I know just as little of. They came to our
ranchería—Nana's village, that is—only a short time before
Pelón. Besh, who does all the talking for both of them, said
only that they came as representatives of their people and
were present to discuss the matter of the secret of Sno-ta-
hay. What it was they had to discuss we never learned, for
the pack of Pelón arrived to interrupt us. When Besh
learned of Pelón's mission to pursue old Enh, he said not
one more word except that he and his giant friend would
go with Pelón's band, since their mission shared a common
interest with that of the outlaws."

She broke off her story to peer over Mackenna's head,
squinting into the rising sun.

"If you want to know anything else," she muttered,
getting up and reaching for her battered rifle, "you will
have to ask Pelón. Here he comes."

By the time Mackenna found his feet, he could hear
the rattle of the unshod horses' hoofs on the flinty rock of
the trail. Next moment, Pelón and Hachita came into view,
both riding double. The bandit leader had the white girl
mounted up behind him, while, in his great arms, Hachita
still carried the grotesquely stiffened form of old Enh, the
dead Apache Prairie Dog.

Behind the bearded prospector, Mal-y-pai mumbled an
apology and struck him wickedly in the back of the head
with the butt of her Winchester. Mackenna saw bright
whirling suns and upending yellow mountains, and that

was all. He went into the gray dust of the fireside as silently as a hammer-struck steer.

"A thousand pardons, Blue Eyes," said the old lady,
bending over him and unlocking him from the drag log,
"but you see it is that Pelón told me not to let you loose.
Now I shall have to tell him a black lie that you struck
me and seized the key. *Ay de mí!* The terrible injuries to
one's honor that must be suffered!"

11

The Crazy Niece of Nana

MACKENNA BLACKED OUT only for a few moments. The blow from Mal-y-pai's riflebutt had been a glancing one, more shocking than wounding in its effect. When he did recover, it was because the deerflies were biting him. The attentions of the black and white insects were like the jabs of a hundred hypodermic needles, except that the flies, once injected, would not withdraw their syringes until satiated with blood, or until the victim mashed them on his arm or face. Mackenna awoke cursing and pawing at himself. Between swipes at the camp pests he felt of the back of his injured head and stared blinkingly around the meadow.

He was chained to the pine tree once more. By the fire, Pelón drank coffee. Mal-y-pai attended him. Across the fire from them, the white girl sat dejectedly and forlorn upon the pine chunk to which the old squaw had fastened Mackenna. Pelón was explaining the return.

"It was this damned girl," he said to Mal-y-pai. "She could not stand the heat out there in the rocks. She began to get pale and when she had vomited two times, I knew that I had better get her back here to the shade. I did not care to lose her, of course. Not until Mackenna takes us to Sno-ta-hay."

"How about the Mimbreño?" asked the squaw, hunching a shoulder at Hachita, who was sitting under a pine apart from the fire, still holding old Enh as though he were a sick child rather than a mortifying corpse. "What the devil was he doing with you? Watching you for the damned Chiricahua? I don't trust those two. They know something."

"So do I," said Pelón. "That Hachita is no older in his brain than a baby. He won't let go of that body. He says either we wait while he takes it back to Nana's band, or he quits. He doesn't care. But as soon as his friend, Besh, gets back from Gila City, he is going to take the old man's body back to Nana's *ranchería*. Now, that's bad. It could mean real trouble."

"Yes, that's so," agreed Mal-y-pai. "With a simpleton like that, who knows what he would say about us and our trip to Sno-ta-hay? By God, Pelón, he can't be allowed to do it. With his wandering tongue, he might have half the Indians in this part of Arizona tracking us down. Not to mention the soldiers and the sheriff from Gila. *Ay, Dios!* Here, lend me your pistol, Pelón. My rifle's hammer is broken and it won't fire."

"I suppose, you stupid old magpie," replied Pelón, "that you mean to blow out his skull?"

"Of course. What else is there to do?"

"And his friend, Besh? You would shoot him, too?"

"Why not?"

"Well, for one thing, their people know that they came to Nana's village to see you. Their people also know *why* they came to see you. On the other hand, Nana's band will certainly tell those people that Hachita and Besh went

with Pelón López to see if they could not find old Enh and
torture the secret of the gold of Sno-ta-hay out of him."

"*Ih!* So what of that?"

"So this of that, old woman: if it is your idea of a
smart thing to do, to have the Chiricahua and Mimbreño
Apache learn that we shot their messengers Besh and Hachita, then I must say that you are a female jackass."

"A female jackass? How could that be? A female
jackass is a jenny. A jackass is always a male. As well, a
male is always a jackass. All males. Including you, Pelón
López, you baldheaded half-breed bastard."

"Well, lovely one," shrugged the outlaw leader, "just
be thankful you are of the pure blood and beautiful. Do
not try, also, to show brains. Leave that to Pelón, eh?"

"Bah!"

"Bah all you want. Wasn't it you, brilliant one, who
let Mackenna get away from you?"

"It wasn't fair, he struck me while my back was
turned."

"You mean the same way you struck him at the fire
just as I returned?"

"Sure, but he's a white man. They're not supposed to
act like an Indian."

"True."

Pelón nodded the concession and both he and the old
woman sat frowning and thinking their separate thoughts.
Chained to his melancholy pine, Mackenna did the same.
Slumped upon her wooden hassock, the thin white girl no
doubt had an equal disposition. It was very quiet in the
outlaw camp.

12

Old Friends and Greedy Dogs

IT WAS sunset of the second day. By Pelón's reckoning, his men ought to have returned some hours sooner. Sánchez, his apparent second-in-command, shared the uneasiness. If the giant Mimbreño Apache, Hachita, was also concerned, he did not show it. He sat by a big rock downwind of the fire, where Pelón had ordered him to remove himself. It had been another very hot day and the odor of Enh was grown to a formidable stench. Mackenna, freed from his pine tree that he might come to the fire and feed himself, most surely joined the outlaws in their unrest. If the Gila City party did not return, or if it returned but did not bring Seiber and the other white men—well, there was little profit in such ifs. Mackenna could put it far more simply: the Gila City party had better return, and return with Seiber and Company. The option to this was a long hard trip to Sno-ta-hay alone with Pelón and Sánchez.

Such a trip was, in turn, a certain guarantee of serious trouble from the American Apache bands. Pelón was extremely unpopular above the border by virtue of the army troops and civil-law officers stirred up by his periodic visits.

These raids led inevitably to innocent U.S. Indians getting killed or injured in the excitement over Pelón's invaders. It followed that unless Pelón's present party stayed intact, and strong, all six of its original members remaining loyal for the entire journey to Sno-ta-hay, the local Arizona Indians would almost surely annihilate them somewhere on the trail of the sacred canyon.

However, it was not this prospect of his own death in the desert which consumed Mackenna's thoughts. It was the danger to the girl. She, at the moment, was wisely off in the shadows beyond the fire. Earlier she and Mackenna had risked some guarded effort to exchange fleeting looks or small hand signs. But the contacts had been too costly. Each time that Pelón intercepted one of the attempts, he would command the ancient squaw to beat the girl. It was a crude device, and potent. After the second beating, both Mackenna and the girl kept their eyes on the ground, using only peripheral vision and what acuity of hearing they had to keep track of one another. In itself, this was a trying thing. Added to the general tension over the delayed return of the Gila City messengers, it bore heavily upon the two white captives. Another hour went by. The strain of the waiting grew intolerable. Pelón spoke.

"I think we had better start to discuss what will occur if my men and yours do not come back," he said to Mackenna. "I will not abandon my purpose. My instincts tell me that you have it perfectly in your memory how to go to the canyon and find Adams' gold. You will take me there if I have to ride on your shoulders and drive you with my spurs. My friend Sánchez is in agreement. Hachita doesn't matter. Indeed, I wish to God he *would* leave. I can't stand much more of the fragrance of that dead Indian."

Mackenna waited a moment, then shrugged.

"There is nothing to discuss," he said. "We are in a game of cards. You hold the deck."

It was now Pelón who looked at Mackenna.

"Do you remember," he asked, "that time that I came upon you in that Mescalero *ranchería* some years ago?"

"Perfectly," replied the white prospector, wincing. "The remaining toes of my right foot thank you eternally."

"I bought you from those Apaches for a small sum and I took you close to San Carlos and set you free and told you to remember the service. Is this not so?"

"Yes," admitted Mackenna. "And you will likewise recall that some summers after that, there was a certain cavalry patrol which had cornered a fugitive in a box canyon down on the Salt Fork where a certain prospector was washing for color. You may bring back in your memory the fact that this prospector hid you in his cabin and lied to the patrol of soldiers and said to them that he had seen no other human beings than themselves since the spring melting of the snow. Is this not also true?"

"Damn, yes!" said Pelón vehemently.

"Well, then, we are quits."

"No, by God, that's not the way I see it!" denied the outlaw. "The way I see it is that we are old friends come together again by good chance and bound upon the same mission. As well, I see it that we are on our honor as men of conscience and good will."

Mackenna responded to this entreaty by staring hard into the blackness of the desert night.

"What the devil are you looking for?" demanded Pelón.

"I am waiting for the lightning," answered Mackenna.

"What is that? What lightning?"

"The lightning of the Lord," said Mackenna. "I am waiting for it to strike you dead on your haunches."

"Do you say that I lie?"

"Of course."

"All right, then, we are both greedy dogs sniffing out the same hidden bone which some other greedy dog has buried long ago. Does that suit your stomach better, *amigo?*"

"You must have some point to make," said Mackenna. "The only difficulty is that you are not jabbing me with it hard enough."

Pelón moved with deceiving quickness for one so coarse and heavy. He seized the white prospector and slit the buttons from his shirt, top to bottom, with his knife. The cut went through the thin cloth and opened the skin in a twenty-inch razorline which left Mackenna gasping with pain. When, in the following moment, the bright blood welled up from the shallow incision, the half-breed nodded with satisfaction, stepped back around the fire and sank again to his haunches.

"My point is that we are in this hunt as partners, Mackenna, not as enemies," he explained. "If you want me to jab you harder with that point, I will do it."

"No," gritted Mackenna, "once is sufficient. But I'm curious, Pelón. If we are such ancient and honorable associates, how is it that you feel compelled to attack me all the while?"

The outlaw hunched his shoulders.

"If I attack you," he replied, "it is for your own benefit. Remember, *amigo*, that I have also saved your life during this same time. Or do you think Monkey was playing with that rock he raised over your head?"

"I'll admit you puzzle me," said Mackenna. "All right, let's have your discussion of the missing Gila City people. I'm ready now."

"You are very stubborn, Mackenna," scowled Pelón.

"I don't understand you. You could have let me go ahead to begin with, and saved yourself that scratch on your belly. What is the trouble with you? Are you stupid, after all?"

"No," said Mackenna, "I'm Scotch."

"Are they anything like the Irish?"

"Cousins, you might say."

"Aha! I thought so. That Laguna Cahill is by an Irish father, and he also has a head like a granite cannonball."

"Thank you," said Mackenna gravely. "What about the matter of those Gila City people?"

"Yes, excuse me," nodded Pelón, "here is the way that I view the problem . . ."

Whatever the way was that he envisioned for the continuance of the search for Sno-ta-hay without the Gila City party, it remained unstated. As he began to speak, a desert coyote yammered suddenly and in a peculiar pitch from the barren slope of the Yaqui Spring trail. Instantly, Pelón leaped to kick the fire into a dozen scattered brands, which old Mal-y-pai beat out with her blanket. The meadow was dark in ten seconds.

"*Quién es?*" whispered Mackenna nervously.

"It's Besh," growled Pelón. "But be still and listen. *That's our signal for soldiers coming.*"

13

The Buffalo Soldiers

THE CRY of the coyote came several times more, each time closer to the camp. Mackenna, old as he was to the Apache arts, marveled anew at the absolute reality of the yapping going forward in the rocks below. Had not Pelón said so, not even Mackenna could have said if these were animals or men approaching.

Suddenly, startlingly, Besh appeared out of the night and stood within ten feet of Pelón. His deep Indian voice said, in Spanish, that the situation was all right for the moment and that he had given the warning because he could see the fire's reflection halfway up the trail and he was not entirely sure that it might not, also, be visible from Yaqui Spring, where the soldiers had stopped.

"*Ih! gracias!*" said Pelón. "Next time, let the bastards come. You frightened me with your damned ki-yiying."

"Better that than to lose that hairless scalp," answered the Apache. "These are buffalo soldiers, Pelón."

"What? Colored men? I don't believe it!"

"Wait until morning and see for yourself. Those black soldiers are hard to see at night."

Mackenna grinned. Watching the tall young Apache, he was not certain that it was a small Indian joke, but he wanted to think that it was. He liked this Besh. There was a cleanness and direction about him which did not go with the rest of the renegade band. But Pelón, if he, too, saw the joke, was not amused by it.

"Damn," he said, "that's a dismal thing! You know, I don't like those *Negroes*. The white soldiers laugh at them and say they are no good in a fight. That hasn't been my experience. They fight like hell."

"Once they are aroused," agreed Besh, "they are very mean fighters. They will not quit. They are hard to start, it is true. But once they have their blood up, they will kill you. And I think these may have their blood up. They are the same ones which chased us from the *rancho* where you took the girl."

"Damn," said Pelón again, and was silent.

Besh let him brood a moment, then said unexpectedly, "I have the white men with me; do you want me to bring them on up now?"

"What? You do? Why the devil didn't you say so?"

"You didn't inquire."

"Oh, you crazy Indian! I assumed you had failed when you appeared alone out of the darkness. Do you play with me, Besh? I remind you, I am not playful."

"I remind you, also, that I do not fail. I will go and get the white men." The Apache paused, frowning. "There is only one thing," he said. "I could gather but three white men. Seiber was not at the meeting place, but sent another man. This other man was agreeable to us, and so we allowed him to find two others. He did this. So I bring three, rather than the five of the agreement with Mackenna."

"*Jesús María!*" exploded Pelón.

"Also there is one more thing," said Besh. "I have lost

Laguna Cahill. He disappeared into the front door of that cantina by the river and we never saw him again. We would have known nothing whatever of him except that this other white man who came in Seiber's place, he found Monkey and myself waiting out in the sagebrush and said Laguna had told him we wanted to see him. This white man speaks Apache better than I do. He told us that Laguna had stolen two horses in Gila City and fled across the river for Mexico with this girl from the cantina. So now that's all of it."

"My God," raged Pelón, "it's certainly enough! And, by the way, congratulations. That's the longest speech I ever heard from you. I didn't realize you knew that many words."

"Thank you," said Besh gravely. "I will go and get the white men. Monkey is watching them and I would not care to be away from them too long."

"*Santos!*" shouted the outlaw leader. "Go!"

When the Apache youth had faded from sight, Pelón turned to Mal-y-pai. "Make another very small fire," he ordered. "Set it in under the overhanging rock, there. That way its light won't get directly into the sky and won't be seen farther than we can afford. My God, I've got to have some coffee, buffalo soldiers or no buffalo soldiers."

To Glen Mackenna, he growled, "I hope these white men from Gila City are good ones. I don't like it that Seiber couldn't come. I smell something."

"I think we all do," broke in the old squaw. "It's that damned flyblown Enh, over there with Hachita. If that Mimbreño fool does not bury that carrion by sunrise, I myself will shoot him between his stupid eyes and put him in the same hole with the old man."

"A good idea," said Sánchez, the silent Mexican sergeant-deserter. "I will pay you two pesos for the job."

"Shut up, both of you," ordered Pelón. "I was talking to Mackenna."

"As you will, *Jefe*." Sánchez shrugged. "As you know, I am interested in but one thing, the Adams gold."

"Well, for the love of the sweet Christ!" snapped Pelón. "Do you suppose that I came up here to smell dead old Indians, or shoot skulling rocks out of the hands of stupid crazy Yaqui monkeys, or send half-bred Irish Mexicans to Gila City so they can run off with cantina bitches, or to fight buffalo soldiers? I, too, have visions of the gold, you damned fool Federale dog!"

"Gently, gently," soothed Sánchez. "You were talking with Mackenna, *amigo*."

"Oh, yes. Well, Mackenna, as I said, I don't like it that Seiber didn't come. There isn't another white man in Arizona who I would trust, or who these Apaches with me will trust. I agreed because it was Seiber you said would come. No other will do."

"There must be one other," said the white prospector quietly. "Besh brought this new man back, did he not?"

Pelón looked at him and blinked.

"Well, yes, he did. I hadn't thought of it that way."

"Then, think of it. The answer is quite simple."

"Yes?"

"Of course. There must be another white man in Arizona whom the Apaches will trust. One that both you and I have forgotten. Could it be anything else?"

Pelón pulled his long Colt from beneath its serape hiding place.

"It had better not be anything else," he said.

"*Cuidado!*" warned Sánchez. "Don't shoot too quickly. Let's see who it is first."

Pelón withered him with his gargoyle's scowl.

"You Mexican dog," he said coldly, "do you think I

am a man who kills for nothing? I always see who it is. My
father was of the old Spanish blood undiluted. He was a
man of honor, as am I. Only Indians and Mexicans will
shoot a man without seeing his face."

"If you say so, *Jefe*."

"I say so!"

"*Bueno*. Here they come. I wonder who it will be."

Sánchez's curiosity was a common one with the group
waiting about the tiny new fire being fanned alive by Mal-
y-pai. Each of its members, for his own reason or hers,
leaned tensely forward peering into the surrounding darkness. Suddenly Besh loomed again out of the nowhere. Behind him this time came three dark-hatted white men, followed by the crouching Yaqui, Monkey. The central of
these three visitors moved as silently as his Apache guide.
He was a tall man of strong build, neither young nor old,
and possessing a memorable smile which lit up his sunburned brown face as with some inner burst of candlelight.
He was, of course, the only white man in the territory who
could have come for Al Seiber, and none of them had
thought of him. Characteristically it was Pelón López who
recovered first, and happily.

"Benito!" he cried, throwing out his thick arms in
genuine welcome. "Before God! why did I not think of
you? It must be as Mackenna has said, that I grow old."

The grinning newcomer shrugged easily. He accepted
the outlaw chief's bear hug, neither rejecting nor returning
its vehement grip. When the powerful half-breed had released him, he gave a little wave of greeting to the others
and sat down to the fire.

"Well, Pelón," he said, "if you won't invite a man,
he must invite himself." He turned his remarkable smile
upward to the hovering Mal-y-pai. "*Café, por favor,
Madre*," he said. "None of us is as young as he was in the
better days. . . ."

14

Good-bye in the Belly

THE OTHER two men with Ben Call—the tall quiet-eyed smiler—were Vachel and Desplains. Vachel was a small, rat-faced man, who had been on the same prospecting odyssey as Mackenna for twice as many years. He was hard and dried-out, and tough as a mesquite root, and he would get to Sno-ta-hay if any of them would; but he had a bad eye and Mackenna did not trust him. The other, Raoul Desplains, was a beefy, florid French-Canadian, more adventurer than prospector, and seemed oddly out of place in the arid Southwest. He did not harbor the shifty look of his companion but he was obsessed with the material idea of wealth and showed the French strain in his eternal, grasping shrewdness, and Mackenna found in him an equally unfortunate choice of comrades.

Ben Call he knew by reputation and from having seen his picture in the various territorial newspapers over the past decade. That he had been a scout and mule packer for General George Crook in the Apache wars, he knew; also that he had worked with Al Seiber at San Carlos. He was possibly, next to the latter, the most respected of white men by the Apaches, both tame and renegade bands regarding him very nearly as one of their own race. As well, he had worked as a local law officer in Arizona, serving as deputy sheriff in at least two counties.

There were, too, of course, the other tales about Ben Call: the dark whispers which held him to be more cow thief than Indian scout, more pot-shooting hired gun than honestly employed deputy. But Glen Mackenna could not afford such delicacies of distinction. Call's possible feet of clay would have to wait a more moral place. The fireside of Pelón López was not the ideal site for debates on saintliness. Under existing circumstances, and on balance, Call was welcome.

The latter's two companions were unknowns, and more or less self-elected. When Call had tried to solicit interest in going after the Adams gold, he had drawn only queer looks and hostile stares. The Gila Citians kept their boots on the bar rails. Ex-officers of the law, dishonest or otherwise, were not honored men in the cantinas of the border.

Moreover, old maps and Indian secret ways to Sno-ta-hay, the long lost canyon of the doddering crackpot Adams, were about as rare as rustled beef and bed lice in those parts. Call himself, by grinning admission to Mackenna, would have laughed at the Sno-ta-hay story had it been referred to him by anyone other than Al Seiber. But, since he had agreed to substitute for the German scout in the matter, there had been no course for him but to pick up two men, or three, or four, or even one, and go with the Indians to meet Glen Mackenna "somewhere in the Yaquis." He told the latter quite frankly that he had no more faith in his companions than Mackenna might have, but that they were white and did even up the scale a little. Which scale, Call had added, glancing around the dark-

faced ring of Pelón's followers, would seem to be in dire
need of evening up. To this idea, Mackenna could only nod
his tacit agreement, bringing the brief discussion which
Pelón had permitted them to its close and returning the
parley to its general purpose and problem—the journey to
Sno-ta-hay and the finding of the incalculable treasure of
the Lost Adams gold.

Mackenna and Call had held their acquainting talk in
Spanish, where they did not wish Vachel and Desplains
to understand it, and in swift English where they wanted
to lose Pelón and his intent pack. It was, in fact, this latter
maneuver which caused the bandit chief's ugly face to
cloud over and which led him to his barking order to
"callate!" or "shut up," as they were making his men nervous. Moreover, it was time to decide what they would do
about the buffalo soldiers and about going on to Sno-ta-
hay. He, Pelón, did not have unlimited time in the area, as
they would understand. Call, in especial, would be sym-
pathetic since, as a deputy sheriff, he had helped chase
Pelón upon the occasion of El Jefe's most memorable visit
above the border. That would be the raid in the autumn
of 1887. The one which went all the way up into Yavapai
County. Did Benito remember that visit? But of course.

Ben Call was merely nodding pleasantly to all of this,
in no way committing himself. Watching and listening to
the sometime deputy sheriff, Mackenna felt himself growing uneasy. Call smiled too often. His shrugs and grins and
nods were all evasions. Could it be that the other side of
the "Call story," the side which defiantly claimed he was
a rustler, a hired gun, a turncoat smalltime thief and Indian-
lover (gun smuggler), was the truer version? Again, it
could not matter to Glen Mackenna.

No white man in the position of the redbearded prospector could fail to be happy over the arrival of the calm,

quiet-faced man who was such a known and good friend to
the Apache people. He was certain Call would not be willing party to any physical harm coming to either Glen
Mackenna, or the captive white girl. But where a man has
been labeled half-hero, half-outlaw, and by responsible per-
sons for both allegations, that man had to be kept under
closest watch.

While these suspicions were beginning to grow in the
place of Mackenna's first excitements over seeing Ben Call,
Pelón drove on with his concerns as to the departure for
Sno-ta-hay and the proximity of the buffalo soldiers at
Yaqui Spring.

"Now," he said, concluding his friendly remembrances
with "Benito" Call, "we must decide quickly what it is that
we will do tomorrow. Or, rather, how it is that we will do
it. Of course we are going to Sno-ta-hay."

"Of course," said Sánchez.

"Of course," said Besh, the young Chiricahua.

Ben Call shrugged and smiled. Glen Mackenna did
nothing, said the same. Pelón parted his scarred lips to continue. Monkey forestalled him.

"I believe," said the brutish Yaqui, "that I will quit
and go back. I am homesick. Besides, when I have a chance
to be alone with some white men, you send along people
to watch me. Anyhow, I have this short scalp and this long
one"—he held up the grisly forelocks of the foster parents
of the white girl—"and they will do for my needs. This
country has changed. The white men are everywhere now
and there is no decent chance to kill them as in the old
days. I think that I will go home."

When he had done, Pelón held up a warning finger.

"Don't make trouble, Monkey," he said. "Don't do a
foolish thing like that."

Monkey's eyes glittered. The wild look came into

them. Mackenna tensed. So did Ben Call. Pelón did not appear to do so. The rest of the wolfpack only leaned in a little, waiting.

"I came for hair," said the Yaqui. "You promised me that. I don't care for gold. That a *yori* fault."

"I have enough trouble," Pelón told him patiently. "Please do not add to it, Mono. All right?"

"No," said the Yaqui, throwing down his coffee cup and getting to his feet. "I am tired of all of you; I am going back. Good-bye."

He started at once toward the grazing ponies, out beyond the fire's tiny throw of light. Pelón López did not bid him to stay. Neither did he stand up. He just pulled his Colt from beneath the serape and called out quietly to the deserter, "Monkey—" and then, when the Yaqui had stopped and turned about and said, "Yes?" he nodded to him and called, "Good-bye," and shot him in the belly, low down.

There was a silence, then, which was a physical presence and could be felt, like fog, or smothering heat.

During it, Pelón got up and went over to where Monkey lay writhing soundlessly in the grass. Picking up a melon-sized rock, he crushed the Yaqui's head and returned to the fire.

"Ammunition," he said, "is scarce."

Ben Call, to whom these Indian ways were perhaps less dismaying than they were to the other white men present, palmed his hands.

"Yes," he said in Spanish, "but you should not have used even that one bullet. The soldiers will surely hear it."

"But of course they will," smiled Pelón. "And when they have, among all these rocks and these craggy hills and rotten stumps of yellow mountains, where will they agree that it came from? Here? There? Everywhere?"

"True," said Ben Call. "And then they're also buffalo soldiers and it's nighttime. They're afraid of the dark, you know, just as many Indians are."

"Yes," nodded Pelón, "and many white men."

Sánchez, the politician, waved his hand and added, "Sí, amigos, and even some mejicanos, eh?" and there was a lone small laugh from Pelón at this, and the outlaw chief felt warmed to continue along a more comradely line.

"Let us look upon the happier side of such an unfortunate thing," he suggested. "A man does not like to lose a good fighter such as Monkey, but we must be honest; he would have made trouble among us sooner or later, with his unending hatred of the yori. Once it had been shown to me that our party would travel on from this camp part white and part not-white, then, naturally, Monkey was dead." He held up his hands defensively, as Mackenna and Vachel and Desplains registered unfavorable grimaces. "Do not be so quick to judge the matter, my friends," he said. "Could we have let Monkey ride out of here, knowing what he knew of our plans? Would any of you want such exact information to reach, let us say, the authorities in Gila City? Or the army officers stationed nearby? You, Benito," he said, singling out Call, "would you be pleased to have your name listed with mine in this little adventure? I mean to imply, after such an affair as that whereby we had the trouble at this white girl's rancho?"

"No," answered Call simply. "Not quite."

"I would think not. You know too much about ropes already, eh, Benito?" He uttered his quick barking laugh at the remark and Call, who was a rodeo competitor and certainly one of the finest cowboy ropers in the Southwest, nodded again and said unsmilingly, "Yes, amigo, I do; a man can get hurt playing with ropes."

"Aye," said Pelón, "particularly if they are being carried by others, eh, *compadre?* And perhaps thrown up over a convenient tree limb? Just above your own saddled horse? With a sliding noose on the dangling end? All very playfully, of course."

"Of course," said Ben Call.

"We understand one another then?"

"If you mean do I understand that they might hang me for what you did at the Stanton Ranch, if they catch me riding with you, the answer is yes. It's a good point that you make, too. I only got to Gila City yesterday. I could have trouble accounting for the day before. Go on."

"Well then," shrugged Pelón, motioning to Mackenna and the white girl, "as these two friends of yours have the same stake in the gamble as you do—their lives—there can be small argument over the need to destroy the Yaqui. Besides, it was *pundonor* with me; a point of honor."

"Oh?" said Ben Call. "In what way?"

"My agreement with Mackenna," replied Pelón López. "He had my word that we would go on from this camp with one white man on his side for each of my *muchachos.* When you could find but two men to come with you from Gila City, it created an awkwardness. As *jefe,* I had to face it squarely."

Glen Mackenna put down his coffee cup. Even after his eleven years of life among the Apaches, the coldness of the implication was startling.

"Do you mean to say," he interrupted carefully, "that you killed that Indian to even up the sides of our party?"

Pelón raised his wide shoulders apologetically.

"Well, Mackenna," he inquired, "you can count, can you not?"

"I can."

"Then count with me: assuming that Hachita would do as he promised and take old Enh to Nana's *ranchería,*

that left my side with five men. Now, Benito appears with
two gringos, and that made only four on your side. Five
and four are not equal. So my friend Monkey offers to
solve the problem by leaving us. I only made sure that
he did not change his mind and, hell, there you are, it is
four and four. The *pundonor* is accommodated and Pelón
has kept his word. What more do you want?"

The question was clearly rhetorical. But Besh, the
slender Chiricahua descendant of Cochise, was not schooled
in such niceties of style.

"One thing," he answered in his wonderful voice.
"You must count again."

"What?" said Pelón, getting up. "Count again? Whatever for?"

"For Hachita," answered Besh. "He is not going to
Nana's *ranchería*. He is going with us to Sno-ta-hay."

With the words, the Apache youth also stood up. He
and the half-breed bandit leader measured each other across
the fire's light. It was Pelón who broke the new silence.

"But it was Hachita who said he would go to Nana's
ranchería. I didn't ask him to go."

"I speak for Hachita. Ask me."

"All right. Will you permit Hachita to go with the
old man's body to Nana's village?"

"No."

"Why not?"

"I can't tell you."

"That is your last word on it?"

"That depends."

"On what?"

"On what you do with that pistol you are now cocking under your serape?"

"Whatever do you mean?"

"Pull out the pistol and see."

"Oh? Suppose I did so. What would I see?"

"I don't know," said Besh, "because I don't know what a man sees when a hatchet is buried in his skull from behind."

Pelón grew a sickish gray. All eyes, save his, flicked toward the night's darkness behind him. He could see the looks of startlement on the faces of Sánchez and the others.

"May I look?" he asked Besh.

"Yes, very slowly."

Pelón pivoted his huge head with infinite care. Behind him, gleaming ax poised to split that head from bald pate to beard-blue jawbone, waited the Mimbreño giant, Hachita. How he had gotten there with no one having seen or heard him, was not easy to imagine. Pelón López was not equal to the question, and returned his face to Besh with the same caution he had shown in having his look at Hachita.

Shrugging, he smiled with empty eyes at the handsome young Apache.

"So it is that your friend Hachita will go with us to Sno-ta-hay," he said. "Had the wind been right, it might have been otherwise."

"Yes," said Besh, "you would have smelled him."

"I might *still* smell him," said Pelón.

Besh said nothing.

15

Decision at Surprise Grass

OF COURSE Pelón had freed Mackenna and the girl before the arrival of Ben Call and the Gila City men. He no doubt felt—indeed he told Mackenna as much—that it would not look right for one partner in a venture to be in chains and the other not in chains. The new partners might get the wrong impression of the entire arrangement.

Thus the council which now went forward about the coffee fire was held in physical freedom. Even the missing Indian women, Lupe and Sally, who had been on guard in the rocks, were called in with signal yelps to join their campmates in the battle planning. There was an immediate disagreement, however.

Mackenna, belatedly moving to take charge of "his men," went up to Ben Call. "You must have had a pretty good guess," he said, "at what you were getting into."

"Yes," said Call. "It's not a standard business agreement when its messengers are *bronco* Apaches. Besides, I know Pelón."

"I, too." Mackenna sighed.

"It was because of Seiber that I came. He's in the hos-

pital at Prescott with that bad foot of his—the one the
Apaches shot up for him at San Carlos years ago."

"It never did heal," said Mackenna. "That's too bad.
It never will now, I daresay."

"Indian lead," said Call, "never does heal right."

Mackenna ignored the superstitious statement, and
asked Call if he understood that he, Mackenna, was to head
the white men on the trip. Call shrugged and grinned dis-
armingly, as he did to nearly everything, and Mackenna
took that for an agreement. He then told him about the
Stanton girl, to which, surprisingly, Call replied that Besh
had already told him of the murders at the ranch and the
fact of the girl having been carried along as a hostage.
"You might say," he smiled, "that seeing her here comes in
the same category with meeting that dead Yaqui and Besh
out in the brush past Gila City—it's not precisely the place
you'd look to find a proper young lady of our tribe. Put
another way, it's plain to me that we can either make a
fight to free you and her, right here, or go along to Sno-ta-
hay on Pelón's terms. As for a fight, we can't count on
Vachel and Desplains and I think that to start anything now
would be suicide."

"I think likewise," said Glen Mackenna. "It's decided
then? We'll vote to go on?"

"Yes."

Mackenna looked at Ben Call, wondering how much
of his reasoning was common sense, how much of it his
great knowledge of renegades, and how much was his
normal white man's greed for the fabled wealth of the Lost
Adams Diggings. He thought to put it to him, straight out,
then decided this was not the time and place. So he nodded
his acceptance of Call's "yes" and turned to Pelón and said,
"All right, *Jefe*, my side is ready." It was here that the
difference of opinion ensued.

"Good," said the outlaw leader, "you sit on that side
of the fire; we'll stay over here." He motioned his men to
flank him. They did so, silently. Old Mal-y-pai and Sally
also drew in. Lupe, the fat Pima captive, sat dumbly on a
rock by herself. Her day with Sally in the hell's heat of
the hills had nearly killed her, and there was nothing left
in her save the desire to draw one more breath. The Stanton
girl hesitated, as Mal-y-pai left her side. Seeing her do so,
Mackenna went over to her quickly and took her hand.

"Come on," he said, "you heard El Jefe. He said our
side sits over here."

At once, Pelón moved forward.

"Wait," he said. "That wasn't my statement at all. I
said my side sits over here and your side sits over there. I
didn't say one word about the girl. You know very well,
Mackenna, that we agreed to leave the women out of it."

"We did not agree to that," denied the bearded prospector. "We agreed not to count the women when divid-
ing the sides."

"Well, what's the difference?"

"The difference is that she *is* on our side and *of* our
side. She is white. She goes with the white side."

Mackenna did not know why he had suddenly made
the hard stand, when he had just agreed with Ben Call
not to do it. But something had happened to him when he
had taken the girl's hand and she had looked at him and
squeezed quickly back with her slender fingers. That contact, that perfectly normal reflex of her grasp returning
his, had sent a defiant power surging through him. Now,
having delivered himself of its ultimatum and seeing the
look of flaring anger it brought to Pelón's brute face, he
wondered why in the name of a reasonable providence, he,
the sensible, realistic, hard-headed Glen Mackenna, had
uttered such a patent invitation to violence and disaster.

In the clumsy quiet which followed his rash challenge, however, he received unexpected support.

"Of course, she's with our side!" snarled the rat-faced man, Vachel, confronting Pelón. "What the hell do you expect us to do? Let *you* have her?"

Even though the small prospector did not know Pelón López personally, and did not, thus, realize the deadly danger he had stepped into, his act had to be accepted as one of Western frontier honor, and nothing less.

Ben Call didn't move, nor did the big Canadian, Desplains. Glen Mackenna did. Easing up to side Vachel, he said softly to Pelón, "Well, *Jefe*, what do you say? You're the leader."

The gnome-bald half-breed glared at him. But it was a cunning glare and the bearded prospector saw the cupidity and avarice in it, and struck at the weakness swiftly.

"While you are thinking whether to kill us here, or to keep us alive until we have taken you into Sno-ta-hay," he said, "think also about all that gold up there lying free and fat and brightly glittering in the grass-roots. Think very hard about that."

Pelón obeyed the injunction. The side of him which was not Apache was too strong for the red blood. The greed for gold which came to him from his Spanish father's people, four centuries line-bred, could not be submerged in the pagan regard for the beauty of the land which was the religion of his mother's wild race. The seed of the con-quistadores was too potent for the thin Apache soil. Pelón López threw back his wrinkled, ugly head. His explosive, humorless laugh burst jarringly to end the quiet. He threw his thick arm about Mackenna's shoulders.

"Mackenna! *Hombre! Amigo!* We are partners! But of

course the girl may sit on your side. Do you not enjoy a small joke?"

Mackenna, releasing his breath with an audible sigh, considered the question.

"Yes," he finally decided, "I guess that I do, Pelón. Many thanks."

"It is nothing," waved the gracious host. "Come, let us return to our talk. *Amigos, muchachos, hombres, mujeres!* We are bound for Sno-ta-hay and all the gold of the Lost Adams Mine! Come sit with Pelón López, your poor and humble *jefe*, and tell him how it is that you wish him to conduct himself on the happy trail ahead . . ."

Mackenna went back to the Stanton girl and took her hand once more in his. They didn't talk and didn't need to talk. The clasp of their fingers said it all.

16

Colt Smoke and Serapes

THE IMMEDIATE PROBLEM was the buffalo soldiers. Surprise Grass, the secret Apache oasis in the Burnt Horn Desert, was in reality a siren resting place. The tortuous trail which plummeted downward three miles to Yaqui Spring was the sole entrance and exit to the lovely meadow negotiable to saddle mounts and pack animals. This, of course, as Pelón now pointed out to his listeners, was the reason that the Apaches did not use the retreat as a regular watering place. Once the secret of its trail was discovered by an enemy, the oasis became a trap. Pelón, and others, used it only in times of no pursuit and of presumed absence of any white men from the vicinity. The unexpected arrival of the Negro cavalry so close upon the heels of the Gila City returnees thus created a crisis of singular urgency.

"Comrades," said Pelón, spreading his hands, "those damned black soldiers camped down there at the spring must be attended to. When daylight comes they will be looking for what happened to Besh and the others that they were chasing from Gila City. And they won't be fooled for long. Don't forget that they have a smart white officer leading them, and that he has a mongrel dog of a quarter-white Apache with him as a scout. Some of us know this particular scout; we know him all too well. His name is Young Mickey Tibbs. His father was the original Mickey Tibbs, a half-white, half-Apache, whole son-of-a-bitch from the old days. His mother was a full-blooded Mescalero squaw. She was once wanted for murdering two white men in their blankets to get an old mule and a side of bacon away from them. It's the best *hesh-ke* breeding you could find, and this Young Mickey is meaner than a mustang stallion. He's only a boy, true, but he's a hell of a boy. He will find this trail into Surprise Grass when the sun rises tomorrow. He probably already knows of it from some miserable drunken Mescalero relative, who sold it to him for a pint of *tulapai*."

Pelón sighed and shook his head.

"Ask Besh," he suggested to the others. "He will tell you as I have told you—those buffalo soldiers have got us trapped in here. We could get away on foot, but we can't go to Sno-ta-hay on foot. So there you are."

"Are you saying," asked Sánchez, "that we must fight the soldiers, or flee through the high rocks on foot?"

"No," said Pelón, "we could ride down in the morning and surrender with good feeling all around. Of course, the feeling wouldn't be so good when the soldiers got us back to the fort and put those ropes around our necks."

Mackenna, watching the outlaw leader when he said it, could see no hint that he had intended it for humor. Yet, he felt again that twinge of instinct which told him that somewhere deep in this murderous outlaw from Sonora lurked the faint spark of human response lacking in most habitual criminals.

"You *are* saying that we must fight or flee, then,"

accused Sánchez, himself certainly no victim of a sense of the lighter side. "Do you deny it?"

Pelón turned his shoulder on him and said to the rest, "Forgive him; he's a Federale. They don't fight unless they have a hundred men to your ten."

"What do you suggest, *Jefe?*" asked Mackenna. "You can't expect my white men to fight those soldiers down there. Is there another way?"

"Yes," answered Pelón quickly. "Would you like to hear it? Never mind. You will hear it anyway."

He paused, studying them all. Mackenna thought that he devoted even more consideration to his own followers than he did to those on the white side of the fire. It was evident that whatever he was about to propose held the element of high risk, even the seeds of outright revolt perhaps. The red-bearded prospector tensed himself.

"We must," said Pelón, "separate yet more of the chaff from the grain."

"What is that?" demanded Sánchez sharply.

"There are still too many of us. Losing Laguna and Monkey was not enough. More must go."

"Do you say," said Besh, the Apache, "that there must be more killing?"

"Not at all. I never used the word."

"Never mind the word," nodded Besh. "How about the thought?"

"The thought," replied Pelón, "is simply this: some of us will start for Sno-ta-hay; others of us will not."

"This is where we were when Hachita stood behind you with his ax," said Besh.

"No, no," denied Pelón, hurriedly glancing behind his as he spoke. "You don't gather my idea at all. I mean that we shall *agree* on who sets out and who does not."

"How will that be done?" muttered Sánchez.

"Easily," said Pelón. "I will decide it."

"*You?*" broke in Vachel, using English deliberately, although he spoke Spanish as well as any native. "I wouldn't let you decide how many hairs there was on a billiard ball." He gestured quickly to his white companions. "*We'll* decide any deciding that's done, you understand?"

Again, Pelón shrugged and spread his hands.

"Fortunately, small one," he said, "we have no argument. I was thinking of my own side being too numerous."

At once, Besh and Sánchez came to their feet, and the giant Hachita came, unbidden, to stand with his friend, Besh. Neither of the Apaches said anything, leaving it to the Mexican army deserter, Sergeant Venustiano Sánchez, to state the common curiosity.

The latter came most uneasily to the task. It was only minutes since Pelón had crushed the skull of Monkey. It was only minutes since Hachita had poised his blade to cleave the skull of Pelón. There was death all around in the darkness of Surprise Grass. Sánchez nodded grayly.

"And who would you eliminate?" he asked.

Pelón watched him a moment, then broke into his unnerving laugh. When he could control his merriment, he put a friendly hand to his Mexican comrade's shoulder, and said affectionately, "Venustiano, old companion, do you think that I would include you in such an unfortunate number? You, who have been with me on a dozen trails? You, who mean more to me than any natural brother? Before God, how can you stand there and doubt me?"

Sánchez's face grew even grayer. His voice shook.

"You *do* mean to eliminate me, then," he whispered.

"But of course!" said Pelón gaily. "How could you ever have suspected otherwise, old friend?"

He permitted his Mexican lieutenant another moment of sickness, then unexpectedly embraced him.

Sánchez did not know whether to laugh or cry, even so. But when Pelón had released him and stepped back, the outlaw's upper lip was drawn into that knife-cut grimace which all knew by now to be a smile.

"However, dear comrade," he amplified, "the separation will not be permanent. It will not even be painful. You are a professional soldier, Venustiano. You know how it is that, occasionally, an order must be obeyed with which one might not be in strict accord. Am I right?"

"Always," gulped Sánchez. "What is it you would have me do, *Jefe?*"

Pelón waved his bearpaw of a hand to the others.

"Gather in here more closely and attend," he directed the whole group. "Everyone should understand, as there must be no mistakes. Such treasures as that of Cañon del Oro are not won without great risk. That deception which we must now employ upon the buffalo soldiers carries with it some small chance of failure."

"This means," said Ben Call quietly, "that someone is apt to be killed?"

"Benito, I am surprised. *You*, to ask that question?"

"Excuse it," grinned Call. "I didn't mean to think ahead of you."

"Thinking ahead is what makes you charming, Benito," said Pelón, not with the entire cordiality of the earlier exchanges with the tall white man. "Be so kind as to hear me out, however. That's a lot of gold we're talking about up there in Sno-ta-hay. It's worth a lot of risk."

"Agreed," nodded Ben Call, and fell silent.

"Mackenna," said Pelón, "are you also still with me? Do you likewise still hunger for the Adams treasure?"

"Pelón," answered the bearded prospector, "I have no hunger but to go on living. Therefore, I am still with you."

"Spoken like a crafty man," said the outlaw chief. "I will watch you as carefully as I watch Benito," he promised, "but for different reasons."

"For God's sake," snapped Vachel, "lay off the fancy Spanish chatter! If you've got a plan for sneaking us out of this pine pocket and down through that cavalry camp without getting us all shot to hell, then spill it!"

"Impatience is costly," chided Pelón. "Don't make a 'monkey' out of yourself, Vachel."

Mackenna and Ben Call looked at one another. Both had caught the inflection Pelón had put on the word "monkey." Both understood the renegade's reference.

Vachel, apparently, did not.

"You go to hell!" he rasped, ratlike features contorted defiantly.

Pelón López moved his wide shoulders with eloquent Latin submissiveness.

"*Después de Usted,*" he murmured politely, "after you."

With the graceful gesture of his left hand, the right hand tightened upon the worn walnut butt of the big Colt beneath the serape. He shot Vachel from a distance of no more than eight feet, from under the serape, and without visible change of position or facial expression.

The small prospector fell slowly over backward, coffee cup still held in his hand. As Glen Mackenna moved instinctively to lean over and determine the site and seriousness of the wound, Pelón waved the smoking barrel of the Colt and said calmly, "Do not concern yourself, my friend; that one has gone to the place of his own invitation."

17

Sonora Stand-off

PELÓN WAS right, and Vachel was dead. In the silence which followed Mackenna's confirmation of the fact, Ben Call stood up slowly. He had not, since coming into the outlaw camp, put down his Winchester. He held it now, by one brawny hand and on the full cock, his thumb hooked over its hammer as though the weapon were a revolver.

"*Amigo*," he said quietly to Pelón, "a time has come."

That was all he said. There was no hint of what time had come. But the bandit leader understood the meaning.

"Benito," he said, "you cannot be serious?"

"Yes I am, believe it."

"All right." Pelón still held the Colt. It hung in his right hand by his side, as the Winchester hung in Ben Call's hand by Ben Call's side. "I believe it."

Call nodded, very carefully, very slowly.

"I'm going out of this camp," he said. "You're not reliable any more. My turn might lie next beneath that serape. I don't care to wait for it."

Pelón appeared deeply hurt.

"But, Benito," he complained, "what could I do? I am the leader."

"Not for me," said Ben Call. "I'm going."

Pelón studied the situation. Call, he had reason to know, could handle the short Winchester carbine with devastating effect at such a belly range. Mackenna was not armed. Desplains was. Behind himself, Pelón knew, the two Apaches were ready with knife and ax. But ready for whom? *That* Pelón did not know. He thought that they would stand with him. The young Chiricahua had said they would. An Apache usually kept his word. A pure-blooded Apache, that was. But in such a division as now threatened, no man could be sure. The Indians also thought highly of Ben Call. And he knew—Pelón did—that Besh, at least, respected Glen Mackenna. There was, too, that business of the Stanton Ranch killings which had angered the young Apache. Pelón hesitated and was not certain: it looked like an impasse.

"Well, Benito," he said with a shrug, "go ahead. You came of your free will. Leave the same way."

Ben Call shook his head and smiled his soft smile.

"No," he said, "I'll not leave the same way that I came, Pelón. I'll take the Stanton girl and Mackenna with me. Desplains can come or stay, as he likes. I don't speak for him."

"Benito," said the bandit plaintively, "you dishonor our friendship. What was that Vachel to you? A ragged packrat of a man. Nothing. A bad-tempered mongrel."

"You killed him for nothing, Pelón. Him in this camp. Desplains in the next. Me in the third. You're not to be trusted these days. Mackenna is safe because he knows the way to Sno-ta-hay. The girl is safe because if anything happens to her, Mackenna won't play your game. Ben Call

is safe because he has his Winchester pointing at your belly.
You gave good advice to Vachel. Take some of it yourself.
I'm no 'monkey.' "

"I know that, Benito. Put away the gun. Let us talk."

"We're talking."

"Put away the gun then."

"I will," said Call, "when I'm down there in that
cavalry camp."

"And you think I will let you go?"

"I think so."

"And Mackenna and the girl with you?"

"Why not?"

Pelón glanced around at his group. He had not yet
played his hidden card, and was only being sure that it
still lay buried in the deck. Besh and Hachita stood im-
mobile. They neither nodded nor shook their heads when
Pelón looked around. But they were not the outlaw's concern just now. He was looking at his women; at old Mal-y-
pai and at Sally. The two Apache squaws sat hunched
atop their sitting stones out on the edge of the firelight.
Both were huddled in their dirty blankets against the set-
tling chill of the night. As Pelón looked at them, both gave
him a small, almost imperceptible nod. He turned back to
Ben Call. Pelón was smiling and, watching him, Mackenna's
heart sank.

"You ask why not?" the half-breed said to Call. "I
have two good reasons for you. *Mujeres,* show him."

When he gave the order to the women, each seemed
barely to shrug her blanketed shoulders. But the movement
was enough. It parted the filthy coverings sufficiently to
reveal the old Model '73 Winchesters each squaw had
hidden under her blanket and held trained upon the white
group the entire time of the talk by the fire. Those rusted

but well-oiled rifles now stared at Ben Call unwaveringly. The big white man, his raise checked, stood stock-still. Even his grin was motionless.

Pelón shrugged apologetically.

"I don't know anything about those two Apaches," he said, pointing with his left hand to Besh and Hachita. "But, I know all about *those* two." He gestured toward Sally and Mal-y-pai. "One is my sister and one is my mother, and they will shoot to kill you as surely as we stand here smiling at one another."

Call looked at the Apache women. "*Ya lo creo.*" He nodded, grin fading. "I believe it."

"Believe this, then," said Pelón. "I really do have a good plan to divide our force so that we may all get past the buffalo soldiers. As for whether it will certainly succeed, only God can say. But if it does work, then there will be no bloodshed and we will only be fooling the soldiers. That's no crime, is it?"

"No," said Call. "At least no more than most of us commit every month we live. But shooting Vachel was a crime, Pelón: we call it murder."

"I know, I know," soothed the half-breed, "but you will admit that Vachel was a troublemaker. So was Monkey a troublemaker. If I shoot my own man, why would I not shoot yours? Am I the leader, or am I not the leader?"

Call looked at Mackenna. He shook his head slightly in a way that the latter understood to be some sort of signal, and his heart dropped again. But he got ready to fight. If Call were to start shooting there was nothing he, Mackenna, could do to stop him. And once he had started firing, there was nothing he could do but join with him in the attempt to break free of the renegade camp. But he had misread Call's sign.

"Pelón," the latter now conceded, "perhaps you are

right in a sort of Apache way. At least, let me talk with
my side and see what they want to do."

The bandit chief scowled a moment.

"You may talk with Mackenna," he decided. "He's
your leader."

Mackenna, who had been feeling anything but a leader
the past ten minutes, flushed deeply. Two men had been
brutally murdered in front of him, and he had done nothing, not even by word, to intervene or to complain after
the fact. He had only stood dumbly by and watched it all
happen, trying in some clumsy way to shield the girl and
to stay by her side, and that was all. Now, knowing that
she was watching him, with the others, he nodded belatedly
and said to Pelón, "*Gracias*, but it is Ben Call who leads for
our side."

Pelón's scowl deepened.

"What is this, Mackenna?" he asked. "I said you were
the leader of the whites. Benito is your second, as Sánchez
is mine. That's the way it is, do you understand?"

"Of course, he understands," said Ben Call quietly.
"Why do you think I want to talk with him if he isn't the
leader on our side?"

"All right," nodded Pelón impatiently. "Go on, have
your conference. Just remember that my two women are
watching you with the Winchesters."

"Sure," smiled Ben Call, "and you do the same; you
bear it in your mind that my Winchester is watching you
and your two women. Do we share the confidence?"

"Yes, for God's sake!" snapped the outlaw. "Go
ahead!"

Call, his carbine continually trained on the renegades,
stepped backward to where Mackenna stood with the
Stanton girl. "What do you think?" he asked, low-voiced.
"Looks to me like a Mexican stand-off."

Mackenna squared his shoulders, jaw jutting stubbornly. "I hate to admit it, friend," he told Call, "but I haven't been able to think of a thing."

The tall, careful-eyed man looked at him. His watchful regard neither condemned nor accused. It was just an expression of acceptance of that which could not be altered in any event. It seemed suddenly to Mackenna that Ben Call here found himself in the place most natural and familiar to him—the middle. But if Call was indeed playing both ends of the game, his next words gave no hint of such strategy.

"You think we ought to fight, Mackenna?" he said.

The bearded prospector scowled, thinking desperately. "No," he finally said. "The odds are all wrong. If it went the best possible way for us, one of us might make it away, unwounded, but Miss Stanton would still be held by these devils. It won't wash, Call. Not for me."

At the reference to herself, the girl moved silently forward, placing herself between her two defenders.

"Miss Stanton's name is Francie," she announced with a wan smile. "That's short for Francelia."

Call and Mackenna glanced at one another.

"It helps," said Ben Call, "to have a lady with your kind of courage in a spot such as this, ma'am. We surely do appreciate it. There's no telling how much trouble you've stalled off by keeping your mouth shut and not pressing any of us for attention."

"I'm like Mr. Mackenna, Mr. Call," she said. "It's not that I'm brave; I just haven't been able to think of anything to open my mouth about."

"Sure," said Ben Call, "I know how it is, ma'am."

He and Mackenna talked quickly. As quickly, they agreed that to fight would be useless and more than useless. If they were, any of them, to come out of the experience alive, let alone unharmed at this advanced point, it would be a miracle *without* adding any weight to their tombstones by starting to shoot their ways out of the Winchester stalemate presently obtaining between Ben Call and the two Apache squaws.

There was no doubt, whatever, that Call could do more damage than the two Apache women. Also, there was no doubt that the remainder of the renegade side would get Call, regardless. The mathematics of it were simply unavoidable.

When Call had gambled to bluff his way out of the camp minutes before, it had been with the idea of staying with the Negro cavalry and scouting with them to run down Pelón López and force a handover of the girl and Glen Mackenna. Now that thought was as dead as Vachel.

They would have to make some dicker with Pelón, Call estimated, which would keep the shaky status quo a little while longer. To his, Call's way of thinking, this meant accepting the bandit chief's plan for eluding the cavalry, even if that accepting rendered them accessories to any possible succeeding fact of war on the U.S. Government. If Glen Mackenna had any better hunches on how to get more gracefully away from Surprise Grass, his companion concluded, now was the time to come up with them.

"What do you say?" he asked Mackenna, warm smile turned frostily cold. "Do you want me to tell Pelón we'll go along with him?"

Mackenna started to say yes. Then, noting Francie Stanton's eager face, he changed his mind. The thin youngster wasn't looking to Ben Call, as he himself had been looking to Call in this moment of white-lipped decision; she was looking to him, Glen Mackenna: she had those compelling, wide gray eyes fastened on him as entirely as though there weren't another male human being within a hundred miles of that wolfishly silent outlaw pack watching them from beyond the dying embers of the coffee fire.

Mackenna shook his head and stood tall. "No," he said quietly to Ben Call, "I'll tell him."

18

The Decoys
of Venustiano Sánchez

"WE HAVE got to hurry," worried Pelón. "That damned moon is rising by the minute. Sánchez is far enough ahead now, too. We must start out. How is it going, Mackenna? Are we ready?"

"I think so, *Jefe*," nodded the bearded prospector. "Call, you all set?"

"All set," replied the latter, coming forward.

The three men paused, briefly surveying the remaining mounts, saddles and baggage which they had assembled.

In the already departed Sánchez group had been Lupe, the Pima squaw captive, and the French-Canadian drifter, Raoul Desplains. The latter was chosen for his place because he was unknown to the soldiers. So was Venustiano Sánchez and, presumably, the Pima woman. Thus, the three could realistically portray their roles of escapees from the camp of the renegades. Sánchez and Desplains were to ride into the soldier camp at Yaqui Spring, with Lupe. In the excitement of their arrival, the outpost pickets of the camp would be drawn off-guard. Pelón and the others, following as closely as they dared behind Sánchez and Desplains, could then rush by the camp of the buffalo soldiers and escape into the open desert. They would then skirt the Yaqui hills north to an Apache waterhole known as The Skulls. The fat Pima slave girl, Lupe, was to be abandoned in the soldier camp. Sánchez and Desplains would seek to make their exits later in the night, when the camp had gone back to sleep. Aiding them, of course, would be the fact that, Pelón and the main band having already escaped, there would be less need for an alert guard by the buffalo soldiers.

Lupe, quite clearly, was the weak part in Pelón's plan. But no scheme is without its risks, as all the band understood and agreed. And Lupe did not, in fact, appear to pose too great a threat to the gamble. She was a stupid woman, made still more dumb and senseless by her brutal experience as a captive of the Mescalero. She did not speak a word of English and almost no Apache. In Spanish, her conversation at once revealed the pathetic lacks of her mentality. The white lieutenant in command of the black cavalry patrol would scarcely pay serious heed to such a creature. The risk was mainly that Young Mickey Tibbs might be able to get her to talk to him, as a fellow Indian, and so get a coherent story from her. But he would hardly have the time to do so before Pelón and the others rushed past the soldier camp to freedom. As for Sánchez and Desplains, they were old campaigners and could be depended upon to look out for themselves.

"Well," said Ben Call, breaking the silence, "if we're going, let's go. As Pelón says, that moon is no friend of ours, and we don't want our decoys getting too far ahead."

"Wait," protested the outlaw leader. "I want to check

that white girl again. I must make sure those ropes and that gag are tight. If she should cry out, or work her hands free, I would have to shoot her."

"Yes," said Call, "and then I would have to shoot you and there's no saying where it would stop."

Pelón didn't answer him but went down the line to examine Francie Stanton's bonds. Her horse was positioned behind that of Besh and in front of that of Sally. Pelón rode first, with Mal-y-pai and Ben Call behind him, ahead of Hachita. Bringing up the rear came Mackenna in charge of the camp's packstring of three scrawny mustangs.

"All right," said Pelón, returning. "Now we will go."

Call and Mackenna only nodded and went quickly to their mounts. Swinging up, the latter called up the line to Pelón, "Go ahead, *Jefe*," and the bandit leader clucked a guttural Apache word to his pony and led the cavalcade through the growing moonlight to the head of the Yaqui Spring trail.

Five minutes before, Sánchez had started down that trail with Desplains and the simple-minded Pima woman. They were already out of sight among the black boulders of the plunging track. Far below, the desert lay waiting in the white moonlight. From the brink of the Surprise Grass drop-off, Mackenna could see it lying silently beautiful out beyond Yaqui Spring. He could see, too, the shadowed gray depression, not yet invaded by the climbing moon, which was the canyon of the spring. At that distance and upon such a clear, still night, any fires in the soldier camp would have been visible from the high hills. And they were. Mackenna plainly saw them burning in the murk of the Yaqui Spring bivouac. As Pelón had predicted, the buffalo soldiers were not entirely asleep.

There was not, happily, much opportunity in the ensuing descent for bona-fide fretting over that discovery.

The trail itself absorbed nearly every art and instinct of survival. Its unbelievable steepness and heart-stopping narrow width required the ultimate in canyon horsemanship. The little Indian horses seemed, half the time, to have their outside hoofs treading thin air beyond the edge. Insofar as he could, however, and still stay with his mount, Mackenna considered his situation.

Three days ago he had been a wandering and contented dweller in the deserts and mountains of Arizona. He had owed no man, known no woman, owned only one horse and one saddle and one rifle and one ragged blanket in the world. He had been the friend of the nomad red man, and of the scattered handful of hardy whites who ranched and prospected the ranges of his wilderness home. Upon occasion, he would find a small trace of color in some creeklet's gravel, or the dry sand of a desolate, unknown wash beneath the red and ochre walls of some unmapped canyon. These scant grains and, infrequently, a few larger nuggets of gold had kept him in flour and coffee, bacon, tobacco, beans and ammunition. With his rifle he had provided steaks of venison and antelope, when required or encountered, and this diet had kept him well and strong. He had been in the field through the blazing heat of summer and the sharp cold of winter for his entire eleven years in the territories, never taking a permanent home nor feeling the want of one. He had been, to his educated mind, a happy man. The West was an escape for him from his early life of school and cultural forcing and the cloying confines of settled urban life in the large population centers of the East where his restless physician father had practiced for the nineteen years which Mackenna had spent under his roof.

Now this peace and this freedom were threatened with annihilation. The Indians, the Mexican, the half-breeds, he could cope with. Pelón, he felt reasonably sure of. The odds in the strange company were now balanced. The renegade force, reduced to the baldheaded bandit leader, Sánchez, Besh and Hachita, was no more than a sporting match for Ben Call, Raoul Desplains and Glen Mackenna.

Indeed, white men of their caliber could well expect to get to Sno-ta-hay and come back on no worse than even terms with an egocentric half-breed outlaw, a Mexican army deserter and two Arizona Apaches, one of whom was only half-bright and the other well disposed toward fairness.

But, good God, the girl! What in the name of hell was Mackenna going to do about her? Mackenna didn't know. What he did know was that if something did *not* happen to remove her from his life, he had spent his last summer in the Mogollons and his farewell winter in the sun-drenched canyons of the Salt. He would marry Francie Stanton and give up the old lonely ways, if it was his absolute final act.

He knew one other thing with the same utter certainty. If something should now *try* to remove her from that life of his, he would tear out its throat with his bare hands.

19

The Yaqui Spring Blockade

THERE WAS a gaunt cluster of shielding rock six hundred yards above the soldier camp at Yaqui Spring. Here Pelón halted his party, ordering its members to fall out of single file and bunch their mounts, with his, ready for the dash past the cavalry encampment below.

"Remember," he told Mackenna and Ben Call, "that my sister's rifle will be watching the white girl."

The two men looked back. They saw Sally holding her pony, flank-on, with Francie Stanton's. The Apache squaw had her Winchester jammed past the front sight into the white girl's side. The latter was doing what she might to sit quietly and to keep her nervous mount from bolting. But with both hands roped to the saddlehorn and her feet lashed under the animal's belly, the painful jabbing from the rifle was creating a clear danger of stampede.

"Sister Sally," said Ben Call softly, "you had better quit pushing that rifle barrel so hard. If you make that girl get the horse upset, we will all be hurt."

At these words to the noseless squaw, Pelón cursed angrily and turned his mount back and struck his half-sister with the flat of his hand across her mouth. The sound of the blow was sodden. Mackenna did not have to peer very hard to see the dark blood coming in the moonlight. The squaw neither moved nor spoke in response to the blow, however. Pelón came back to the head of the group still cursing.

"Yosen take her!" he growled. "She's like a damned bitch-wolf."

Mackenna nodded, tight-lipped. "We can be thankful," he said, "that her mean spirit was not inherited by you."

Pelón pressed his mount against the prospector's. "Do you joke with me again?" he demanded.

"Do you want to discuss it, just now?" countered the red-bearded prospector.

Pelón grinned. "No, I suppose not. The more I know of you, Mackenna, the less I trust you. It's those damned blue eyes and that harmless look that you have. They keep deceiving me."

"Again we are fortunate," replied Mackenna. "In your looks we can have complete trust."

"How do you mean that?"

"Precisely as I said it."

"Mackenna, I warn you!"

"I accept the hint," said the white miner.

"Here's another hint you had better accept—both of you." Besh broke in, speaking for the first time since leaving Surprise Grass. "Lower your voices and watch for Sánchez and Desplains down there close to the spring."

"That's good advice," said Pelón quickly. "Can you see them down there yet, Besh?"

The young Chiricahua was leaning intently forward, black eyes glittering.

"Yes," he said. "I just now caught the wink of the

moonlight off their rifle barrels. We had better hope that
Young Mickey Tibbs is not on guard right this moment.
His eyes are as good as mine."

"Where are Sánchez and Desplains positioned?" asked
Pelón.

"In that brush clump up the slope from the soldiers.
They ought to call out to the camp soon."

The words were scarcely uttered before they were
implemented from below. They all heard Sánchez's voice,
followed by the French-Canadian accents of Desplains,
hallooing the encampment. Then they heard, as plainly,
the galloping hoofs of their companions' ponies thumping
out of the brush clump toward the watch fires of the patrol.

From their blankets, the badly startled Negro cavalrymen blundered to their feet, as their pickets began yelling
to them not to shoot, that the incoming horsemen were
friends, or, at least, not Indians. At the same time, Sánchez
and Desplains were crying out, the one in Spanish, the other
in his broken English, for the soldiers to perform the identi-
cal favor and for the same reasons—they were not Apaches
and they thanked God in heaven to see the American
soldiers there.

This completely disorganized the camp. The pickets
were yelling at their trooper comrades to hold fire, the
white lieutenant was shouting for his first sergeant to tell
him what the situation was, and three or four of the colored
soldiers were firing their carbines regardless of the pickets'
pleas not to do so. A better turmoil could not have been
arranged with a month of planning and a year of pure luck.

"Let's go!" cried Pelón López triumphantly to his
waiting followers. "My God! We could walk on foot past
those black soldiers the way they have obeyed the alarm
of Venustiano!"

"Could be," said Ben Call in English, "but I'll ride all the same."

"Hang on, Francie!" Mackenna heard himself calling to the Stanton girl. And then, even in the wild gallop down the slope, he realized it was the first time he had used her name. He was so struck by this victory over his bachelor's wariness that he rode past the milling camp of the black cavalry patrol and half a mile into the desert beyond it before he remembered to worry about the soldiers greeting him with a cut-down volley of carbine fire.

Indeed, Pelón's escaping band all made the rush without incident. It was a fine, exciting, even a brilliant maneuver. Yet its total victory was still in the making. Sánchez and Desplains, seeing the disruption wrought among the Negroes by the shrill Apache yells of Besh and Hachita, added their own brash bit of outlaw cunning to their chief's bold coup.

Leaving Lupe, the Pima squaw, in the midst of the crowding circle of admiring colored troopers seeking to help her down from her mount and relieve her supposed fears, the two rascals led their own ponies quietly on into the boulders and out past the soldier watch fires. There they mounted the little brutes unhurriedly and loped off through the fine desert moonlight to rejoin Pelón and the others just as they were circling back into the hills north of the cavalry camp.

No leader could have played in better luck. Not a person had been hurt on either side. No member of the band had been seen closely enough by the soldiers to be identified, except Sánchez and Desplains, who could always claim their ponies had bolted. The plan of Pelón López had borne the golden fruit of bravery, and ahead of the half-breed's galloping band now lay only the parched

and pitiless miles of the land itself. That was all which
stood between his remaining *muchachos* and the incalculable wealth of the Lost Adams Diggings. The buffalo
soldiers had been made utter fools of. Young Mickey Tibbs
had been still yawning in his blankets when Sánchez and
Desplains deserted the cavalry camp. Bright as the moonlight was, the army scout wouldn't be able to do a thing
about following them until daylight. There was too much
rock and hard sandstone the way they were headed for
even Young Mickey to decipher without full light. Pelón
allowed himself the luxury of his barking laugh and called
out for his comrades to slow their horses and to go at a
comfortable jog. At such a saving gait they could still reach
The Skulls by dawn. They could water their mounts and
lie about resting several hours, knowing that the buffalo
soldiers and Young Mickey Tibbs would only be starting
out from Yaqui Spring as they were arriving at The Skulls.

"By God!" Pelón cried, reaching out and slapping the
sore shoulder of Glen Mackenna who, with Ben Call and
Francie Stanton, he had called up to ride with him in his
moment of supremacy. "Even for me this was a fine night's
work! Those poor colored men! Did you see them running
around in circles like run-over dogs? And shooting their
guns up into the air? And rolling the whites of their funny
eyes like crazy broncos fighting the rope? *Ay de mí!* Can
you imagine Pelón López ever thinking those black apes
might make him trouble?"

Neither Call nor Mackenna answered him. His great
naked head swung about menacingly.

"What is this?" he challenged. "Still sullen over your
failure to outwit me, Benito? You, Mackenna, my friend,
do you also hold it against me that my brain is superior to
your own in this game?"

"Oh, never, *Jefe*," denied Mackenna, catching the

ugly gleam in his eye. "It is only that we are overwhelmed."

"Well, I can't blame you. I am remarkable."

Glen Mackenna looked at him and nodded. "You're too modest," he said.

"More jokes, Mackenna?"

"No, *Jefe*, but 'remarkable' is such a mean, small word. You deserve something better."

"You have such a better word, perhaps?"

"Yes. How about 'loathesome'?"

The outlaw chief straightened and sat proud in his saddle. "I knew," he said loftily, "that one day you would have to recognize my true nature."

"It was inevitable," admitted Mackenna.

They rode on through the night. It was a lovely night. The desert smelled as only the desert can smell after an enormously hot day. The sun's heat had baked out of each stone and grain of sand and tiny arid-leaved plant its entire fragrance. Now, with several hours of cooling darkness to soften them, these earthen odors and these pungent scents of sage, beargrass, prickly pear and Spanish dagger were rising to meet the nose in a delight of horse-stirred dust, sweated saddle leather and acrid, biting tang of pony droppings. It was the sort of wanderer's wine which men of Mackenna's and Ben Call's lone breed drank heavily.

Pelón and Sánchez, murderer and deserter, were likewise victims of this spell of the hot sands and cool moonlight. So, too, were slim Besh and silent Hachita. Even the gaunt Sally and the mummy-faced Mal-y-pai breathed deeply of the night. Francie Stanton felt it, as well. She was strangely excited, rather than frightened, and was astonished to find that she did not even feel tired.

It was the kind of thing, that nighttime desert air, to make poets of peasants, boys of men, girls of women, and the reverse. It even made philosophers of Sonora half-breed bandits. And debaters of red-bearded gold hunters and suspect ex-deputy sheriffs. The feeling of the ozone and the influence of Diana got into all of them. Mal-y-pai was moved to ride with Mackenna and Francie, off Pelón's flank, and spin, for the blue-eyed mining engineer, the full pedigree of El Jefe, together with the true story of Sally's father—not white, but a full-blooded uncle of Nachez, the great warrier—and the details of the sad misunderstanding through which the younger squaw had lost her nose. Mackenna was not surprised to learn, through this fable, that Sally was, like her half-brother, Pelón, "a good girl." She had not been unfaithful to her husband at all, but had merely attempted to demonstrate for a would-be lover that her charms were not available. In the process, unhappily, the husband had happened along. Not understanding that Sally was discouraging the other man, he had refused to listen but insisted that it was no way to dishearten a suitor by showing him what he was missing, and had whipped out his knife and put the mark of misery upon his faithful wife.

It was such hasty mistakes as this, said the old lady, which made of life such a complicated matter. If men would only listen, instead of leaping for knife or rifle, there would be a deal less trouble in the world.

Mackenna, on the point of inquiring politely into the question of possible additional half-brothers and sisters of Sally and Pelón, was embarrassed to see riding just behind them the hot-eyed squaw of the story just completed. Clearly she had heard every word recounted by her mother and had been watching Mackenna throughout. He felt her burning eyes strike into him, now, with a force of animal intensity. He wondered at this glare, not understanding its reason. Then, of a sudden, the gaunt squaw shifted her gaze to Francie Stanton for an instant, before returning it to

Mackenna, and he knew what it was that made Sally's eyes show fire in the moonlight. It was not only predatory hunger for him but hatred for the white girl. He realized, then, that he must never allow Francie to be alone with the Apache sister of Pelón, after that night. Nor must he let the sensuous Indian woman get him, Mackenna, soparated from the rest. It required no experience with women for him to comprehend that Sally had the feeling for him. Her whole shrikelike, hovering tenseness proclaimed it dangerously. That she would kill the young white girl to come at him was a cold fact which did not seem reasonable in the soft context of the desert night and the new friendliness which its beauties had set in motion within the strangely assorted band. But Mackenna knew that it was reasonable to an Apache.

He broke his eyes away from those of Sally and returned to ride with Pelón and Ben Call and Venustiano Sánchez. Sally dropped back with the other Apaches, Besh and Hachita. Mal-y-pai, left alone with Francie Stanton, who had been freed of her gag and bonds by Pelón's order, nodded to the white girl and mumbled, "It's too bad you don't speak Spanish, *muchacha;* I would tell you something about that flat-nosed bitch back there. I like you a little bit. You're skinny and tough, like me. But you're pretty. I was never pretty. Maybe that's why I like you. Maybe it's the thing that I know Mackenna has the real love for you, which guides my heart. It's no matter. I still wish you could understand what I am saying, you poor damned little fool. *Ih!* Why should I bother? You would probably spit in my face for my trouble. After all, you're white and I'm but a dark, ugly brownish red, like an old cowhide long in the sun. The hell with you! I hope Sally cuts your ovaries out—!"

She wound up the Spanish anger with a guttural

Apache curse, but Francie Stanton smiled, reached over and patted Mal-y-pai's wrinkled talon of a hand. Mal-y-pai hissed like a snake and withdrew the hand as though it had been scorched by a brand from the fire. But, in the moonlight, the white girl saw the gleam of the tears in the rheumy old eyes of the mother of Pelón López, and she smiled again and said, in quiet, low tones, "I don't think you would hurt me. I don't know what you said, but somehow I'm not afraid of you." She frowned a moment, trying to think how she might convey to the old lady what she herself felt and meant. Finally her gray eyes brightened luminously. Reaching out, she touched the ugly squaw on the breast above the heart. Then she placed the same hand over her own heart, and said the one word, "Friends."

There is a sound to that word in any language, in any land, which is like no other. The old lady looked over at her, startled. Their eyes met and spoke together, then broke away.

"I don't know," muttered the old lady in Spanish, "I don't know . . ."

20

Something
Wrong at The Skulls

"IT's ONLY a little way now," said Pelón. "Ay!
Just smell that dawn wind freshening! What a night this
has been." He waved an arm expansively, blessing Mackenna with his expressionless grin. "Admit it, old friend,
you know I'm right. You're as excited about the Adams
gold and getting away from those stupid buffalo soldiers as
I am. That Young Mickey Tibbs! *Ih!* He's nothing like
his father, the old man. I thought he was. But you can't
hope to make two men as crafty and wicked as Old Mickey
Tibbs."

He paused, drawing in a breath of the desert air,
smacking his wide lips as though it were good to the taste.

"You see, *amigo*, it's this way. If, as I have said before,
the Old Mickey was a whole son-of-a-bitch, then, ha, ha,
ha! I guess you would have to say that the young one is
only half a son-of-a-bitch, eh? At least, he's only half the

son-of-a-bitch that his father was. What do you think of
that joke, Mackenna? You think it's a good one?"

"Not as good as the one your mother just told me
about your sister Sally," said the white prospector. "But
yes, I'll admit it, you've inherited some of the old lady's
talent for a tale. Why didn't you tell me she was your
mother, Pelón? Is it a secret?"

"Well, yes and no, *amigo*. After all, it does no one a
great deal of good to be known as the mother of Pelón
López." There was a sudden faint echo of seriousness in
his reply, another gleaming of that tiny spark of human
weakness which Mackenna had thought he saw before. "I
told you about Sally, however. You can't say I wasn't
partly honest with you. Besides, what does it matter?"

Mackenna measured his answer. "It only matters,
Jefe," he finally said, "if you are the man I think you are.
I have seen you kill two men tonight, and two times you
have attacked me like a crazy person for no reason, and
you struck Sally earlier up there before we ran by the
soldier camp, all for no good cause that I could see. But
I still think that you are not like Monkey, not an animal
like that."

"What kind of an animal am I then?"

"A bad one, but one which never had the chance to be
a good one. You are too old now to be made over, but I
think the seed of your Spanish father's honor can be
brought to grow in you just the same. Do you know anything about the Spanish religion, Pelón?"

"Hah! I know all about it. The *padres* are a pack of
lying dogs. They sleep with the sisters and they steal the
minds of the little children and they collect all the money
from the poor and send it to the Pope in Rome, and the
whole thing is enough to make an honest outlaw blush
in shame for his own failings as a thief and murderer."

"I see," said Mackenna, that you are a follower of the Revolution; those are the ideas of Benito Juárez."

"My ideas, too," insisted Pelón. "A great man, though, that Benito. A hero. Did you know he was part Indian?"

"He was all Indian," said Mackenna. "Especially in his ideas about the Church. No, Pelón, I don't mean to ask about religion itself; I wanted to know if you were familiar with the teachings of Christ?"

"Christ?"

"Certainly."

"You mean Jesús, the son of María?"

"Is there another?"

"Are you a Catholic, Mackenna?"

"No."

"Why do you ask these things then?"

"Pelón, can you reply to a simple question?"

"Of course. Do you think I am stupid?"

"Never mind that. Stick to the point. Do you know that Jesus Christ teaches that it is never too late for a bad man to become a good man?"

Pelón threw back his huge head and laughed.

"Ah, that Jesús!" he said. "I wish that he could ride in my saddle for a couple of trips. It's like Benito Juárez always said: It's easy to talk good."

Mackenna nodded. He was surprised continually to keep finding these small nooks and crannies of intelligence in the brutal bandit, and the finding bolstered his original hope that he might, somehow, exploit Pelón's better side —if he could locate it.

"*Jefe*," he said, "is there nothing that you feel softly about? No one that you love? No thing that you care for?"

"Certainly!" cried the outlaw chief, smashing him on the shoulder. "I love whiskey and a fine bed and a fat young woman. What's the matter with you, Mackenna? There are many things that I care about."

"No, that sort of caring is not what I mean, Pelón. Is there no person or no idea which will make you feel sad, or make you weep, or make you want to do better?"

"How could I do better, *compadre?* I have outwitted an *americano* lieutenant and thirty black troopers and a young whelp of an Apache bastard-scout and am riding free through a perfectly glorious dawning toward good water and a rest and some hot coffee and all taken with the company of good friends and women along to do the camp work. Why, my friend, you are the one who has no feeling for what is better in this life. If I were to be having better luck than I have mentioned, I could not stand it. And, my God, we haven't even mentioned all that gold up there in Cañon del Oro! Mackenna, you're an old woman. You and Jesús should come to Pelón for lessons. You are the ones who are finding life to be bad, not Pelón López!"

Glen Mackenna shook his head stubbornly.

"One day, Pelón," he said, "I will find your soft spot. I know that you have it. I've believed it ever since first we met. We Scots don't let go of an idea too quickly."

"Neither do we Sonorans," said Pelón. "And my idea is for you to shut up now; you've talked too much already."

"As you will," submitted Mackenna, "but there is one more thing, *Jefe*, which I meant to ask you about. This is business. May I state it?"

"Certainly, go ahead. For business there is always time. I'm a businessman, you know that."

"Yes, well, it's that sister of yours. Do you know what I mean? One doesn't like to be indelicate."

"Sure, I know what you mean. What the hell? You think I'm blind? I told you she wanted to be your woman. Also, I told you you could have her. What the hell is the problem? Are you bashful?"

"That's not what I mean," said Mackenna. "I'm talking about the way that she looks at the white girl. I'm afraid she'll kill her."

"Well, damn it, so am I!"

"Then do something about it, Pelón," said the bearded prospector, surprised at the other's vehement agreement. "You can't let her go on like that. At least order her to stay away from the girl. At least do that."

Pelón shrugged his thick shoulders helplessly.

"*Hombre*," he said, "I can't help you. I don't want any harm to come to that white girl any more than do you. But it is not up to me to protect her. It's up to you. You're the only one who can keep Sally away from her."

"What?" stammered Mackenna. "Me? How? In what way?"

Pelón pivoted his great skull and stared at him.

"One last time, Mackenna," he said, "I warn you not to make jokes with me."

"My God! I'm not joking."

"You must be."

"No, I'm not, I swear it. Tell me how to do it, and I'll do it!"

"Well," said Pelón, shaking his head, "it's difficult to actually believe that a man could have come to your age and not know how it is done, but I suppose anything is possible. All right, here is the way you go about it. First, you get them aside some place. Even a bitch like Sally does better without lookers. That's women for you, you know. They're all whores at heart but even whores like to shut the door, if there is a door. So, the first thing you do is get them out of sight, then you usually put your hand on—"

"That's enough!" cried Mackenna, flushing wildly. "My God, that's not what I meant, you damned fool! Any man knows about *that!*"

"Well, you asked me, goddamn it!" flared the outlaw.

"No, no! I asked you how to keep Sally away from—"

He broke off, belatedly, and Pelón gave his coyote's yelping laugh.

"Sure, *amigo!*" he cried. "That's the idea, see? I knew it would come to you. Now, do you understand why it is that I can't help you? But of course. No man of Spanish honor would think to seduce his own sister. Especially *that* sister! No, it's up to you, my friend."

Mackenna nodded hopelessly.

"How far is it to the water?" he asked wearily.

"Over the next rise and past that point of rocks," answered Pelón, pointing to a sandstone scrap directly ahead and a little to their right. "Our ponies will have their noses in it within another ten minutes."

Mackenna glanced back over his shoulder and saw that Sally was still riding with Besh and Hachita. The squaw also still had her eyes fastened on him unblinkingly. Looking over toward Mal-y-pai and Francie Stanton he saw that the latter was nodding, asleep in the saddle. The old squaw caught his look and nodded to him and gave him a little wave, as though to say, "It's all right, I'm looking after her," and, somehow, he felt comforted by that. Still, all the way over the rise and around the base of the sandstone escarpment leading in toward the waterhole, he rode with a heavy and growing burden of Celtic premonition of evil.

Something was very badly wrong with something. And it wasn't as simple as Sally's animal cravings. Nor Pelón's murderous uncertainties of temper. Nor Francie Stanton's childish trust.

There was something wrong with this time and this place and this utter, deathly stillness which enclosed them all in its muffling shroud.

21 〰️

A Crash of Carbines

THE CRASH of the cavalry carbines stunned the ear. It broke so point-blankly upon the renegade party that its members could smell the burnt powder and taste the bitter grease of the smoke. There was no fight at The Skulls. Later reports of the proud troopers to the contrary, the outlaws did not shoot back. At no time was the affair anything but a trap and a rout. Pelón López did not unboot his Winchester. He did not even fire the famous Colt from beneath the Sonora serape. His only command of the day was for the *"retirada"* and he was turning his horse as he shouted it to his fellows. All of the latter who could followed him. In such a blind ambush, such a blasting away by cavalrymen who had the hated desert Apache where, classically, the hated desert Apache usually had them, there was no chance for friendly identification. The survivors in truth bolted like rabbits. Some were white rabbits and some were red rabbits and some were brown rabbits, but they all ran. All, again, who could.

Ironically, both Mackenna and Call had asked for blankets to ward off the chill of the desert night. The gar-

ments were genuine Indian-issue and the two white men
had them hunched up around their faces and about their
shoulders as shroudingly as any Mescalero or Mimbreño
bronco. Francie Stanton, too, had a blanket given her by
old Mal-y-pai. Hers was a U.S. Cavalry-issue, but she wore
it Apache-style, imitating Mal-y-pai, and in the uncertain
gray light of the morning and with the hot blood of their
savage African ancestors running wild in them, the Negro
troopers did not seek to separate the Government blankets
from those woven in front of some White Mountain or
Sierran *jacal*, or stolen from this dead Zuni or that raped
Hopi, or whomsoever. They just fired at the approaching
renegade ponies and at the blanketed, head-clothed or
sombreroed figures atop the wiry little mustangs. Certainly
they knew that some of those figures were female. But so
long as the consensus of impression, and the sense of the
official report, remained that all were Indians, then a
woman was as good as a man and had there been children
with the party—Indian children—then they also would
have been shot at. So it was that Mackenna turned his
mount and galloped away with Pelón López. And so it was
that Mackenna also reached out, quick-wittedly, and
whacked the rump of Francie Stanton's pony with the barrel of his old rifle, as he came up to the girl's balking
mount. The little horse gave a squall of pain and began to
run. It was in this moment, glancing fearfully back over
his shoulder, that Mackenna saw the bodies sprawled
among the brush and boulders which buttressed the waterhole. There were four of them: Sánchez, Desplains, Besh
and Ben Call. The first three were not moving, but Ben
Call was. He was crawling—scuttling—toward the buffalo
soldiers, waving his hat and calling out, "Don't shoot, don't
shoot; it's me, Ben Call!" The ponies of the dead Mexican
sergeant-deserter of Federales, of Raoul Desplains, and of

the slender, deep-voiced Apache grandson of Cochise were down with their masters in twisting, thrashing heaps upon the hard rubble of rock and sand. Ben Call's horse, stirrups flapping, reins trailing, was galloping free and uninjured off to the right. That was the picture which Glen Mackenna remembered of the fight at The Skulls.

The following instant his mount had swept him around the protecting bulge of the sandstone escarpment. In the same moment, Francie Stanton's horse made the turn and ran swiftly up on his pony's flank. With a common, wild yell, he and the white girl dug in their heels. Bent low and never looking back, they rode as crazily after Pelón, Hachita, Sally and old Mal-y-pai as though born in the same *ranchería* with their dark-skinned Apache packmates.

22

The Halt at Lookout Ridge

UNABLE SAFELY to do otherwise, Mackenna and the girl rode on with the outlaw survivors into the first ramparts of the Yaqui hills. Behind them the sandstone scarp effectively cut off the rear view. For all the white riders could know, the buffalo soldiers might be galloping in hard pursuit not half a mile back. Since there had been no time yet for Ben Call to reach and talk with the troop commander, identifying Mackenna and Francelia Stanton, the proximity of the excited black cavalrymen was extremely dangerous. Indeed, Glen Mackenna reasoned, Ben Call might never have reached the soldiers at all. His wound could have been mortal. He could be lying, right now, a few yards from the bodies of Besh, Desplains and Sánchez, as motionless and still of life as they. In accordance, Mackenna did not argue Pelón's urging for him and the girl to "keep up" and to "ride hard." Neither did Francie Stanton complain when Mackenna passed the order to her. The effect of being shot at in earnest at powder-biting ranges is universal and not confined to men. The woman living more than a few days or weeks in that land under-

stood guns and gunfire—and Francie had been with the
Stantons five months. She was scarcely a hardbitten pio-
neer, yet neither was she a "dude," in the derogatory sense
the Arizonan used that term on newly arrived Easterners.
Hence, when she smiled tightly and waved in response to
his shout, Mackenna was able to experience a double lift of
relief. Not only was Francie Stanton behaving intelligently,
she was still trusting him implicitly. It was a burden of confidence which the lone-wolf mining man found the lightest
in weight of any he had ever borne.

However, the moment's relief was short-lived. When
their panting ponies had climbed the first ridge, Pelón
ordered a halt. From the vantage, they could see over the
sandstone escarpment guarding the waterhole at The Skulls,
and could thus, by a very few moments' wait, determine
the nature of the pursuit.

They all got down to let their ponies breathe. The
Apaches, Sally and Mal-y-pai and Hachita, crowded up to
stand with Pelón, peering intently below. Mackenna stood
a little back with Francie Stanton. It was a strange way and
place to have their first real opportunity to talk. Mackenna,
however, realizing they might never have another such
respite from the eternal surveillance of their Indian comrades, forced the conversation.

"I still say," he began awkwardly, "that some way or
another we'll get out of this, Francie."

He used her name for the second time and did so
naturally. Looking at her in the clear morning light, he
was more than ever impressed with her extreme youth. She
stood no taller than his shoulder. She was so slight of build
and boyish that to see her huddled thus close to him, for all
the world like the child she was, no man could entertain
the former thoughts of her which had overwhelmed Mackenna back at Surprise Grass. Here was nothing more or

less than a very young captive white girl taken by a raiding
Indian and renegade half-breed band of outlaws from
Sonora in old Mexico. He had not previously been close
enough to her, in a good enough light, to see the trout-pool
clarity of her gray eyes and the big flecky spatter of
freckles which lay over her small nose and sunburned
cheeks. It was true that she had a rather wide mouth, with
full lower lip and a certain ready looseness to curve itself
into a smile, which suggested something less innocent than
the eyes and the freckles. But Mackenna knew this was the
sort of imagining that took hold of a man wandering too
long and too stubbornly alone in the wasteland. He dis-
owned it for once and all standing there beside Francie
Stanton in the pure white light of the desert morning. But
as he straightened his shoulders to the resolve, the "little
girl" whose youth and innocence had inspired it, reached
for his hand and took it in hers and gave it a warm squeeze.

"If you say so, Glen," she murmured.

Mackenna shivered to hear his first name.

The only times she had been able to address him previously, it had been Mr. Mackenna. It still ought to be, damn
it, he told himself. She had no right to such familiarity. He
was old enough, or damned near old enough, to be her
father! The thought demanded documentation.

"Francie," he said sternly, watching at the same time
to see if anything were visible beyond the figures of Pelón
and his companions, "how old are you?"

"Sixteen," she answered quickly. "How old are you?"

She looked up at him when she said it and by the way
that she asked it and the way that her eyes hung on him
waiting for her answer, he knew that she saw through his
question to its motive, and that her return query was placed
in exactly the same spirit.

Sixteen she might be. But no child.

"That," he said acridly, "is neither here nor there. But I'm thirty, if you must know."

She nodded and squeezed his hand hard.

"That's not too old," she said, and for reasons which made no sense whatever in connection with the hot flood of the new sun now drenching them from above the Yaquis, Glen Mackenna shivered again and this time so violently that he broke out in gooseflesh.

"What's the matter?" she said quickly.

Mackenna set his jaw and let go a mighty sigh.

"Nothing," he lied. "Be quiet and watch for the cavalry."

As he spoke, Pelón turned and signaled him forward. He went up to the bandit chief.

"They're not coming," the latter told him. "You see down there? There's no dust in the air beyond the big rock between us and the waterhole. Also, they have now had plenty of time to round the rock, had they been coming when we began to watch."

"I'd guess you were right, *Jefe*. Now what?"

"I don't know, Mackenna. I suspect that cursed Benito Call will tell them everything, except, naturally, for his own willing part in the whole business. Then the cavalry will come after us with Young Mickey. Tibbs once more in the lead. That damn Young Mickey. Do you know that he is only seventeen years old? That's right. He was just three when his father went with General Crook down into the Mexican Sierra Madre to try and bring back Geronimo and the Chiricahua. That was 1883. Thirteen, no fourteen, years ago."

Mackenna nodded, frowning.

"I know from my own experience," he said, "that you can't trust these young people. They grow up too fast these days. But don't feel badly, *Jefe*. You're not the only one who has been fooled by a child."

"Well, at least your child is pretty, Mackenna. Did you ever see *mine*—that miserable Young Mickey? He's uglier even than his father, who was uglier than I am. Ugh! *Santa!*"

"They are both trouble," said Mackenna. "What will you do now, Pelón?"

The bandit leader studied him squintingly.

"It is why I called you forward just now," he finally said. "I want to ask your advice. We have come to another bad place."

Mackenna eyed him sharply.

"What you mean is that you no longer have enough men to make sure I won't get away from you, isn't that it, Pelón?"

"Yes, that's it. A new agreement is needed. With only Hachita, who has the mind of a baby crawling on the ground, I cannot watch you and the white girl in a proper way. I will have to watch Sally all the time, too, to keep her from knifing the girl and, well, hell, it just will not work out the right way."

"No," said Mackenna, "it won't. What do you propose?"

"I want to be reasonable with you, *amigo*. Fair and just, as I always am with my friends."

"No, don't do that!" protested Mackenna. "Just be yourself, *Jefe*. What treachery do you have in mind?"

Pelón shook his huge head wearily. "I'm too tired to respond to your insults," he said. "I ought to knock your head off, but I will not do it. What I would like to propose is that we let the girl go back to the soldier camp. But I don't know how to do it in a safe way. Those crazy buffalo soldiers might shoot her yet. Once you arouse them, they're like black hornets; they sting everything in sight."

"If we could only be sure Ben Call reached them alive," Mackenna said. "But we have no way of knowing how badly he was wounded."

"Wounded?" snorted Pelón. "Benito, wounded? Don't make me laugh; it's not funny. That bastard fell off his horse on purpose. I saw him go but I couldn't stop to shoot him. He took care of himself when he could, Mackenna. That's the way he is. You're better off without him for your friend. He always thinks of himself, Benito does. It's why he has stayed alive so long in this country."

"Well, you can't blame him for looking out for himself. That's only human nature."

"Perhaps. But I say he's a bastard all the same."

"Well, Pelón, if Call is safe with the soldiers, then it's safe to let the girl go; she won't be in any danger approaching them at the waterhole with Call there."

"No, I'd feel better about it if we had a guide for her. I have to be able to guarantee her safety, if I am to interest you in the other part of my proposal."

"Do you mean going on with you to Sno-ta-hay?"

"You know that I do."

"Do you think that's a fair offer?"

"I can always kill the girl right now if you prefer."

"No, no, I didn't mean that."

"I didn't think you did. Well, Mackenna, do you have any ideas of a way to get her safely to those soldiers at The Skulls?"

"Sure," said the other, brightening. "You could let me guide her; I know that country between here and there very well. I just rode over it recently."

"Ha, ha, ha!" Pelón laughed raspingly.

Mackenna wisely changed the talk.

"Pelón," he said, "if we can get the girl safely to the soldiers, how do you know that I would honor my word to go with you to Cañon del Oro?"

Pelón stared at him, surprised.

"You're Mackenna," he said.

The bearded prospector accepted the summation. To a human brute of Pelón López's simplicity, things were as they were. The sun rose in the morning. It sank at night. Grass grew. Water ran. Stones rolled if kicked. Rain was wet. Dust was dry. Mackenna was honest.

"All right," said the latter, "I will go with you, if we can safely deliver the girl to the soldiers."

"*Cuidado!*" called old Mal-y-pai from the watch place. "Somebody comes!"

Mackenna followed Pelón back to the lookout.

Over beyond the high rock wall of the escarpment, three black dots of mounted men were crawling out from the waterhole at The Skulls. Pelón turned and barked at Hachita in Apache, demanding to know if the huge Mimbreño could identify the horsemen. Famous, even among his hawk-visioned people, for his great eyes, Hachita peered briefly below.

"Unh," he mumbled thickly. "Young Mickey and two buffalo soldiers. One gray horse, one bay, one brown with a bobbed tail. Good horses. Young Mickey has a big nose."

It was the longest speech Mackenna had heard from the strange giant, and the first words of any length he had uttered since forced by Besh to bury the old man, Enh, at Surprise Grass with Monkey and Vachel. But his mind was not on the broken silence of Hachita; the appearance of Young Mickey Tibbs was what now lighted his blue eyes.

"Pelón," he cried, "there's our guide! Am I right?

What could be safer? The best Indian scout the army has plus two regular soldiers for an armed escort back to the camp. What do you say?"

"I don't know," answered the bandit. "I wouldn't trust that Young Mickey with anything. But it's your girl. If you say it is all right, then I agree. Get her ready."

23

Never Say
the Name of the Dead

MACKENNA TALKED quickly with Francie Stanton. The facts, he told the girl, were plain. This was her chance to get back to civilization, and she would have to go. She made the expected protest against going without him but Mackenna insisted she see it his way. They would meet again, he assured her. He knew Pelón López from many years; the bandit chief would not harm him. Besides, the outlaw was a gold hunter and as subject as any man to the chills and fevers of the legend of the Lost Adams Diggings. Mackenna, himself, could not lie about the spell that the old tale held for him. He *wanted* to go on with the Apache band; he did not care to be "saved" by the buffalo soldiers. But, for her, due to the problem with Sally, there was no other course than to go meet Young Mickey and the Negro troopers. Mackenna would come and look her up when he got back. It was agreed on that basis.

At the last moment, however, Francie hung on to

Mackenna's hand and threatened to stay with him. In this crisis he was given unlooked-for support when Mal-y-pai hobbled over to them.

"By God, wench," she railed at the girl in Spanish, "you do as you are told! Do you hear? Now get out!" Then, as vehemently, she embraced the white girl, stroking her and saying repeatedly, "Friends, friends, friends," the sole English word that she knew.

Francie Stanton showed her first tears then. But she stifled them and told Glen Mackenna that she was ready and would go now on his given word that if he should get free from Pelón, and the old lady would agree, he was to bring Mal-y-pai out with him.

Mackenna accepted the charge and the girl was started down the trail into the desert, mounted on their poorest and lamest horse. They all hung to the lookout watching after her until they saw her, far, far below, meet Young Mickey Tibbs and his black companions. They saw the exchange of gestures between the young Apache breed and the white captive. Then they saw the two Negro troopers turn and start back for The Skulls, escorting Francie.

"That's enough," said Pelón at this point. "The girl is safe and that damn Young Mickey is going to stay on our trail. Let us go on a ways to a good place I know, and there we will wait for him."

"What?" said Mackenna. "Wait for Young Mickey?"

"Certainly. How else may I say to him what I have in my heart for him?"

"Now it's you who joke," accused the prospector.

"Yes," said Pelón. "Like a wolf beside a waterhole."

"Oh. So you mean to ambush him then? Kill him like you did Monkey and Vachel?"

"Oh, no, not like them. Nothing like that."

"What do you mean?"

"With Young Mickey I will take a little time. I owe it to him."

"*Ih!*" broke in Mal-y-pai. "We all do; all the Apaches. He's a damned traitor and the son of a damned traitor."

"Unh!" rumbled the towering Hachita, showing rare emotion. "It was his rifle which brought down my friend."

Mackenna wondered how the giant Mimbreño could have known whose gun it was which had taken his handsome Chiricahua companion. He made a point in his memory to talk with the hulking Apache at the first opportunity. There was something of value in Hachita. Mackenna intuitively sensed it. He had felt, formerly, the same communion with the tall, slender Besh, and now, oddly, the bond seemed to have been transferred to the huge Mimbreño. He had noticed Hachita watching him ever since they had arrived at the lookout, from below, and he knew something concerning Glen Mackenna was troubling the big Apache.

"Nonsense," said Pelón abruptly, denying the allegation about Young Mickey's shot. "No one sees the bullet which strikes his friend. But we won't argue about it. Do you want to go home now, Hachita? It is all right if you do."

The Apache frowned. It appeared as though he were struggling to remember something, and could not.

"No," he finally muttered. "I don't think I better."

"Sure, go right ahead if you wish," encouraged Pelón, showing a sudden interest in being rid of the big Indian. "I think Besh would want you to do it."

"No!" cried the huge Apache, recoiling. "Don't say his name; never say the name of the dead! You know that!"

"Of course," said Pelón, coloring. "A thousand pardons, *hombre*. One forgets the old ways, when he is so many years away from his mother's people."

"Don't forget again," said Hachita, fingering his ax.

But Pelón did not hear him, having already turned to mount up and to urge the others to do likewise. Presently the little string of desert horses set out to snake its way on into the forbidding stillnesses of the Yaqui hills. They were lost to sight in a matter of minutes. Nothing moved or remained behind them to show where they had stood and watched back for the buffalo soldiers, except the cactus sparrows chittering nervously in their quick, flitting attack upon the still-warm droppings of the gaunt Apache mustangs. Oh, and one other thing. Far down on the desert, hidden under the bulging curve of the sandstone scarp, Young Mickey Tibbs lowered his fieldglasses. "*Bueno*," he said, and turned his gray horse around and sent him on a driving gallop back along the tracks of his two Negro trooper comrades and the slim white girl from the Stanton Ranch. For some reason, as he rode, Young Mickey Tibbs was grinning. For a boy only seventeen years old, and who was said to be one-quarter white, it was a peculiar grin. Peculiar and yet familiar. Hauntingly familiar. It was the same grin which marks, no matter the violence of its owner's destruction, the *risus sardonicus* of the human skull.

24 ⋛

Waiting for Young Mickey

THE PLACE which Pelón chose to ambush Young Mickey Tibbs was another of those strange Apache "oases" which allowed the redmen to live in that hostile land. Mackenna always thought of them in that reference term of the desert, although to make an oasis of naked rocks, cacti, Spanish dagger, mesquite and a little mangy patching of stunted trees and gramma grass took some charity. This spot, however, was less forbidding than most, if still nothing like Surprise Grass.

It lay toward the head of a narrow canyon. In this canyon was a typical Arizona stream, now running clear and bright on the surface, now making a small lovely falls, or a deep rock pool, and now invisible altogether as it went underground to course downward through the blind sands below the level of its bed. In a sudden, sharp turning of the trail, Mackenna saw ahead a fall of splashing green water perhaps as high as fifteen feet. Footing it was a fine pool out of which the water ran in a looping s-curve to irrigate a pocket of tough mountain gramma not over two acres in extent and covered, all about its flanks, with a rubble of breakage from the canyon walls overgrown with scrub piñon, madrone, dwarf oak and native walnut. It was a natural trap. As certainly as any horseman traveling this canyon into the yellow Yaquis would come to this watering place, just that certainly he could be shot dead from two dozen invisible firing points within a hundred paces of the halt.

Mackenna nodded as he noted this, and glanced over at Pelón. The outlaw returned his nod.

"Aye," he said. "Here is where we wait."

"It's a good place, *Jefe*. The only trouble I see with it is that the one who approaches it from below must know that it makes a trap for him. I could see it on the instant, and I'm not even one-quarter Apache."

"So will Young Mickey see it," said Pelón. "But the thing is that he cannot circle it. He has got to come to this water, whether he stops or not. There is no other track he can take and stay with us."

"Perhaps he doesn't know this. Perhaps he will try some side canyon to go around us."

"No. He will come here."

"I see. Then you expect him to make a talk, eh?"

"Sure. He's a scout for the cavalry. It isn't his business to do anything but find us. He's not a bounty hunter."

"I've known some scouts that were. You have, too."

"Well, yes, my friend, that is true. In the old days they would bring your head back in a sack if there were any money to be paid for it. But times have changed, Mackenna. The old days are gone. The cavalry doesn't allow its scouts to cut heads off any more. Nowadays there is more honor to the officer who takes his quarry still breathing. The times go soft, Mackenna. Don't you think I know that? Don't you think Young Mickey knows it? Now,

down in Mexico, it's different. Down there I must be careful. But up here in the Estados Unidos? Hah!"

"That's quite a long speech, *Jefe.*"

"I know my subject."

"I hope that you do. Do you think we will have time
to rest a little and relax before Young Mickey comes?"

"We'll make sure. I'll put Hachita on guard down the
canyon a ways. That's the only trouble with this place;
there's no way you can see people coming up the canyon
from here; not until they break right into the little flat, just
as we did."

"That's what I meant," said Mackenna.

"I know, I know, but never mind. With Hachita
watching down below, we can be as safe as babies in a
warm wickiup. For myself, I want a bath. I haven't been in
the water since we left Sonora. Come, *amigo*. Look at that
lovely pool waiting over there across the grass."

Mackenna, too, thought the water looked inviting, although he was not as concerned about bodily cleanliness,
just then, as he was about Young Mickey Tibbs. But, looking at the frowning Hachita, he was reassured. If you
couldn't relax with an Apache mastiff such as that on
guard, there was no certain peace anywhere. He decided
to put his faith in the red giant.

"All right, *Jefe*," he nodded to Pelón. "Let's go."

They set off across the tiny meadow, the woman following. Hachita, at a signal from Pelón, turned back. At
the pool, as was the Apache custom, the horses were first
attended to. When fully watered—the little mustangs
would drink only so much, unlike "civilized" horses which
would founder themselves under the same circumstances
—the mounts were put out in the grass on staking ropes.
The one pack animal remaining of the three original ones

was unloaded and, to Mackenna's surprise, old Mal-y-pai
was put to work by Pelón setting up camp. Sally was ordered to start chopping wood.

"The idea," said the outlaw chief to the curious prospector, "is to assure Young Mickey that we do not expect
him."

"I would guess as much, *Jefe*. The sound of that ax
blade on that hard wood can be heard five miles down the
canyon."

"Yes, if the wind is right."

Mackenna got out his pipe, Pelón found one of the
twisted coal-black Sonora *cigarros* which he favored, and
the two men lit up. A little breeze was working down the
canyon, bringing a trace of cooling air. Under the pungent
shade of the three scraggly cottonwoods marking the pool's
lower side, the resting was good. Mackenna drew in deeply
of the odors of the sun-drenched canyon and found them
good. He thought of old Enh, the dying Prairie Dog, and
of how the Indian patriarch had loved this arid, colorful,
altogether mysterious land. Looking over at old Mal-y-pai
cheerfully laying the midday coffee fire and whistling and
singing to herself, happy as though it were the old times
and she preparing a lunch for Loco, or Geronimo, or
Nachez, he thought again what a wonderful way of life
was being lost with the vanishing members of the old
Apache pure blood. Even the dark and passioned Sally
seemed at rest here in the somnolent perfumes of the
canyon. There was a grace and beauty to her lean form
swinging the camp ax which was not to be found in a white
woman. In the few years only which he had spent in the
country, Mackenna could remember the old Apaches and
the old Apache ways, which already were gone, and it
made him sad, somehow, to sit there smoking with Pelón
López and watching what might be the last sight of the

old Indian free way of life which would come to a white man in that land.

"Pelón," he said, removing his pipe, "I would like to talk. How do you feel about that?"

The outlaw looked at him, great ugly head turtled forward, gross features knotted in a frown.

"That's a strange thing," he answered. "I was just thinking to ask you the same thing. My heart has been touched a little to sit here and hear the sounds of the water and the canyon songbirds and the ring of the ax and the smell of the first wood smoke rising. I don't know, *amigo*, it has just touched me. It seems as though I am saying goodbye to something. Inside of me there is this sadness. Do you feel that, Mackenna? Is it this place, or what? Do you know?"

"No man knows why he feels sad," said the redhaired prospector. "But, yes, Pelón, I feel the thing you do. I was just thinking that it was because in a few years we won't be able to ride and camp in a canyon like this, all alone except for our thoughts and our voices in talk."

Pelón's face turned uglier yet.

"Don't talk like that!" he said vehemently. "That's not what I want to hear. If that is why you wanted to talk, shut up!"

"No," said Mackenna soothingly, "I didn't want to say a bad thing. It's just that this is Indian land and you may be the last Indians to use it this way as it was designed to be used. Does that make you angry, *Jefe?* It should not. Sad, yes. But not bitter with me."

Pelón looked at him a moment. Then he did a strange thing. He put his enormously powerful and hairy hand upon his white companion's shoulder and gave that shoulder a gentle squeeze. Startled, Mackenna saw that there were tears in his slant black eyes.

"Yes," he said, "let us be sad together, old friend."

They sat and smoked in silence for several minutes. It was the outlaw who finally nodded and said, "Now, we shall talk, *compadre*. What is it you would know of me?"

Mackenna had thought to query him on his life and seek, thereby, to come at that soft place in his make-up which he had been so sure existed. But in the present moment of emotion on the murderous outlaw's part, he dared not go into this delicate matter. He sought a diversion and found a natural one.

"Let us speak of the gold," he said, "and of Sno-ta-hay. I have heard many stories of it, but never the story that I believe. Perhaps you would tell me how the tale goes among the Chiricahua?"

"Why the Chiricahua?" asked Pelón.

"Only that Nana, who was in the canyon with Adams, was a Chiricahua."

"Yes, it's true, he was. Later his band split away from the main band, but that's the way it was in the old days when they caught Adams in Sno-ta-hay."

"You have heard the legend, then, from the Indians?"

"Many times, *amigo*. Old Mal-y-pai would spin its mysteries for Sally and me to pass the long winters in the *jacal*, when we were little ones, long, long ago."

"You will repeat it for me, then?" suggested Mackenna. "*Por favor?*"

The half-breed killer studied him a moment, then looked away up the canyon.

"Yes," he said, "I will."

25

The Lost Adams Legend

To BEGIN WITH, Pelón told Mackenna, the time was 1864. That was during the Civil War. Adams, who never had a first name which anyone remembered, was operating a freight-wagon business between Tucson and Los Angeles. He had a good friend who was his partner. The men made money and had two wagon trains, the one going while the other was coming. But when so many of the cavalry soldiers were withdrawn to fight in the war, the Apaches began to get bold once more and to shut off many of the trade routes. It became too risky for Adams' partner in the freighting company. He sold out to Adams, and then it was Adams doing all the driving for himself. Because of this, he would hook one wagon to the other, drawing both with six strong horses. He was warned by the Chiricahua to quit bringing supplies into the Territory to feed the white settlers, but Adams continued driving his freight wagons.

One early dawn the Apaches attacked and ran off his horses. Adams bravely pursued. He pressed the raiders and got back some of the animals—twelve of them. But when he got back to camp, his wagons and all of his trade goods were burned to cinders. The Apaches had drawn him off by running the loose stock, then done what they really wanted to do—put him out of the freighting business.

Adams set off with his twelve horses, his gun, and the clothes on his back—all that he had left in the world. The Apaches had even burned the wooden toolbox of the wagon in which Adams had stored his precious money; over two thousand dollars in gringo paper bills. So he came to another camp which was a village of the Pima people. The camp where he got burned out was near Gila Bend, and the Pima settlement was only a half-day's ride. So we know which village it was; that big one just southwest of Phoenix.

At this point in his narrative, the outlaw paused and asked Mackenna if this beginning agreed with the white legend, and the prospector said that it did. Pelón went on quickly then.

In the Pima village, which was naturally of a people friendly to him, Adams found a big surprise. A score of white miners were already there. They had full prospecting supplies with them, and told a high tale of lost Apache gold in the canyon of Sno-ta-hay. They had good reason for their gold fever, too, as Adams quickly learned.

A young Mexican wanderer had been visiting the Pima village when the white miners came into it from their nearby poor diggings in a Gila River dry wash. The Mexican youth, seeing their thin sacks of ordinary dust, told them he knew of a place where one man might pick up more gold than their total gleanings in ten minutes. The miners, of course, crowded about him with great greed and hunger. They insisted the youth tell them more. He did so.

As a small boy, he claimed, he had been captured by the Apaches. He had been with the Indians to Sno-ta-hay, their secret canvon, where a legend of their people said a great treasure waited. The gold there came in all known sizes, from flour dust, to rice grain, to nuggets as large as burro droppings. At this, the eyes of the white men blazed. Where was this canyon? they demanded.

The young Mexican, who had one ear badly misshapen and was from this called "Gotch Ear," shrugged and pointed to the northeast. "Over there in Apachería," he told them.

It was a grim warning but went unheard. His listeners only wanted to know if Gotch Ear would guide them to this treasure which, in his own words, lay only in the roots of the grass, and no deeper any place than the bite of a shovel blade. Gotch Ear showed as surprising a lack of fear of his former Apache captors as did his eager questioners. He said that he would indeed be willing to guide the white men to Sno-ta-hay, but that the price was clearly beyond them.

When pressed for what this meant, he told them that he wanted a horse to get out of the country on, and that they had not so much as one lame pack mule to offer him. This was true. The twenty men with all their capital of tools and food did not have a single mount. Horses were unknown to the Pimas, and everywhere else in that land which lay about them the Apaches had run off all animals not corralled or tied and guarded night and day by shotgun, rifle and sleepless vigil.

It was at this crushing agony of their greed, where they stood helpless to buy their guide's services for want of a forty-dollar horse, and helpless, also, to journey to Sno-ta-hay without other mounts to carry themselves and their supplies, that Adams arrived in the Pima village with his twelve tough native mustangs.

Immediately Brewer, the California leader of the mining party, offered Adams 25 percent of all gold found, if

he would furnish the expedition his dozen wiry horses.
Since the freighting business had fallen off so decidedly,
Adams quickly enough agreed to the bargain. With Gotch
Ear in the lead, those twenty-one white men and twelve
horses set out to find Sno-ta-hay, called Cañon del Oro, the
Canyon of Gold, by the white men ever since.

Here, Pelón interrupted himself to call over to Mal-y-
pai about some food. Assured that the old hag had a bit of
cold roast mule warming over the fire, and that the coffee
water was coming to a boil, he selected another of his black
cigarros and returned to his tale.

The start was made on August twentieth. Ahead of
them, the land they were to cross held not a single white
resident. Gotch Ear, who had at the last held out for, and
been promised, *two* horses rather than one—and also a rifle,
saddle, ammunition and two fifty-dollar gold pieces—now
told them that the distance to the landmark from which
they could see Sno-ta-hay was eight days. From the landmark, it was four or five more days to the last camp before
the canyon.

Pelón blew a cloud of smoke upward and nodded to
his companion that he would understand this eight days
from the Pima village to the lookout place was a lie that
the Mexican told to insure his employment. No white
party, only partly mounted, could arrive within four or
five days of Sno-ta-hay in such short time. But, no matter,
he and Mackenna understood the true distances.

Mackenna did not disagree.

The journey, continued the bandit chief, went well to
the landmark, a lookout place high on a rocky saddle between two mountains. From here could be seen the sugarloaf peaks, *los dos piloncillos*, which guarded the location
of Sno-ta-hay. But when Gotch Ear took Adams and
Brewer, the party's leaders, up above the saddle next morn-

ing, there was a little hard feeling. Pointing to the twin
sugarloafs, he told his employers that the canyon lay beneath them. Brewer angrily said that it could be as far as
two hundred miles to the sugarloafs. To this Gotch Ear
responded by amending his travel days to "maybe six more,
maybe ten." However, they were too far into Apachería
to turn back. The Mexican had lured them past the place
of possible returning. They had neither the supplies nor the
soundness of their horses for going back. Besides, the cunning Gotch Ear now mentioned that the gold in Sno-ta-
hay was salted in the creek gravel in a size to approach
acorns, and that, in the rocky matrix upstream of the placer
deposits, great smeary chunks of the stuff lay exposed in
the mother lode to the size of turkey's eggs and beyond.
This, naturally, was too much for the white men. Brewer
and Adams ordered the journey resumed. Their fever for
the gold was now hopelessly raging within them.

The count of the days was lost. The country through
which the Mexican led them was terrible in its nature. One
canyon after another cut across their path. All of the white
men became utterly lost in directions and in time. Trying
to think back, even Adams was confused. Had they skirted
the White Mountains of Arizona? Had they crossed but
two streams after leaving the Gila River? Was the second
of those two streams the San Francisco River in New
Mexico's western wastes? Adams could not remember. He
tried, as did every man of the party, and for the same secret
reason—each of them planned to get rid of his comrades
and come back alone some day. But none of them knew
this land and none ever could recall the way that Gotch
Ear took them from the thirteenth day onward.

The Indian version of the Lost Adams legend insisted
that no party of white men, such as that of the Brewer-
Adams party, could go over that deep canyon and little-

water area in anything less than twelve pony rides. So it
had been accepted in the Indian story that it was on about
the twenty-third or twenty-fourth day from the Pima village that Adams and his men came to the last night's camp
but one, from the portals of Sno-ta-hay.

Their excitement was now so great that it made them
sick. Their fever was ugly within them. They could not
sleep, and a watch was set over the guide, Gotch Ear, for
fear he would desert them.

The following day's journey was marked by every one
of them in his memory. Each wanted to know the exact
detail of the approach to Sno-ta-hay for that time when
he would come back without his friends. At once, on leaving camp, they began to climb steeply. Up, up, up they
went. They passed above the altitude of the prickly pear,
the mesquite, and the blue-scaled quail. They crossed a
yawning chasm of red limestone. They came to a military
wagon road, bearing old wheelmarks. "Look at this road
and be sure to look at it hard," Gotch Ear told them. "It
leads to the soldier fort in the malpais country. At the fort
there is a *tienda*, a store. You will be able to buy what you
need of supplies there."

The white men thought he meant Fort Wingate and
they didn't ask him which way they should follow the
road, thinking they knew.

All that day long and until after dark Gotch Ear kept
them traveling. It was later said that he delayed and de-
toured until the sun was gone, so that they would not remember how he got them to that last camp. But finally he
did get them there.

He said there would be no fire. He had "felt" the presence of Apaches for the last three days, he told them.
Since they had seen no human, red or white, and no pony
sign whatever, and nothing but the wagon tracks which

were washed pale by the rains, the sudden mention of the dread redmen was sobering. Nerves tensed.

Yet Gotch Ear knew how to divert the silent fear. With tomorrow's sun, he told them, they would begin the journey into Sno-ta-hay. Before that sun set, they would see with their own eyes, hold with their own hands, the ancient, sacred and incalculable wealth of the Canyon of Gold!

Sleep well, he bade them. You are about to see what no white man has ever seen. *And lived.*

26

Gotch Ear's Gold

"THE REST you know," said Pelón, shrugging. "How next morning Gotch Ear pointed out to them that they had spent the night in the ruins of an ancient Indian village, showing them the old irrigation *acequias*, or ditches, and remarking that the Apaches called this place the Pumpkin Patch, after the few tangled vines of that vegetable still growing there. How he led the party up the canyon through its narrow course, wherein in many spots a mounted man could touch both walls by reaching out his arms. How, after two hours of this hard going, the men had come out upon the upper level of a land which was plainly malpais, volcanic black lava clumps intermixed with patchy timber. How they all swore loudly, at this, knowing that mineral is not found in lava areas, and hence gold could not be there. How they reached, shortly, a mound of piled rocks which Gotch Ear told them was the 'Apache Post Office,' and for them to remember where it was, as they must remember, also, where the Fort Road and the Pumpkin Patch were. Then, how he warned that from certain message sticks set in the rocks of the post office he knew that a large party of Apaches had been here three days before, and would return. How, next, he asked the men to look to the north and, when they had, how they were amazed to see staring directly down upon them *los dos piloncillos,* the two sugarloafs which Gotch Ear had first shown them from Lookout Mountain thirteen or eleven or however many days before. How he explained that the two peaks lay beyond the Cañon del Oro, the canyon where the gold was, and that they marked the end of the trail; that the gold was only hours away; the gold which lay upon the ground and in the grass-roots so thickly that a single man of their number could load a packhorse with it in half a morning!"

Again, Pelón lifted his heavy shoulders, as if to say that Mackenna understood how it went, or how it had to go from that point, as he knew the Apaches. But the white prospector only nodded, not presuming to speak when it was another's story, and the bandit chief nodded back and went on.

"Of course," he said, "the Apaches had been trailing these foolish ones all the way from Arizona. They had not attacked because Nana was somewhat lenient with the whites, and he wanted to be certain the party of Adams and Brewer was going to Sno-ta-hay, as the Indian rumor spreading out from the Pima village had stated. Also, Nana knew Gotch Ear, and he wanted, equally, to be sure that the Mexican bastard was going to betray a trust his Apache foster people had given him. Nana, as you will see, was a very patient Apache; more, he was even generous and reasonable, knowing the weakness of the white men for the yellow metal. But I run ahead of myself."

He chewed his *cigarro,* sniffing the blue smoke drifting over from the noon fire. "The mule is done," he said, "but the coffee has another minute to simmer. We will have just time to finish with the canyon." He spat a shag of tobacco into the palm of one hairy hand, wiped it on his leggins, positioned the *cigarro* between the clamp of his worn side teeth where he habitually kept it, nodded and went on thoughtfully.

"Nana followed the Adams party all that morning until it reached, about an hour after noon, the high wall which held the *puerto*, the place to go in. 'Remember this place,' he heard Gotch Ear tell the whites. 'Its Apache name is Secret Door.' Now Nana could hear this because he and a few of his warriors had circled the Adams party and lain up in the rocks right at the sides of the *puerto*. You see, by doing this, they could be absolutely certain that the party found the door into Sno-ta-hay, and then that they all went through it.

"Well, they did, all right. And, when they had gotten through it, they saw that a tremendously deep canyon yawned immediately beyond it. The trail down into this canyon was in the form of an immense letter Z slashed into the face of the dizzy wall, and going from its very top to the dark trees down in the bottom. Gotch Ear led the way down this trail, which was the worst and most dangerous that any of the men had ever seen.

"But they all got down without accident, and got all their horses safely down it also, and then they still had some daylight left, even so.

"Gotch Ear pointed directly ahead of where the trail came off the canyon wall and the white men saw a perfect green and lush meadow framed by walnut and pine and oak and cottonwood timber and with a clear, lovely stream running through it. To complete this startling vision of cool water, good grass, shade from the hot sun and plenty of burning wood for the fires, there were also construction logs for cabins, sluiceways and mine timbers, should such methods of getting out the gold prove necessary.

"But Gotch Ear had not lied to them, and no mine timbers were required. Nothing was required but to look with the eyes.

"The Mexican traitor told the white men to go over to the stream and look down in the grass. First, though, he pointed out to them an exquisite low falls which the creek made up the canyon from the meadow. 'You must not ever,' he warned them, 'go above the falls. If you do that, disaster will be your only treasure.' But the white men were already running toward the water, and few of them heard his words, and none of them heeded them.

"Of course, the gold lay everywhere in the grass-roots exactly like Gotch Ear had told the men. The white miners went crazy. It is said that in the hour remaining before the sudden canyon darkness, they picked up by hand, running around in the meadow and along the shallow stream like playing children, over ten thousand dollars in nugget gold.

"When darkness fell, Gotch Ear demanded his two horses, his rifle and his two gold pieces. He got them and mounted up and at once started back up the Z-trail to the top of the canyon. He could tell by the crazy way the white men were behaving that death would be drawn down into their camp. What he did not know was that death was waiting also for him, before it attended to the Adams party. It has never been said before what became of Gotch Ear, and in many of the white tales of the Adams Diggings it is said he still lives down in Sonora. The truth is that six warriors, left by Nana at the Secret Door, shot him in the face when he rode out of Sno-ta-hay into the moonlight of the lava beds. Chief Nana himself rode one of the two horses of Gotch Ear for several years after that. But you may be sure the Adams party did not worry about Gotch Ear. They had the gold.

"Next morning, and from the upper canyon, above the falls, appeared Chief Nana and thirty-three warriors.

"This disturbed the white men. Gotch Ear had told them that the Secret Door and the Z-trail were the only entrance into Sno-ta-hay. *Was* there another entrance? Or had the Apaches come down the Z-trail in the night? It did not seem that thirty-four horses and men—not even Indian horses and men—could have gotten down that dizzy wall in the darkness. Or, if they had by some miracle arranged to do so, certainly they could not have managed it without making *some* noise. But, again, they had the gold and common sense was long flown from their heads.

"Nana, they were relieved to note, had not come for hair. He was not hostile, but quiet and serious. He told them they could take what gold they could carry and go quickly and quietly away, and he would not kill them. He told them, also, that if any tried to come back, they would die on the trail inward. He lastly told them that if one man so much as set his eyes above the falls of the stream, all in the party would perish.

"The Adams men did not argue this. They had too much gold to pick up below the falls. So they went to work, some digging for gold, some building a strong cabin for a long stay. The gold, as determined by Nana's scouts, who never quit watching from a secret lookout on the canyon wall above the falls, was all emptied into a hole dug in the ground inside the rising structure of the cabin. Before the cabin walls were closed, the Indians saw that this hole was in front of the fireplace and was covered with a large thin flagstone. Adams, himself, was the one who had charge of this common hoard of the dust and nuggets."

Pelón paused to spit and to shift his *cigarro* two teeth forward.

"Well, the rest differs little from the white man's legends," he concluded. "The whites claim that they only wandered above the falls to look. The Apaches claim they began to mine above the falls, both with pick and pan. The whites say that the Indians were totally treacherous to their word. The Indians say the white men lied like dogs and conducted themselves like rooting pigs.

"Anyway, the camp ran short of supplies. Brewer and six men set out for Fort Wingate to buy supplies. Ten days were allowed for their return. They did not appear on time. Adams grew nervous and went up the Z-trail to the Secret Door to look for sign of the returning party. He found it; five bodies just outside the *puerto*. The supplies the men had brought back were either scattered on the rocks nearby or stolen by the Apache killers. Adams went back down into the canyon, his heart black with fear. He had not found the body of Brewer. This was because Brewer had managed to elude the Apaches. He had hidden in a hole where they overlooked him. Most unusual for Apaches, but Nana himself later admitted that it was the truth. Adams, and his friend Davidson, who had come with him up the trail, were surely not thinking of Brewer's life, but of their own, and of those of their comrades down in the canyon. And well they might.

"When they reached the top of the Z-trail and looked down into the bottom of the canyon toward their cabin meadow, they saw the smoke of the blazing hut and heard the yells of Apache warriors and saw, with their horrified eyes, no less than three hundred half-naked Indians dancing and waving scalps in the meadow about the burning cabin. They knew, then, that no man of their companions lived and that they themselves sat watching on dangerous time.

"At once they turned loose their horses and went far up a tiny side crevice of the trail and hid like foxes in a hole in the rocks under the roots of a giant madrone tree. The Apaches came looking up the trail soon enough, but, like Brewer before them, Adams and Davidson had the luck of their God with them. Again the Indians missed their white prey. Perhaps it was that, finding the riderless horses so near the *puerto*, they thought the riders among those killed on the outside. In any event, and again by Nana's word, they did escape.

"Adams, as you know, in his story, always claimed that he went down into the canyon after dark that night and stole in among the dancing Apaches and tried to get the gold out of the hole under the smoldering fireplace. But he said that the stone was too hot to lift and that he had to go back up the trail when daylight threatened and he still could not touch the heated stone. That is a damned lie, or so old Nana later said. Myself, knowing my mother's people, I cannot think that Adams, who also knew those people, would dream to go back down a canyon where three hundred mixed-band Apaches were holding a scalp dance over the hairless bodies of his thirteen companions.

"Adams, you may recall, supported his lie by saying he had put a big nugget under a stump that same morning. The nugget had been brought back by one of the men from a forbidden trip above the falls. The man had been up there only an hour and had brought back a three-quart coffeepot full to the lip with raw nugget gold of sizes from barley grains to a child's fist doubled. These included the specimen nugget which Adams brought out of the canyon and which he claimed he dug up from the stump burial place. But, hah! That nugget could have been picked up anywhere in the grass of the meadow. You and I know what Adams got for it when he sold it later on in Tucson. You remember, Mackenna? Pah! It was ninety-two dollars they gave him for it! I have thrown bigger nuggets at chaparral birds to make them run for six-shooter practice!

"Well, anyway, *amigo*, that's the Apache story of Sno-ta-hay. The Indians left the gold in the hole under the fireplace. They thought that as good a place as any. Also, it was considered that the Apache people might one day need the gold themselves. So it's still there, according to the tradition of both red and white legends. I think it is there myself, or I wouldn't be sitting here in this fine cottonwood shade waiting for my meat and coffee. My people —my mother's people—say that no white man has found the Secret Door since that time, and that, since old Nana's death, no Apache, even, has been through that door and down into Sno-ta-hay. A watch is kept to see that no one enters, and that's the way the story ends. Adams could never find his way back, and went crazy trying to do so. Brewer kept running and had a fine cattle ranch for many years up in the Colorado country. A hundred men, I think, have died since that time trying to find the Lost Adams Mine. More will die. Maybe even you and me, eh, comrade? Ha, ha, ha! Do you think the Indians still guard the way into Sno-ta-hay?"

Mackenna sat a few moments, not realizing that the outlaw had finished his tale. Then, belatedly, he replied.

"I don't know," he said. "With Apaches, anything is possible. But no, Pelón; I don't think that after all these years, when it is now nearly another century about to begin, that the Apaches still are on watch up there. What do you think?"

Pelón laughed again, and spread his great arms.

"It's nonsense!" he said. "Nana is dead many years.

Adams is dead many years. Who is there left to guard the gold?"

"Ghosts, maybe," said Mackenna. "Thirteen men were murdered down in the canyon. Five died at its top."

"Bah! You don't believe such nonsense as ghosts. You're a white man."

"Also," said Mackenna, "I am a Scot. That's nervous blood where the afterworld is concerned."

"Hell take the afterworld!" snorted the bandit. "What did you think of my story? Does it agree with the white legend of the lost diggings?"

"Almost exactly," said Mackenna. "The differences would not be worth discussing."

"And old Enh's map?" said Pelón, giving his white companion a crafty, sidelong glance. "Do the two stories also agree in the better part with the map which Prairie Dog drew for you in the sand?"

"How the stories agree with the map," replied the red-bearded prospector, "is something which I shall have to think about."

"I thought as much!" said Pelón. "You and your damned sharp mind! Oh, well, come on, let's have our bath and then eat. I'm starved for food."

"Let's just eat," said Mackenna uneasily. "I'm not in the mood to bathe."

The bandit grinned and thumped him on the back.

"You're going to get into the water, Mackenna," he said. "All of us are. When Pelón takes a bath, everybody takes a bath. Mother! Sister! Come on. Mackenna and I are going into the water. You, too, both of you. Off with your clothes! Everybody jump in and have a good time . . . !"

27 ⋛

Sister Sally

SALLY WAS only about Mackenna's own age. For an Apache, she was slender and not short and square in form. Indeed, poised on the rock by the falls, waiting deliberately for the white man to see her before she dove in, she took Mackenna's breath. Had he not known of her disfigured nose and her hawklike boniness of face, he would have thought her the most striking nude of "Pagan Woman by Pool" that it was possible for nature to fashion. Even knowing what he did of her facial deformity, he still held his breath and stared.

Sally knew it. She knew that he was looking at her beautifully curved and uplifted breasts, her rounded yet hard belly, her sculptured buttocks and long trim legs. She knew it and she stood and posed for him until her half-brother, Pelón, seeing her, bawled up to her, "Get in the water, you! What is it you imagine we wish to see? Your bottom is hard and flat as a boy's. Pah, dive in!"

Now, Mackenna heard a startling sound. It was the laugh of Sally. He had heard her laugh before, a sort of feminine copy of Pelón's hoarse bark. But *this* laugh! Mackenna had never heard such a musical sound.

While he was wondering at it, Sally dived into the pool and started toward where he nervously held himself immersed. Too late, he tried to escape. When he moved to crawl out on a mid-pool sunning rock, she seized him by the ankles and pulled him back into the water. There she began to wind about his frantic plunges to elude her as fluidly as if she were of the element of the pool itself. Her grace was positively liquid, compellingly hypnotic. In passing above or below him she managed, always, just to touch him and then glide away so that the motion seemed deliberately erotic, yet entirely attractive and natural. Suddenly Mackenna was helpless. Despite his alarms and his genuine fears of the noseless Apache woman, he felt himself becoming aroused. He could not believe it and yet neither could he deny it, as she drove after him relentlessly, her own passions now plainly rising to a fever pitch within her.

In a final bid to escape her, Mackenna saw a small arm of the pool which was fringed with cattails and which ran off to one side of the falls and to a sandy spit in a side slough of still water. Into this natural retreat he swam strongly, hoping to make land and retreat to his clothes. He got as far as the sand spit, but she was beside him before he could get to his feet and race away through its shallows. There, in the warm, sun-drenched cove, hidden from Maly-pai and Pelón, she threw herself against him, making furious, demanding noises in her throat and offering her body with panting, pleading desperation. With the supreme effort, Mackenna threw her away from him and got out of the water. She was after him like a striking cat, forcing him to seize her upper arms and to throw her violently back and away from him. She fell heavily.

When she came unsteadily to her feet, she was still

panting, still wild-eyed. She glared around the confines of the cattail branch of the pool, then suddenly leaped over the reedy borders of the water into the rocks and brush beyond, and disappeared from sight. Mackenna heard her bare feet pattering briefly, from rock to rock, down-canyon. Then there was nothing but silence and the resumed sweet buzzing of the sage bees and the "talky" calling of the scaled quail above the falls. He swam slowly back into the main pool, got dressed, went to the fire and joined Pelón and the old woman. He had a strong premonition that a bad thing had happened with Sally, and that much worse threatened. But he could think of no way to enter into the problem with Pelón, or with "Mother" Mal-y-pai.

Therefore, he took his piece of high-smelling mule meat and his tin cup of vicious Apache coffee and ate and drank in frowning silence, while the outlaw and the ancient harridan eyed him speculatively and waited for "Sister" Sally to appear.

When, after half an hour of continuing silence in the canyon, she failed to do so, Mackenna grew extremely nervous. Pelón and Mal-y-pai could sense this. They began to watch him more closely, and more with suspicion than with speculation. Finally the bandit chief came out with it.

"Well," he said, "what did you do with her? What happened between you?"

"Nothing!" said Mackenna vehemently. "I swear it."

"What happened?" repeated Pelón.

"I've told you. Nothing."

"She was after you. We saw that. You both swam into that other pool over there. We know her. She tried to be with you. It looked to us as though you had the same idea in your own mind."

"Never!" cried Mackenna. "That woman terrifies me!"

The outlaw watched him, glittering-eyed.

At last he nodded.

"*What happened?*" he demanded for the third time.

Mackenna knew that he must be very careful now. With their savage intuitions they were feeling the same nameless concern that he was. It had grown among the three of them. The old lady was staring at him also.

"I refused her," he told Pelón simply. "She insisted, and I had to throw her back. She fell. When she got up again, she glared at me like a trapped puma, then leaped into the rocks and ran away down-canyon. I couldn't see her go, but I could hear her. That's the way she went."

Pelón shot a hard glance at Mal-y-pai and was the next moment on his feet.

"My God, *amigo*," he said to Mackenna, "you should have told me sooner. Come on, there may yet be time!"

"Time?" said the prospector, arising. "For what?"

"To pull her away from him!" the outlaw said raspingly. "She's gone down to spend what she built up for you on that poor Mimbreño fool. He can't handle a woman like that. He's only a baby in his mind. She'll make him crazy."

He started to swing away from the fire in the dogtrot of the traveling Apache warrior, then stopped short. Behind him, Mackenna also froze in his tracks, staring at the entrance of the down-canyon trail into the meadow.

Coming out of the shadowed maw of the canyon, into the bright sunlight of the open grass, was Hachita.

In his arms, stark-naked and in a posture of hanging limbs and head which could only mean one thing, was the hot-eyed Apache harlot, Sally.

"*Dah-eh-sah!*" cried out Hachita brokenly. "She is dead . . . !"

28

The Seed of His Sire

IN HIS incoherent, stumbling way Hachita told them how it had been. It was a bad story. Pelón had been right about him. Despite his boasts, he had no great experience with women. Indeed, he had no experience at all. He was so big and so stupid and possessed—that horse's face—and was shy and afraid of the women, and so they would not come to him and he could not force himself to go to them. Sally had never so much as looked at him before. Now she came down the canyon, where he had been watching for Young Mickey. She came up to him in the sunlight with no clothes on and with her fine body moving in a way to make a man think of low things.

Even so, Hachita had only said hello to her and asked her to go away, since he was on guard. But she had laughed at him and put her hands on him, and then had helped him to put his hands on her, and, well, the next thing they were down in the hot sand panting and grasping and growling like two animals, and then, all of a sudden, with Hachita's arm about her neck and pulling her to him, he had heard something go "crick." She had ceased to move and lay

there looking up at him with her eyes wide open and the
sun glaring, straight overhead, into her eyeballs. There
was no life in them, and Hachita, even as stupid as he was,
knew that Yosen had taken her soul and that she was dead.

Mackenna, as the Mimbreño giant was recounting his
simple tragedy, bent and examined Sally's limp form. He
raised the head and let it down again. By the way that it
fell back and turned floppingly aside in his supporting hand
and hung, chin-up and grotesquely angled, he knew Hachita had broken her neck in the violence and ignorance
of his love. He stood up, as the Apache finished his confession. Hachita awaited his words, as did Mal-y-pai and
Pelón. In such an instant, such a moment of doubt, all
turned to the brain and training of the white man. The
latter, facing them, was surprised to see that the giant Mimbreño was crying. He had never seen an Apache cry. Neither, apparently, had Mal-y-pai and Pelón. Tears, in the
sense that the eyes grew moist with some emotion, these
were known. But they were unshed tears. They were
things which did not count against a man or a woman. But
weeping? Real falling tears? These were foreign to the
Apache nature. Presently Mackenna could see that Pelón
and his fierce old dam were embarrassed for their Indian
kin, and so he spoke to Hachita, looking away from the
others, as was proper to do in such an awkward case.

"My friend," he said to the huge Apache, "will you
come and talk with me? We can go by ourselves and you
can say what you will to me, or say nothing. We can just
sit and let the memory of this unfortunate moment go
away from you. What has happened to this poor woman is
no fault of yours. I can explain that for you, if you want
to have me do it." He paused briefly, letting the young
giant think, then added, "You know, Hachita, that your

friend who fell back at The Skulls trusted me. Is that not a true thing?"

He gambled here. He did not know how Besh had felt about him, but Indians are extremely sensitive and he was certain that the dead Chiricahua youth had returned his own interest and *simpatía*. He was right, and the gamble was a good one.

"Yes," said Hachita, raising his enormous head and brushing his hand across his eyes to disperse the tears, "that is a true thing. My friend who fell back there told me I should trust you, if anything happened to him. He said you were a good white man. There was something else he told me; it was not about you, but it was very, very important. I have been trying to remember it ever since he fell. But you know how it would be, *Patrón*, with a poor mind such as my own."

"Your mind is not poor," said Mackenna. "It is only that you do not worry so much as some of us do. You are happier. You ought to be glad. Come on, now, let's go over there under the cottonwoods and have some coffee."

Hachita nodded obediently, and they started off.

But Pelón had recovered.

He came swiftly up behind them and said to Mackenna in a rasping voice, "Wait a minute! What the hell do you think you're doing? You haven't told me about my sister yet. What killed her?"

"The neck," said Mackenna. "He broke her neck in his passion. It's as limp as a wrung chicken's. He couldn't know what he had done. He's innocent."

"I know, I know," grumbled the bandit. "My God, you don't have to tell me that!"

"Pah!" It was old Mal-y-pai, scuttling up to join the council. "Innocent! You men are always innocent. God-damn it, what do you do with a mean stud horse who

doesn't know how to mount a mare without first killing her
with his hoofs, and love-play with the teeth biting the neck
arch, and such things, eh? What do you do with a horse
like that, I say? Damn your eyes, you bastards! You kill
him, that's what. You take the son-of-a-bitch out in the
brush and you put a rifle ball through his stupid, blunder-
ing brains!"

Pelón dived for her in time. He wrenched the old
Winchester from her grasp, as she raised it to fire at
Hachita's head.

"Curse you!" he cried. "Would you fire your gun up
here in this quiet canyon when we are expecting—"

He broke off the reprimand. His brutal face blanched
with the memory which his anger had stirred.

"My God!" he said. "We have forgotten Young
Mickey!"

He threw the old lady's gun back to her and reached
down to retrieve his own carbine propped on a rock by
the coffee fire. As he did, a mocking voice from behind
them froze the little group. It came from the opening of
the meadow into the down-canyon trail. It was a high
voice, almost like a girl's, but carrying a warning sibilance
akin to the burring "wwhhhrrrrr" of a rattler's buzz.

"Sure enough," it said in Spanish, "you have forgotten
Young Mickey—but Young Mickey hasn't forgotten you."

Pelón López stood up very slowly. He left his Winchester on the rock where it was. In a low voice, he told
Mal-y-pai to put her rifle beside his. The old squaw did it
without question, an eloquent tribute to the reputation of
Young Mickey Tibbs. Mackenna simply stood as he was,
facing up-canyon, away from the speaker across the
meadow. Hachita stood with him. Neither of them turned
to look at the visitor. Under such circumstances, Indian
manners forbid rude staring or uninvited curiosity. Put

another way, none of them dared turn around until told
to do so. Hachita, however, still had his Winchester in his
hand.

"You," called Young Mickey. "The big bull there. Put
your gun down on the ground like the others."

Hachita did not move. Mackenna, watching him
anxiously, could see that he was thinking very hard. He
was coming to a resolve of some sort, and it had to be a
decision about his rifle still being in his hand. Mackenna
suspected that he meant to use it, but didn't want to see
the big *inocentón* killed needlessly.

"Don't do it, *amigo*," he said. "There's no need."

Hachita looked at him, sidelong, and shook his head.

"There is a need, *Patrón*. I will turn and shoot him to
make things even for the woman I have harmed."

"No!" warned Mackenna tersely. "Stand still and put
down the gun as he told you."

"Big Bull," said Young Mickey in his thin cutting-
knife of a voice, "I heard what you grunted. Before you
try to shoot at me, let Pelón and the white man turn
around and see my war shield. I don't think they would
like to have you putting bullet holes through it."

"Hachita!" ordered Pelón, "stand still. There is something very wrong here. All right, Mackenna, let's turn."

They came around to face Young Mickey, ready, they
thought, for anything up to a half-company of cavalry, or
a loaded mountain howitzer, or a dozen enlisted Apache
Government scouts.

But they had underestimated the son of Old Mickey
Tibbs. The seed was the equal of the sire. His "shield" was
Francie Stanton.

29

The Grave
at Birdsong Meadow

"IT WAS pretty easy," said Young Mickey Tibbs, in the bastard "cowpen" Spanish of the land. "I just waited until I saw through the fieldglasses that you were gone on up the canyon, then I trailed back and shot those two dumb troopers and took the girl."

The professional aspects of it intrigued Pelón.

"How did you dare do that?" he asked. "Won't the white officer suspect something? Two shots coming so close to your departure, and then finding the two buffalo soldiers shot in the back? And you gone?"

"Bald One," said Young Mickey, "you don't have the proper regard for me. First, I didn't shoot them in the back. I rode right up to them, smiling, and shot them from in front, precisely as if they had ridden into an ambush set by you. I also shot them with the Winchester of that Chiricahua we killed at the waterhole. I picked it up from the rocks on my way out with the two soldiers to trail you. With the two soldiers dead, no one will question an ambush. The fact that I am gone will puzzle them, but when I return I will merely say that I was taken prisoner in the same ambush. Your pony tracks are all over the ground back there. None of them will ever guess the truth, and none of us will tell it to them, will we?"

He paused, watching Pelón.

In the moment's impasse, Mackenna moved forward and started taking the gag from Francie Stanton's mouth.

"Don't touch her!" hissed Young Mickey. "Baldie and I have not reached our understanding yet."

"You go to hell," said Glen Mackenna, dead level and in English. He loosened the gag, pulled it away. "Come on," he said to Francie. "You look like you could use a cup of Mal-y-pai's poison. Mother, pour a cup for the girl," he added, back in Spanish again. "You see, God is good. He takes away one daughter and brings back another."

The old squaw glared at him, then said something mutteringly in her own tongue, and took Francie roughly by the arm and dragged her over to the fire. Mackenna relaxed.

"Well," he said to Young Mickey, "let us hear your proposal. Be quick with it. We have business waiting."

The boy looked at him. Mackenna took the pause to return the favor. Young Mickey Tibbs, he decided, was not as ugly as Pelón López. But there was an air of depravity about him which went beyond the outlaw chief's ignorant brutality. Pelón was mean like a mean horse or a mean steer or a mean bear. This boy was wicked. He had a weak mouth, a snaggling, single wolf's tooth protruding like a fang from his upper lip, and mismated eyes which were walled slightly and which he could not command to bear upon any object at will. They kept wandering off, and his constant effort to keep them focused gave his whole thin and skull-like face a look of vacancy which was literally frightening.

"Well, now," said this child of darkness, hissing his words because of the interference of the wolf's tooth, "you're pretty brave, aren't you?"

"Not very brave," answered the red-bearded prospector. "Ask Pelón."

"Asking Pelón," nodded the boy, "is exactly what I intend to do. And if you mix in with our talk one more time, you are as dead as those two buffalo soldiers down there on the other side of the sandstone cliff."

"Don't mistake my ambitions," said Mackenna carefully. "I'm only working for this expedition. I'm the hired guide, precisely as yourself for the cavalry down there."

"You're smart and talk smart, and I hate smart white bastards like you!" snarled the boy. "Pelón, you better tell him about me."

"He knows about you, Mickey. And he is not very brave, as he says. Ignore him. It's true that I've hired him to take me to this certain place. It's a business arrangement, nothing more."

The young Apache breed's face contorted itself sneeringly.

"Yes," he said, "a business arrangement I know all about. That's why I'm here. I just brought the damn girl along with me so that you wouldn't shoot me before you heard me out."

"You're bluffing. You don't know a thing."

"I know everything."

"Tell me how."

"Because of that fat Pima slut you dumped into our camp at Yaqui Spring. I knew her from the days when the Mescalero had her. She remembered me. She was so glad to see a friend that she talked like a schoolteacher."

"You lie! That girl had no brains. She knew nothing."

"She had eyes. She saw. She had a tongue. She talked. You want to waste time having me prove it by going all the way back to old Enh, and to this white mongrel, Mackenna, and Monkey and that white man Vachel you killed up in Surprise Grass and Ben Call and all of that?"

Pelón looked at Mackenna. The white prospector shrugged. What was there to say? It was plain that the vile boy had gotten the story out of Lupe. It was the weak link in the chain of Pelón's plan, and it had snapped. Now they had real trouble with them.

"I don't know what to say," the outlaw grumbled truthfully. "You have me where it is tender. I can't move."

"My position is simple," said Young Mickey. "There's gold enough for all, up there in Sno-ta-hay." He pointed to the northeast. "The stories I have always heard say that Adams and his men put a quarter of a million dollars under that fireplace stone in ten days—the first ten. Who knows how many days they mined after that? Who knows but what a million dollars, or even two, lie up there waiting for us? I ask only to go along and share. My price is not killing the white girl before your eyes."

Again, Mackenna and Pelón exchanged looks. Behind them, to Mackenna's terror, Hachita growled and moved forward. "Don't do it!" the white prospector cried to the Apache. "Remember that your dead friend told you to trust me!"

Hachita hesitated, his slow mind groping. Finally he nodded and put down his rifle.

"That's good." Pelón sighed. "He isn't a good enough shot to have risked it. Not nearly so."

Mackenna nodded toward Young Mickey Tibbs and said to Pelón, "Tell him we take the offer, we agree to the price. He's right, anyway. What's one more share of the gold mean to us?"

"Well, for one thing, it means a hell of a lot more to me than that skinny girl of yours, Mackenna. But I, too, am a businessman. And it is clear to me that Young Mickey must come into our little company."

Glen Mackenna shook his shaggy red head.

"I wish that I might see it as easily as you do, Pelón," he said. "But the truth of the thing has gotten so confused I can't follow it any longer."

The bandit, too, shook his head, but he was grinning now.

"Why, it's very clear, *amigo*. If you try anything funny, I will shoot you, or your girl. If Mickey tries anything, Hachita will bury his ax in his skull, because Mickey is the one who shot B—" He caught himself, and said, "Who shot his Chiricahua friend. Then, if I try anything, you or Mickey will shoot me. On the other hand, if Hachita sees me threaten you, he will come for me, as his friend told him to trust you. Then, of course, if he comes for me, my sainted mother will shoot him, and, well, hell, you can see how it will go, Mackenna."

Mackenna shook his head again, harder.

"If you say so, *Jefe*," he admitted ruefully.

"All right," called the outlaw to Young Mickey. "Uncock your gun and come on over and have some coffee."

Young Mickey nodded slowly.

"First," he said, "take your right hand out from under the serape and put the pistol on the rock by the fire."

"Jesús María!" Pelón grinned, his scarred upper lip stiffly lifted. "That damned Lupe *did* tell you everything!"

"They all talk," said Young Mickey, "when they're on the blanket. Put the pistol on the rock."

Pelón did as he was bid. They moved to the fire and Mal-y-pai poured the coffee into the tin cups. Francie

Stanton sat with Mackenna, her hand holding tightly to his arm. He could feel her shaking.

"There is one thing to remember," said Young Mickey Tibbs. "In the matter of our new partnership, something special has been added; something you don't know about yet."

"Go on," said Pelón. "We're always delighted to be told fresh woes."

"Well, this is bad. What has happened since you did those ranch killings is that everybody down in that part of the country is all stirred up against the Apaches and the Apaches are hiding out like coyotes. The word has gone through all the tribes that you are headed for Sno-ta-hay and that this new trouble is all your fault. At least a dozen bunches of Indians are out looking for you, Pelón, trying to cut you off from Cañon del Oro. They figure they're doing it to show the whites they mean good, and they want your bald scalp as badly as the Government does. But I figure they're doing it for the same damned reason we are."

"What do you mean?" said Pelón López.

"They think if they can find you, they can find Sno-ta-hay. They're just as bad today as the white bastards. There's not a one of them under forty years old who wouldn't cut his old mother's throat to get at that gold. Hell, they're not stupid any more. They don't trade for beads or mirrors any more. They're out for blood."

"My God, this is a horrible thought!"

"Well, not so bad. Not in one way. In one way it makes the choice easy. There's only one way for you to go, Pelón. You can't go back."

"He's right, *Jefe*," said Glen Mackenna. "We've got to keep running."

The outlaw chief considered it only briefly.

Then he tossed away the dregs of his coffee, rinsed the cup with clean sand, handed it to Mal-y-pai.

"Put it away with our other treasures on your pack-horse, Little Mother," he said. "We are going to Sno-ta-hay."

While the old lady and Francie Stanton packed the camp things, the men buried Sally deep in a rocky crevice beyond the pool. Boulders were wedged in atop her blanketed figure, assuring that no animal, nor bird, would disturb her sleep. There was no excess of sentiment, but neither was there any talk or joking or light thoughts during the interment. While the grim work went forward, Mackenna tried to catch his thoughts up to the moment of the fact.

Where in this whole chain of circumstances had he made his gross mistake? Which turning of the trail had offered the last best chance for him to gamble with the lives of Francie and himself? It seemed to him that he had passed many opportunities by. Yet, truthfully, there had been no time when a move of violence, or desperation, might not have killed Francie Stanton; or, nearly as bad, maybe worse, when such a move might not have injured or killed him, thus leaving her at the mercy of the outlaw band. Nowhere had there been a decent opening to get free. He resolved to go over this same ground of reasoning with Francie at first opportunity, so that the girl would understand his past behavior, as well as knowing how to conduct herself from this camp forward. Their soundest move was to keep traveling with the pack of Pelón, until some future turning of the trail should provide the avenue of escape so far denied them. It was still a long, long way to Cañon del Oro. There was almost certain to be a time and place between Sally's grave and Sno-ta-hay where he and the nervy sixteen-year-old could make their reasonable break for freedom.

Meanwhile, the answer was to play the game of outlaw with Pelón López; to keep alive that slender element of *simpatía* which the outlaw killer had shown to him from their first meeting so many years ago; to keep searching, too, for that brute's weakness which he *knew* the bandit possessed, and through which he still believed he would be able finally to outwit and vanquish him.

As for the addition of the boyish murderer Young Mickey Tibbs to the band, this was a dangerous thing in its own right. He felt sure the youth was criminally unsound, the same as Pelón López, but without Pelón's saving grace of "inner spark." Young Mickey was to be watched in every camp, at every rest and water stop, on each mile of the ride between. It was a certain assumption that, among him and Pelón and Hachita, there would be no hour in which the lives of their two white "partners" were not in jeopardy.

Coming to Hachita, there was again the matter of the unsound thought processes of the savage mentality with which to cope. He seemed to want to stay with Mackenna, but he continued to frown and to look at the white man as though there was something he had to remember about him which was not entirely of a happy nature. This regard made the bearded prospector quite sensitive. To have such a huge shadow at one's elbow was more chilling than comforting. Still, as with Pelón and Young Mickey, Hachita had to be tolerated.

Indeed, even at the moment, with Sally's grave closed and the party finding their mounts to leg-up and leave the small death meadow, the giant Apache was continuing to haunt Mackenna and to hang to him.

Pelón noted the fact and ordered Hachita to come up

in front of the pony line and ride with him. To this the
Apache said no. His dead friend had told him to trust the
white man with the red hair. He would ride with that
white man. Mackenna quickly assured Pelón that he did
not mind the company. He also, and wisely, made the same
assurance to the scowling Hachita.

"*Schicho*," he said to the Mimbreño in his own tongue,
smiling, and put his hand to the Indian's tensed bicep.

The word meant "friend," and, after frowning over it
a minute, Hachita smiled and put his great paw on Mackenna's arm and said rumblingly, "*Schichobe*," which was
even better, meaning "old" friend.

The agreement was good enough for Pelón. He seemed
to want no friction with the big Apache and he was,
additionally, becoming very concerned about getting to
Sno-ta-hay.

"Hurry up," he said quickly, "let's go."

He put his own horse in the lead, placing Young
Mickey behind him, then old Mal-y-pai with her rifle be-
tween the cavalry scout's shoulder blades, followed by
Francie Stanton, Mackenna and Hachita.

As the latter two swung into their rear-guard positions,
the Apache hesitated a moment, frowning back down the
canyon toward its lower reaches and the distant, silent
rocks of the fatal waterhole at The Skulls.

"I wish," he said plaintively to Mackenna, "that I
could remember what it was that my dead friend down
there charged me with. It was something to do with why
we two came along with these dogs; with why we went to
the *ranchería* of old Enh and Mal-y-pai, in the first place.
I wish that I was not so stupid and slow. My friend down
there would be unhappy with me if he knew I had forgotten what it was that he told me I must remember."

"It will come back to you," said Mackenna reassuringly. "Just keep trying, and it will pop into your mind one day as easily as nothing at all. You'll see. Come on; your friend trusts you. He knows you'll remember."

The huge Apache nodded and seemed content.

"Thank you, white friend," he smiled. "My friend told me to believe you, so I will. Come on; here we go!"

He kneed his little pony and, together, he and Mackenna set off up the narrow canyon after the others.

As they went, Mackenna, too, was smiling. It made a man feel good to be still alive and to have Francie back and to win a friend like the simple-minded giant at his side, all in the same hour of a lovely Arizona day.

Especially was it gratifying to have been able to help a poor suffering brute like Hachita, simply by a pat on the back and an assurance that he would one day, and easily, remember what it was that Besh had told him.

Could Glen Mackenna have known, in that passing moment of satisfaction, what it was that Besh had told Hachita, the warm glow would have gone ice-cold within him. As it was, his blue eyes shown more brightly than they had since the first squeeze of Francie Stanton's hand back at Surprise Grass, above Yaqui Spring, and his heart, for no reason at all that would make sense in a thirty-year-old man, beat as carefreely as a cactus sparrow's.

"Aha," he said to the sober-faced Apache, "this is a glorious day! If I could sing, I would make this canyon ring with happiness."

Hachita looked at him wonderingly.

"What do you have to be happy about?" he asked.

It was an excellent question. Mackenna knew that. The only difficulty was that he didn't have an excellent answer for it.

30 〰

Sugarloaf Peaks

THEY WENT on through the Yaqui hills to strike
the upper Salt River. Following that stream toward its
headwaters, they sneaked past San Carlos and Sawmill and
proceeded eastward across the Fort Apache Reservation
into the Sitgreaves Wilderness west of St. Johns, Arizona.
Here, on the sixth night, they made camp in a high saddle
between two unnamed mountains. At this point they could
see ten thousand-foot Greens Mountain to the north, and
eleven thousand-foot Baldy Mountain to the south. The
view, east and northeast, was blocked by the seat of the
saddle. It was not a comfortable camp, being windy and
lacking firewood and water. Complaints, however, were
small. They had made good time, the horses were all sound,
no bad frictions had developed. Neither had any chances
of flight shown themselves to Mackenna and Francie Stanton. But their companions, if they had not relaxed their
surveillance of their red-bearded guide and the young
white girl, had treated them with less crudity than dis-
played prior to the ambush at The Skulls. Something, almost, of camaraderie had developed in the ride through the

arid highlands of Natanes Plateau and the Kinishba Indian country, and then into the beginning timber of the Sitgreaves and Apache Forests. Mackenna, with his love of the land, had been able to imbue Francie Stanton with a spirit nearly the equal of his own. For the last two rides, especially, the girl had begun to "smell the sunlight" and to "hear the trees grow," as the Apaches put it. She had taken strongly to the old squaw, Mal-y-pai, and the latter, after a suitable period of gruff denial, had given in and admitted, with a show of her four teeth, that she and the "skinny chicken" were *simpático*.

Now, in this sixth camp of their journey, with the New Mexico line not over forty miles distant, no signs of pursuit to the rear, and none of blockage to the front, the entire company—except for Young Mickey Tibbs, who sat always to one side with his rifle cocked—seemed tame as a band of summer tourists inbound for a fortnight of roughing it in the "high and wild."

The tiny, clear-flamed fire which Mal-y-pai had built from kindling packed along on the horse from the lower slope of the saddle, glowed like a pink jewel in the blackness of the gusty mountainside. Its warmth felt good at the altitude. There was a supper of broiled venison, Apache bread—corn tortillas—and black coffee. Pelón told some chilling tales of his life, Hachita performed a Mimbreño rain dance, and Mal-y-pai offered a Gila River chant which she assured Mackenna meant that from this camp forward it would be suitable for him to sleep with the white girl if he so wished. The chant made the girl ready. Mal-y-pai guaranteed it.

Mackenna didn't bother translating this bit of good news for Francie. Indeed, he thought that upon this high note it would be a favorable maneuver to call it a night. He suggested that, since a very important decision might arise next morning, they all seek their blankets and get a good night's sleep. If his calculations had been correct, all would be well pleased that they were fresh and strong to travel when that new sun came up.

At this hint of something to come, Pelón narrowed his eyes and Young Mickey moved in out of the darkness. But Mackenna dismissed their interest. "We're all tired," he said. "We can talk some more in the morning."

They were agreeable to leave it there. Making thirty and more miles per day over rough country by ponyback for almost a week was sufficient to weary even Sonora outlaws and mixed-breed Apache cavalry scouts. The camp slept.

With first light, Mackenna led Pelón and Young Mickey to a viewpoint several hundred feet above the camp, and pointed northeastward. His companions stared incredulously.

"*Madre!*" gasped Pelón. "The Sugarloaf peaks . . . !"

"Yes," said the red-bearded prospector. "There they are."

Until that instant, Mackenna himself held no real belief in the sand maps of old Enh. He had been struck the night before with the similarity of their camp in the "high saddle between two mountains" to that described in the Adams legend and he had known that they were certainly in the area of the legend's consistent location. But until this moment of Pelón's indrawn oath, he had not dared to think that daylight would show them the fabled Sugarloaf peaks.

But there they were, looming dark against the dawn and precisely to the north and east as Adams had seen them those thirty-three years gone when Gotch Ear had taken him to perhaps this very point of rock, and said, "*Mira!* There they are!"

He looked at Pelón, and both men nodded. It was a strange feeling, Mackenna suffering its fever no less than the murderous bandit. They had found the first of the Adams landmarks. They were standing on Lookout Mountain. The white prospector felt his pulse race. In his mind was the inescapable vision of the Lost Adams gold lying in the grass-roots of Sno-ta-hay.

"My God!" he heard himself mutter. "Come on; let's get going!"

From that moment, there was no thought of escape in his mind. He was seized as certainly by the disease of greed to find the treasure as any man of the hundred said to have died from it since Adams came out of the canyon infected and raving from its toxin. He was, in that windswept pause, transformed, or reduced, to a level no different from that of any of the scores of men, white and nonwhite, good and bad, sane and insane, who had for over three decades littered the dry washes and pitiless desert canyons of Arizona and New Mexico with their bleaching skeletons in tribute to the virulence of Lost Adams fever. From that instant of the leaping, stumbling rush back down the lookout slope to the camp below, Glen Mackenna was as sworn to go to Sno-ta-hay as were Pelón López or Young Mickey Tibbs, or any other murderer willing to kill or be killed in the cause of Cañon del Oro.

31

The Pumpkin Patch

FROM THE saddle of the lookout, they angled up the Zuni River into New Mexico, passed south of Gallup, circled old Fort Wingate, drove due north between Bluewater and Smith Lakes into the Chaco Canyon badlands. At sunset of the thirteenth day they made camp in the bottom of a U-shaped canyon. Upstream of the site, the canyon's walls drew in sharply, and there was an opening just wide enough to pass a mounted man on the rocky bank of the creek. "We'll go through there tomorrow," said Mackenna. "If we're still right, we will see something that Gotch Ear saw thirty-three years ago."

Pelón got off his horse. Young Mickey, watching as he always watched, followed him down. The boy drew his carbine from its scabbard and went over and sat down on a rock. None of them paid him any heed. He had not helped at a single camp, nor had he been asked to. It was agreed between Pelón and Mackenna that the best course was to leave him alone. His behavior on the trail, the eternal guarding with the cocked Winchester, the refusal to become a part of the camp, and his continually deepening silence, all led to a confirmation of Mackenna's original suspicion that the youth was mentally deranged. The idea was to keep him quiet.

"Now," Pelón said, replying to the white prospector, "I don't like it here. Which camp do you make of this one in the old legend?"

"Pumpkin Patch," said Mackenna.

Francie and Young Mickey did not know the story of the Lost Adams Diggings in its traditional detail. It was another matter with the Apaches. Both Mal-y-pai and Hachita, as well as Pelón, showed interest.

"Hah!" said the old lady. "Then, when we go through that narrow place tomorrow, we ought to see the irrigation ditches and the tumbled walls of the old Indian village?"

"Yes."

"And the pumpkin vines?"

"Yes, and the vines."

"Well, then, why don't we go up there and look through, tonight? There's light yet for looking."

Mackenna shook his head at the squaw's suggestion.

"I'd rather not," he said. "The tradition says that Gotch Ear looked through there before the sunrise, and you know what happened to him."

"Mackenna is right," agreed Pelón quickly. "Be quiet, old woman, and go boil the coffee. Leave these things to the men."

"Yes," rumbled the giant, Hachita, breaking in unexpectedly. "Don't disturb the spirits. We are close now. I can feel it. I am afraid in some way." He frowned, shaking his great head. "I wish that I could remember what it was that my friend told me to remember. The nearer we get to Sno-ta-hay, the more I think about it."

"Be at ease," smiled Mackenna. "Remember what I told you; you'll think of it when the time comes."

Hachita said nothing, only continued scowling and shaking his head. Young Mickey spat disgustedly, and called over from his guard rock.

"Spirits. Warnings. Traditions. You're all a pack of old women. My God, let's have something to eat. I'm starved. What is there to eat, old lady?"

"For you," said Mal-y-pai, "snake droppings and toad dung."

The boy's face was instantly a mask of hatred.

"For you," he cried, features contorted, "there would be a bullet in your damned old spleen! You're lucky we have to keep our rifles quiet. Remember me, Mother! I'm going to do something for you when we have the gold and are going out."

"You're like a colt full of green grass, ugly boy," said the ancient squaw. "All bloat and blowing from the back end. I spit on you."

She did, too, and the wall-eyed scout had to leap quickly to avoid getting splattered. He clubbed his rifle, choking with rage. He would have brained Mal-y-pai but for Mackenna's desperate dive to knock the old lady out of the way. He and she went to the ground together, and Young Mickey's rifle butt whistled overhead. It struck the boulder in front of which Mal-y-pai had been standing, badly splitting the wood of the stock. Seeing his gun so damaged, the boy turned dead-white.

"Goddamn you," he said, "I'll kill both of you for that."

Whether he would have, remained unsolved. As he hipped the broken stock to fire down at the sprawled figures, he was swiftly lifted free of the ground and up into the air. Hachita held him there, helpless as a rat in a hawk's claw, measuring the back of his head for the best place in which to bury his belt ax.

"No, no!" shouted Mackenna, from the ground. "No more killing, Hachita! Your friend wouldn't want you to do that. Put him down, now. Gently, gently . . ."

The huge Apache nodded in mute submission. But as he lowered the runted cavalry scout to earth, he wagged his head slowly. "I don't know, I don't know," he said uncertainly. "There was something about killing in what my friend told me. I remember that now. But what was it?"

"What I've just told you," said Mackenna. "Not to do any more of it. Now, that was it, wasn't it, Hachita?"

"I don't know, white friend. Maybe, if you say so."

"Sure. Come on now. We're all in the same camp."

"Yes," said Pelón, "and it's the last one before Sno-ta-hay. My God, think of that, *amigos!* We're almost there!" He hesitated, a shadow crossing his gross features. "Damn it, Mackenna," he said, "I am suddenly worried about something. If this is the Pumpkin Patch camp, then we missed another landmark we should have seen today."

"The wagon road," nodded Mackenna. "We should have crossed the wagon road sometime this afternoon."

"Yes, yes, that's it. Damn it, I don't like it. It makes me think we are wrong. The Adams story is so certain on that point of the wagon road to the fort. We're lost, I think. I'm going up there and look for those pumpkins."

"With the spirits of Gotch Ear and the others?"

"Damn the spirits!"

Mackenna did not want to stir the camp that night. He wanted it to sleep, and to sleep soundly and well.

"Wait," he said, "use your intelligence, Pelón. Do you remember why it was that Gotch Ear had Adams and Brewer look so carefully at the tracks of that wagon road? I will tell you. It was because, even then, it was an old road, little used, and its wheel tracks were so faint that only an Indian could see them without having them pointed out. Now, here we are, with the sun and the rains and the sandstorms of more than thirty summers—and the snows and blizzard winds of as many howling winters— passing over this land and tearing at it and eroding it away since that time. Come, now, *Jefe.* How could it be that the old road would still be visible? Of course we didn't see it; it isn't there to see any longer."

Pelón was but partly convinced. But the old crone who had brought him into this world of outlaw troubles and travails called over, just then, that the coffee was poured and steeping, and for all who were hungry to find and sharpen their own roasting sticks and come and hang their pieces of flyblown deer loin into the fire and burn the maggots off it.

This more logical argument ended the renegade's indecision. With the others, he gathered toward the fire. But, in doing so, he pointed up-canyon.

"Those pumpkins had better be there in the morning," he said. "And you know what I mean, dear friend."

"Of course," shrugged Mackenna, smiling confidently.

And then he sat there wondering how many pumpkins they would find after thirty-three years without any irrigation water in the ditches of the ancient Indian village.

32 ⋙

Thirty-three Years from Fort Wingate

THERE WAS another thought gnawing at Glen Mackenna's mind that suppertime in the campsite outside the
Pumpkin Patch—or where he had assured Pelón López the
Pumpkin Patch was waiting. The other thought had no
connection with pumpkins. It concerned Francie and himself, and a desperate resolve which had been growing in
his mind all of the long afternoon. The struggle had not
been easy. Mackenna knew where they were. Also, he
knew *if* there were dried pumpkin vines and dusty irrigation ditches beyond that canyon wall. And the excitement
of the knowing made him weak. But the certain knowledge
of what Sno-ta-hay would mean to the girl and himself,
what it *had* to mean for them, had been returning to him
with compelling power the past hours.

At shortly before eleven o'clock that morning, they
had passed a place which Mackenna recognized and which,
because they were not looking for it where he was, his
companions had not seen. They had ridden past it without

a glance, their eyes and their imaginations fastened on vistas of nuggets and gold dust far ahead—indeed, near ahead, at this time—and so they had only kicked up their little horses and trotted on across the indescribably faint traces in the rock and brush of the old military wagon road to Fort Wingate. *But Mackenna had seen those traces.*

It was this secret edge which he held over his dangerous comrades that now centered his thoughts. This was the last camp. Beyond lay one more day's ride. If he and the girl were, belatedly, to depart the company, this night must be the time. Once through the Secret Door and into Sno-ta-hay would be too late.

Of course, he had known this for a long time. But his own gold hunger had forced the grim fact to recede. He had ridden nearly four hundred miles with his brutish "friends," knowing that they would turn upon him and kill him the moment he had led them to the gold. And yet he had kept riding. The pull of the Lost Adams gold was that irresistible. Not even the safety of Francie Stanton had been able, for the past two weeks of incredibly hard trailing, to take his mind from the prospect of that fabled meadow of rice gold at the grass-roots, and that incalculably rich ledge above the falls, with its nuggets nested big and thick as turkeys' eggs and its smears of the raw gold as long and as thick as a man's arm. But now, hard up against the last night, and the last fire, Mackenna knew reality.

He had not lost his nerve. He had only found his heart. It was being on the trail with Francie these last few days from the lookout. It was watching her learn to love the land. It was seeing her experience the same discoveries he himself had made when first he saw the silent canyons, castellated mesas, dark high timber, gleaming water and sky-vaulting naked rock of the inner ranges. It was this change in the girl which had finally worn down his consuming eagerness for the treasure; yes, and replaced it with the even greater longing and need to save Francie Stanton. He trembled, now, watching her across the fire, to think how near he had come to leading her into the death trap of Sno-ta-hay. But that was behind now. He still had the terminal chance to redeem himself. He could still prove to himself that he was neither glutton nor coward, but that he had the raw courage and the good common sense and, yes, the cunning skill, to get the youngster out of that evil camp and set upon the wagon road to Fort Wingate, the settlement of Grants, New Mexico, and safety.

The immediate problem, the food being finished and the coffee being rationed around for the last cups, was to get Francie aside and informed of their last-ditch plight and of his determination to get them out of it. To his surprise, Pelón made no objection when he asked if it would be permissible for him to speak with the white girl in private for a few moments. He wanted, he told Pelón, to put to her the proposal advanced by old Mal-y-pai some campfires back, that she begin sharing her blanket with her red-bearded friend. "Good, good," nodded the bandit, lifting his mirthless grin, "I was wondering when you were going to take her. I think she would be willing. With you, I mean, naturally. You understand that, *hombre?*"

"Of course," said Mackenna. "*Mil gracias.*"

He took Francie by the hand and led her away to a cluster of rock where they might sit and still be in the firelight, yet far enough away from the others to risk a low-voiced conversation in English. She smiled, not comprehending his motive, and snuggled her slim body close to his, as they walked. He heard old Mal-y-pai cackle at this. The crone's laugh gave him the idea to further her illusion, and apparently that of Francie Stanton, that he

meant to romance the young girl. He awkwardly slipped his
arm about Francie's shoulder. It was a long arm and not
used to being put about such a small companion. Its bony-
knuckled hand fell too far and brushed accidentally
against the shifting firm young buttocks. The hand was
pulled immediately away, but not immediately enough.
The girl's own slender hand seized it and placed it back
where it had been.

"I like it there," she whispered up to Glen Mackenna,
and the latter felt a weak and wild moment of suffocation
which drove all thoughts but one from his racing mind.

Then he recovered and was himself again. Pushing her
roughly down on the rocks, he said, "Now sit there and
act as though we were talking just the way we were
walking. But don't believe it. What I've got to say to you
is a matter of life and death, Francie, and I want you to
listen like you never listened in your life before. . . ."

Swiftly he told her the truth about their situation,
explaining the deadly danger, the opportunity offered by
the old wagon road to get out to civilization—the last
chance, presented by the camp they were now in, to make
a strike for that road and for freedom. When he had concluded the preliminary sketch and was launching into the
detailed plan he had formulated for their getaway, the
sixteen-year-old interrupted him, smiling excitedly.

"But Glen," she said, "I don't want to run away! I've
been talking with old Mal-y-pai the past two days, and I
wouldn't miss finding all that gold in that canyon for
the world! Why, it's the most thrilling thing I ever heard
of. Real gold. Lumps and chunks and sand drifts of it. It's
all over the place up there, Mal-y-pai says. And just think!
Nobody has set foot in there for over thirty years. Now,
we're almost there and the gold is ours. All we have to do
is go down into the canyon and pick it up. We'll be rich,

Glen! We can get married and have as many kids as we want, and send them all to school, and even to college. And you say you want to quit? This close to all that money? All that *gold* . . . ?"

The way that her voice rose, the way that it under-lined the word "gold," made Glen Mackenna shiver.

This girl, this crazy little sharp-breasted nubbin of a frontier brat, had the fever. She had it as hard and as bad as it came. Francie Stanton was sick with the Lost Adams sickness.

"My God, Francie," he said hoarsely, "you can't mean it. You can't actually believe that it's just a simple matter of going down into that canyon and picking up gold in the grass-roots! Listen, for the love of God, don't let that idea linger in your mind another minute. Throw it out, Francie. It's no good. It's a damned dirty, deadly lie. Don't you know that? Haven't you heard a word I said? These people we are with will kill you. You've seen them at work. They'll cut your throat, or split your head, or put a bullet in your belly or through your back, as quick as they'll say *'buenas días'* or *'adios.'* Now, you *know* that! *Think* about it!"

Francie looked at him, gray eyes on fire.

"Glen," she said, "I want to see that gold. I want to get my hands on it. I want to feel it. I want to have it. You go on. Get away. Mal-y-pai surely won't let Pelón hurt me. I'll be all right."

Mackenna wagged his head, let his red beard sink in defeat upon his chest.

"No," he said, "Mal-y-pai won't let Pelón hurt you, and neither will I. We'll go on."

He saw her eyes light up with pleasure at his capitula-tion, and he could not prevent the thrill which rushed through him when she reached and grasped both his hands in hers. It might still be all right, he told himself. He might still think of something. In the next moment, a remembered rough voice was advising him that he had better do so.

"Well spoken, *amigo*," said Pelón, strolling from behind the rocks upon which they sat. "You made the wise decision there. And many thanks to you, *chiquita*." He bowed to Francie. "You have more brains, really, than your friend. I am disappointed in you, Mackenna."

Mackenna swallowed his anger and his fear and his embarrassment in one dry-throated gulp.

"I am disappointed in myself, Pelón," he said. "I took my eyes off of you. That's a bad thing to do."

"Always," said the bandit.

They eyed one another.

It was Pelón, finally, who spoke. "Let's go back to the fire," he said. "You will be more comfortable there through the chill of the night with the leg irons on."

Mackenna, who had started toward the fire, stopped short. "The irons again?" he said.

"But of course," answered Pelón. "What else?"

At last Mackenna's blue eyes iced over.

He came forward to stand quietly in front of Pelón.

"This else," he said. "If you try to put those leg irons on me, you've taken your final step toward Sno-ta-hay. You take the lead tomorrow. You show the way to Adams' gold. You find the Secret Door. You find the Z-trail. I won't go another foot with you."

"There's still the girl."

"It's the girl I'm thinking of."

"What are you thinking of her?"

"I'm thinking of saving her."

"How?"

"By the same way in which Gotch Ear thought to save himself."

"Do you mean it? That's your deal?"

"Yes. I'll take you to the Secret Door. You'll give us two horses and a rifle. You take the gold. We'll take the road to Grants and Fort Wingate."

Pelón studied him for a long, uneasy minute.

He shook his head, unable to believe the facts.

"You would trade your share of the gold for this skinny thing? This scrawny pullet? This bony child who thinks Mal-y-pai will defend her?"

"Yes."

"Mackenna, dear old friend, you are crazy."

"No, I'm *not*. That's why I make the deal."

"What? Do you still think I would harm you? You, who have taken me almost to the Adams gold?"

"What's your answer, Pelón? Two horses and a rifle. When we have reached the door."

"We could find it anyway."

"Go ahead then."

"I could trick you. Promise the horses and the gun. Then not give them to you."

"They will be given in the morning. Before we start out."

"But then *I* would have to trust *you!*"

"Of course."

From the fireside, giant Hachita arose and began to drift over toward them. Out of the shadows, by the picket line of the horses, lounged Young Mickey Tibbs, also easing in their direction.

"All right," said Pelón quickly. "I will do it. No need to tell the others, eh?"

"Not until tomorrow. But I get the rifle tonight."

"You drive a merciless bargain."

"No, only mindful of my fellow merchants."

"True, true. All right, it's agreed. Come on."

They went back to the fire and Pelón had Mal-y-pai
dig Mackenna's rusted old Spencer Carbine out of the pile
of campage stowed on the packsaddle. The wrinkled squaw
came over with the weapon and gave it to the prospector
with a nod. "I'm glad to do it," she told him. "It's those
damned blue eyes."

"What's the idea?" demanded Young Mickey, shifting
his grip on his Winchester's crudely repaired stock.

"We are equal partners," said Pelón, raising his own
rifle.

Young Mickey thought it over.

Glen Mackenna, in the stillness, pulled the loading
tube out of the Spencer's butt and checked the cartridges.
None had been removed. He pushed the tube back in.

Young Mickey uncovered his wolf's tooth.

"Sure," he lisped. "Isn't that just what I said back in
the Yaqui hills?"

"Precisely," said Pelón López.

"All for one, one for all," murmured Glen Mackenna.
"*Vivan los tres mosqueteros.*"

33

Apache Post Office

THEY RODE for two hours. The sun was just beginning to get into the top of the canyon. As in the legend,
the canyon trail was so narrow that a long-armed rider
could touch both sides by reaching out his hands. Already,
with the dawn start, they had ridden through the box
entrance and found the pumpkin vines and old irrigation
acequias and tumbled footings of the adobe walls of the
ancients. Now all were peering hard ahead for the next
landmark: "Apache Post Office."

Excitement crawled among them. The canyon floor,
going steadily upward since the start, now took a sudden,
very steep upward pitch, and they looked at one another
and all hearts beat faster. Was this the "stiff climb" which
Adams told of, which topped the canyon trail out into the
malpais? Would they break free of this deep hole at its
top and see what Adams and Brewer and Davidson and
the others had seen thirty-three years before? The stud-
ding of a large open flat with black lava outcrops? With
stunted pine timber? With the flinty ground's surface up-
heaved and rumpled as an old unmade bed? Would it be

like that, or would it be only another tangle of chaparral
and beargrass, such as to be found at the topping of a
thousand canyons in that country? Minutes, now, would
tell.

Francie, riding at his insistence in the lead with Glen
Mackenna, was beside herself. She was flushed and her eyes
shone. Her breathing was quick and shallow. Mackenna
found his own breath coming harder with each climbing
step of the Apache ponies, and it was not the altitude which
bothered him. It was the Adams Fever.

He glanced back, making certain that the line of
march was remaining as he had demanded it should. He
well knew that each landmark identified this day increased
the danger of Pelón's deciding he could go the rest of
the way without the help of Glen Mackenna's memory of
the sand map of old Enh. And, from the look of the open
light Mackenna could now see showing above him, they
were coming to the topping-out of Apache Post Office
precisely as Adams had reported it. His surveillance of his
followers reassured him only for the moment.

Directly behind Francie and himself rode Hachita,
interposing his enormous bulk between them and the guns
of Pelón and Young Mickey. Behind Hachita came Mal-y-
pai with the packhorse, then Young Mickey, and Pelón
bringing up the rear where he could drop the traitorous
cavalry scout with a single pistol shot, if need be. Against
the "need be," the Sonora outlaw rode with his right hand
constantly hidden beneath his infamous serape.

Satisfied, Mackenna stood in his stirrups and waved
down to Pelón. The bandit returned the wave and called
up, "*Hola!* Do you see anything yet?" And the white
prospector, eyes shining nearly as wildly as Francie Stanton's, shouted back, "Come on; follow me; see for yourself . . . !"

With this he put his heels into his pony's ribs and sent the little animal digging up the last few yards of the trail. In a moment, he burst out above. The others came crowding out of the canyon, their mounts bumping and jamming each other in the rush to see what might be seen above.

It was something to see, too. The land, up there, lay wrinkled and disturbed and broken as the face lines of a ninety-year-old man. Yet the general surface elevation did not vary thirty feet, and had an overall "flat" effect. Everywhere the black and gray-black eruptions of the steel-hard volcanic rock thrust upward among the thin grasses and the gnarled dwarf pine.

This was it; this was the malpais.

But wait. Something was missing. Something was wrong. Pelón spurred his pony up to the side of Mackenna's mount.

"For a moment," he growled, "I thought that you had been right again. But I don't see it. Where is the Apache Post Office?"

The white prospector shook his head. "I don't know," he answered, peering hard himself. We ought to be able to see it. Wait, maybe Hachita can find it. He's got the eyes for it. *Hola!* Hachita, come up here!"

The big Mimbreño rode forward and studied the lava outcrops. He shook his head. "*Nada*," he said, "nothing. There's no heap of message rocks out there."

"Wait, now, wait!" said Mackenna, seeing the dark rush of blood to Pelón's face. "There has got to be something we've overlooked in the legend . . ." He thought furiously, not so much frightened by the threat of the outlaw's explosive temper as swept away by his own hot excitement. His eyes sparked then, and he uttered a Spanish oath, and cried out, "Of course! That's it; Adams mentioned an elevation—they saw the post office from a slight elevation. Look around, look around . . . !"

"There it is!" hissed Young Mickey Tibbs. "Off to the left. You see it? Shaped like a wolf's head. Those two pines for the ears. That spit of lava for the tongue. Come on!"

All joined in the rush to follow his pony across the jumbled roughlands to the dark outcrop. A natural path led to its low summit. From its crown, a view was opened into a huge bowl of land sloping away to the west and hidden completely from the topping-out place of Pumpkin Patch Canyon.

"*Alli! Alli!*" cried Hachita, even he caught up in the game. "There is the message place!"

They all saw it an instant later and galloped their mounts down to it, all yelling and war-whooping like purebloods. When they came up to it, they were shaking with excitement. Nothing had altered in thirty-three years. Even some whittled message sticks still protruded from the stones of the ancient post office. Everyone began to laugh with relief. Except Hachita. The giant Mimbreño was frowning.

"That's strange," he muttered. "Those sticks look like they were freshly cut."

At once a stillness fell among the laughers.

"What?" said Pelón. "Surely you joke."

"I don't think so," put in Glen Mackenna, sliding off his horse. "He means it." He went over to the pyramid and bent over it. He touched one of the sticks, but did not remove it. He rubbed his thumb ball with the tips of his forefingers. There was a stickiness.

"They *are* fresh cut," he said. "The sap still runs from the ends. Keep your horses back. Maybe we can figure out the tracks of whoever put these here."

But the red-bearded prospector was wrong. They

could not figure out the tracks. The reason was not far to
seek. Other than for the single line of hoofprints made by
Glen Mackenna's horse in coming to the pile, there were no
pony tracks around that Apache Post Office.

34

This Place Smells of the Other World

"WHAT DO the sticks say, Hachita?" asked Mackenna.

In this moment, the white man had the say. The superstitious half-breed, Pelón López, and even the three-quarter bred Young Mickey Tibbs were feeling their Indian blood. Old Mal-y-pai was muttering an Apache prayer as fast as she could. Hachita, too, was vastly uneasy and did not want to talk. But, with quiet patience, Mackenna got him to do so.

"The sticks say, 'Apache was here and will return,'" he finally told the prospector.

"That's all?"

"No, one other thing. They say, 'Remember.'"

"'Apache was here and will return—remember,'" repeated Mackenna softly. "The two ideas seem related and yet unrelated. Who could have been here, Hachita?"

"I *know* who was here," said the huge Mimbreño.

"Who?"

"I can't say his name. You know that."

Mackenna's eyes narrowed. The towering Apache was talking about his dead friend Besh, whose name was forbidden to be spoken by Apache law. He was thinking that the hand of the dead man had placed these warning sticks at the last legend-mark before the Secret Door. The idea was absurd, but Mackenna did not dare make light of it.

"Yes," he agreed, "I know the law. But suppose it was not him, but someone else. Is it not possible for another Apache, or for some other Apaches, to place these sticks? After all, they know we're in the country, and we know they're looking for us. With their skill at erasing their tracks, they could have come into this message pile without leaving any sign the average eye would pick up. Are you absolutely sure, Hachita, that you see no such sign with your great gift of eyesight?"

Hachita stared down at him.

"No, white friend," he said, "there is no such sign. I told you who left those sticks."

"All right. But how are you so certain?"

"Because of that last word, *Patrón*."

"You mean, 'Remember'?"

"Yes. You should know that I do."

It dawned on Mackenna then. The Apache was referring to the injunction that Besh had given him about not forgetting what it was that he, Hachita, must do, should any harm befall Besh. The big Mimbreño was convinced that the ghost of Besh had planted the message sticks to remind him to remember. It was fantastic. Utterly pagan. And yet . . .

"Yes," Mackenna told the huge Indian, "you're right. And I do recall it now. But the sticks say nothing of not going on. They don't forbid us to proceed. Don't you agree to that, Hachita?"

The latter nodded his immense head.

"Yes, I guess that I do. But I wish that I could remember what it was that my friend swore me to. You see, he knows I have forgotten it. That's why he put those last sticks there."

They had been talking a little aside from the others, but now the latter recovered their composure.

"Come on!" called Pelón. "*Arriba!* Let's go. Those sticks don't mean a damned thing. Some crazy coyote of a New Mexican Apache sneaking around on foot and playing tricks. Pah! Who fears such nonsense?"

"That's so," snarled Young Mickey. "To hell with the red bastards. They don't scare me."

"Yes, yes!" croaked old Mal-y-pai. "Come on, let's ride again. I don't like this place. It smells of the other world. Hih! I'm afraid. Hurry up."

Mackenna swung up on his mount and nodded to Hachita.

"Are you ready?" he asked. "Do you feel all right?"

"Yes," mumbled the slow-minded brave. "My friend said to trust you. Here we go. Damn! I wish I could remember."

They rode for hours then. There was very little talk, almost no laughter. The sticks in the message pile were bothering them, but the lure of the Adams gold would not be long intimidated. By late afternoon, spirits had picked up and Pelón was telling dirty stories of his past, and old Mal-y-pai had quit praying and was singing a corn dance chant in her wonderfully terrible and cracked soprano. It was four o'clock when Young Mickey discovered ahead of them, and to the left, a high and evidently blank wall of red sandstone. "Could that be it?" he asked Mackenna, and the prospector, studying the formation and checking it against the angle of the sun and his memory of the map of old Enh, answered, "Yes, that has to be it."

They galloped toward the wall. Even at one hundred yards, even at fifty yards, they saw no sign of a break in its perpendicular rampart. Pelón was beginning to curse and glower again. Young Mickey was snarling silently and licking his wolf's tooth with nerves. But the tradition and the sand map and the unerring memory of Glen Mackenna were not to be denied. At ten yards, point-blank against a seemingly blind cliff of solid rock, Hachita suddenly grunted and pointed to the right.

"*Allí*," he said, "there it is."

And there it was. La Puerta Escondida. The "hidden" or "secret" door to the enormous riches of Cañon del Oro and the Lost Adams Diggings! They had found Sno-ta-hay.

"*Santa!*" gasped Pelón López. "My God, it is true!"

35 𝌆

Through the Secret Door

THE "HOLE-IN-THE-WALL" was hidden by a sheet of rock which protruded from the floor at the foot of the cliff in the manner of a bull-ring barricade. This stone shield had been expressly described in the Adams legend. Its discovery by Hachita let the entire company understand that it stood just outside the immense treasure of the lost canyon, separated from the gold in the grass-roots and the turkey-egg nuggets of the waterfalls ledge by no more than the descent of the fabled "Z" or "zigzag" trail. Each member of the band now endured the throat-closing excitement of this knowledge.

Mackenna, watching his companions for the first sign of any move to negate the agreement to allow Francie Stanton and himself to go free, could not keep his mind on this danger regardless of its likelihood.

The lure and the aura of the legend were not resistible. No man standing thus at the threshold of the greatest of all the secret mines of the Southwest could place such a mere thing as his life above the overpowering pangs of the gold hunger. It was only concern for the safety of Francie Stanton which, even for the moment, held Mackenna alert. Then this human compassion was also swept under. Indeed, the white prospector was so far disordered by the resurgence of his greed that he actually led the rush toward the hole-in-the-wall.

But he was not alone in this selfishness. Francie's pony was the next behind his in the brief dash. The girl appeared to be as suddenly possessed as her bearded companion of no more urgent ambition than to be right up with the outlaw band as it broke into the sacred canyon of Sno-ta-hay. Of the two, it was Mackenna who first recovered his sanity.

"Wait!" he shouted to Pelón. "I demand that you wait! Our agreement is being forgotten!"

The bandit, surprisingly, at once clapped his hands together and commanded his followers to control themselves and behave as proven friends of the trail who had now come to an honorable parting with their trusted guide, Mackenna. The white man, he said, had fulfilled his part. He had taken them to Sno-ta-hay. Now it was the time for them to show their own good faith, and to give him the two horses and the girl, as promised.

As if to cement his high meaning, Pelón got down from his mount and came over to Mackenna, smiling and holding out his hand.

"Old friend," he said, "here is my hand. Take it and let us exchange grips. We have had some hard times, but my heart has been favorable to you all the while. Surely you have understood this?"

Mackenna nodded, putting down his own hand.

"Of course," he replied.

"Bueno!" cried Pelón, uttering his barking coyote's laugh. "You see? Didn't you always say that I had the good light shining within me? Didn't you always say that it would burst forth one day? That you would see it before we were done? *Ay de mí,* but you are a clever one, Mackenna!"

Their hands came together and Mackenna knew, at the instant of their closing, that he had made a terrible mistake. The crush of the bandit leader's stumpy fingers took in his extended hand like the steel jaws of a dredging shovel. The smile on Pelón's scarred face changed within the instant to a snarl. He whirled and threw Mackenna out and away from the saddle and down to the rocky ground with a force which drove the breath out of the bearded miner. It was a full half-minute before the latter could force his lungs to work, another thirty seconds before his spinning brain could be brought to a standstill. By this time the outlaw chief was bending over him, helping him to his feet. He even, with seeming compassion, brushed off the rock dust from Mackenna's shirt and returned to him his crumpled black hat. The look of regret upon his heavy features was a thing of wonder.

"It's a sad thing, *amigo,*" he said quietly, "but there is little gain in discussing it. Get back on your horse and let's go on. You know, of course, that there could be no real consideration of our parting."

"Of course," nodded Mackenna, after a moment. "But would it be beyond decent courtesy to inquire why not?"

Pelón shrugged.

"I know that you are a mining man," he answered. "I know that you have been to the school where such things are taught, and that you are very learned in the matters of all the minerals. I am aware, also, that you have devoted eleven years of your knowledge to the search for gold in this same land. You know this land. If there is some question down in that canyon," he pointed through the door, "as to where, precisely, the dust and the nuggets may lie, then you could tell us the answer. None of the rest of us know how to look for gold. Now, don't you consider it fair that you should go on with us until the treasure has actually been found? I give you my word, Mackenna, that once you have shown us where the gold lies, you can go. You and the girl. Exactly as we agreed. After all, that's the tradition, that's the legend, Mackenna. That's the way it was with Gotch Ear and Adams. Do you tell me that I lie? Didn't that damned Mexican have to go all the way down into Sno-ta-hay before they gave him his two horses and the gun?"

The mention of the gun caused Mackenna's eyes to flick to the ground where his battered Spencer lay in the rocks. Nodding slowly to Pelón's statement, he reached down. The bandit's booted foot drove into his extended wrist with shattering force. Mackenna's fingers, just closing on the carbine's grip, flew apart. The weapon fell again into the rocks. Pelón picked it up and handed it to Mal-y-pai.

"Come on, *amigo*," he said. "Isn't it true what I say? That Gotch Ear had to take his party all the way down the zigzag trail?"

"It's true, yes."

"Well, then, let's go. You have my word. What the devil more could you ask?"

Mackenna walked stiffly over and climbed back upon his mount. He looked at Francie Stanton and the others.

"Forgive me, *Jefe*," he said, reining the mustang about and pointing him through the shadows of the Secret Door. "For a moment, only, I forgot your reputation as a man of honor."

"Please to remember it," said Pelón, and followed him through the entrance.

Inside the wall, they stood upon the head of the trail. The view down into the canyon was dizzying. The drop,

Mackenna figured, was seven hundred or eight hundred feet, and vertical. Below, from this first vantage, nothing could be made out on the floor of the declivity because of the tree growth choking the bottom.

"*Cuidado,*" the prospector called back to Pelón. "The decline is fiercely steep."

The canyon turned to the right, just beyond their viewpoint. All could see the gigantic "Z" which the thin line of the trail slashed across the face of the wall. In many places this tracery against the blank rock assumed an angle approximately forty-five degrees. It appeared to be impossible of negotiation on horseback, or even afoot, leading horses. But the legend said that the Adams party had taken their horses down to the canyon floor. The others now looked at Pelón, who, in turn, nodded back to Mackenna.

"All right," he said, "but let the Indian go ahead of you. If someone must fall, let it be him."

Hachita, if he heard the reference to himself, made no sign that he resented it. When called, he pushed his pony forward and led the way into the first elbow, or hairpin reversal of the trail, without comment. Behind him came Mackenna, then the others, with Pelón riding last where his hand under the serape could watch Young Mickey. The unstable youth had fallen into another of his sullen moods of silence, and would bear particular attention because of it. But, as Hachita before him, he gave no sign that he felt any undue scrutiny or discrimination. He rode, as he had ridden from the start, with his Winchester unbooted and on the cock.

Below, and just below, the first zigzag of the trail, there was a lookout spot which jutted from the sheer wall of the cliff in a balconylike bulge of the native rock. It afforded the only "view place" in the precipitous plunge of the wild track, and the adventurers, dismounted now and leading their horses as Adams and Brewer and Davidson and Gotch Ear had undoubtedly done thirty-three years before, instinctively took pause to gather their courage for the remaining, major descent. Hachita, with his hawk's vision, was again the first to see a sign far below which defied the normal eyesight of his companions.

"*Miran*," he grunted, pointing. "The small house."

Pelón and Mackenna and Young Mickey were instantly at his side, peering down. The cavalry scout uncased his fieldglasses. The saliva was running from the corners of his mouth. As he raised and focused the glasses, his tongue flicked the spittle away, sluicing it across the snaggled wolf's tooth. "Jesus Christ!" he lisped in English, lowering the glasses. "It's the burnt-out cabin. You can even see the fireplace."

Mackenna took the glasses from him. He looked briefly, passed them to Pelón. "It's all there, *Jefe*," he said. "The cabin, the hearth, the meadow, the stream, the low falls up the canyon. See for yourself."

Pelón focused the glasses, cursing and growling in his excitement. When he saw what the others had seen, he could not contain himself but began to dance about on the ledge in the manner of a crazy man. Mackenna thought swiftly of how simple it might be to give him a shove and send him over, ending it all, right there. But the idea had no sooner entered his mind than the bandit leader was over his exultation. There was, moreover, the matter of Young Mickey Tibbs, who was watching both Mackenna and the Sonora renegade with quite probably the same solution in mind for the two of them. All three men appeared to draw away from the ledge in the same uneasy moment.

"Come on," shouted Pelón. "Why do we wait?"

"There's a question here," Mackenna replied to him. "Or, at least, there may be one. It occurs that now you have seen the diggings with your own eyes. Everything is down there, waiting, precisely as described by Adams so many times. Why would it not be allowable for the girl and myself to take our two horses and turn back here?"

Pelón laughed his rabid laugh, and was, in the same instant, scowling black as the thunder summer lightning.

"Damn you!" he snapped. "Did you see gold down there? Could you make it out with your own eyes, or with the *binóculos?* You damn fool! Don't play with me. You know our bargain. You lead us to the gold. The *gold,* do you hear?"

There was a bad sound in his voice and Mackenna quickly gave in.

"I hear, *Jefe.* Let us go on down, Hachita."

The huge Apache frowned and shook his head. "I wish," he said, "that I could remember. I seem to feel that it had something to do with this place. You know, I mean what it was that my friend told me not to forget."

"Yes, I know. But go ahead. Your friend did not say to stay out of Sno-ta-hay."

"That's true. I think . . ."

They went on down, Hachita leading the way. Again and again it seemed that one of the sliding, hunching ponies must go over the edge, but none did. It was approximately one hour later that they reached the floor of the canyon. Gathering at the foot of the trail, they stared out over the darkening meadow and meandering stream which all knew to be the end of their long journey.

Mackenna looked up at the tops of the canyon's walls, eight hundred feet above, his gaze squinted.

There was just the least rim of yellow light staining the east wall's crown.

"Sundown," he said softly aloud. "The same time, to the hour, that Gotch Ear brought Adams here."

"*Spirits!*" croaked old Mal-y-pai suddenly. "God blast us all in our tracks, we of red blood! What have we done? Where have we brought these cursed white people? *Ayi, ayi!* We stand in a sacred place. This is Sno-ta-hay! *Ayi, ayi, ayi . . .*"

She began to chant in Apache, eyes closed, scrawny body swaying from side to side.

"*Callate!*" rasped Pelón, shaking her with his huge hand. "Do you hear me? Shut up, Mother! Do you want to awaken every dead son-of-a-bitch whose bones lie in this canyon, or up on its wall there?" He pointed to the trail they had just come down, cursing foully in Spanish, but the old lady kept moaning and groaning and swaying crazily. Young Mickey Tibbs came up to her and struck her across the mouth. The blow was heavy and brought blood. But it stopped the ancient crone's outburst, and Pelón seemed in no way disturbed by this violence to his dam. "You see, you bony old hag? I told you to shut up. I would have hit you myself, except that I am an honorable son of an honorable father. God in heaven! You Indians. You're all crazy! Come on, Mackenna. Which way is the gold in the gravel?"

"Yes, goddamn it," said Young Mickey, "there is still light to see the gold. *Arriba!*"

"As I recall the map in the sand," said Mackenna, "the main place should be in the S-loop of the stream on this near side of the meadow. Do you see where the gravel bar makes a sickle moon in the water?"

"Yes, yes."

"Go look there for the gold in the grass-roots."

Pelón and Young Mickey exchanged fleeting, suspicious glances at one another, then both broke into a run for the graveled bank of the creek. Francie Stanton dropped her horse's reins and went with them. So did old

Mal-y-pai, still muttering Apache prayers between clutches
at her bothersome skirts to hoist them free of her knobby
knees for better running to where the "rice gold lay in the
grass like little snowdrifts."

Only Hachita and Mackenna remained at the foot of
the zigzag trail.

"What the old woman said, just now," mumbled the
giant Mimbreño, "there was something in what she said.
Curse me, why can't I remember?"

"Don't worry about Mal-y-pai and her spirits," said
Mackenna. "She sees spirits everywhere. You know that."

"No, it wasn't the spirits I was worrying about."

"Well, forget it, my friend, whatever it was. It will
come to you. Haven't I promised you that?"

"Yes, all right. Let's go see the gold, white friend."

They went, then, over to the gravel. Before they
could reach it, Pelón and the others, Francie Stanton with
them, were yelling and scooping up handfuls of the gravel
and throwing it about with total abandon. Crouching in
the shallow, wispy grass, Glen Mackenna sifted a handful
of bank sand and bar gravel and knew the cause of their
crazed elation. That sand and that gravel, even mined ex-
tensively by the Adams party three decades gone, still bore
enough raw gold, rice and flour and pinpoint nugget, to be
seen in one scooping of a bare hand in fading twilight at
the bottom of an eight-hundred-foot canyon with the
naked eyes and held at arm's length.

"*My God*," he muttered, "*it's true, it's true . . .*"

And he stood up slowly and stared off through the
deepening eerie gloom, not consciously aware of the irra-
tional yells of his companions rebounding madly within the
narrow walls of Sno-ta-hay, knowing and thinking but a
single repeating thought of his own, caring no least whit

for the thoughts or the sounds or the absurd gyrations of his five partners in the sharing of the Lost Adams gold.

I'm rich, I'm rich, I'm rich, I'm rich, was all that ran through the brain of Glen Mackenna.

It was all that mattered, all that meant anything. He was rich. He had struck the great-grandmother of the legendary mother lode.

"My God," he said again, *"my God,"* and went down upon his knees and began to grovel and clutch in the sand and at the gravel, as senseless and as mindless as a child gleaning bubbles from the soap froth of its bath.

36

Cañon del Oro

"COME, NOW, we have it almost free—lift harder!"
Hachita nodded and bent his great back to the order.
Mackenna, watching with the others, recalled how Adams
had told in his story of crawling back down off the zigzag
trail after the murders of his companions by the Apaches
of Nana. The legendary finder of the Lost Adams Diggings
had said that, in the darkness, he came to the smoking ruins
of the cabin fired by the Indians and worked among the hot,
charred timbers of the fallen structure to free the hearthstone and retrieve some portion of the buried dust and nuggets hidden thereunder in the fabled "clay *olla.*" He had
claimed, then, that the stone was too hot to touch. Later,
when this was doubted, he had said that he waited for the
stone to cool and that, just as it had, a big log—the very
centerpole of the cabin's roof—had fallen again, shifted
downward another few feet and so blocked the hearth that
the stone, then opened and pried up a few inches by
Adams, could not be raised enough to reach the *olla.* He
could see the clay pot and its gleaming heap of gold, but
was helpless to retrieve any least portion of the "color"
which had cost the lives of eighteen of his companions.

Mackenna had always balked at this part of the tradition. No man would go back down into a canyon full of Apaches—three hundred of them Adams had estimated!— to attempt the rescue of a few hundfuls of gold dust. To any prospector of Adams' experience, the logical move would have been to mark the place by mapping, then get out and come back with help. But now, as Hachita strained to lift the ridgepole on Pelón's command, all doubt of the Adams story disappeared. Knowing how much of raw dust and rice gold and turkey-egg nuggets must lie heaped in that legendary earthen pot only inches beneath his trembling feet, Glen Mackenna also knew that he, too, would have dared any number of Apaches to get to that incredible treasure and to bear off with him whatever amount of it he might stuff in the saddlebag pouches which Adams said he had brought down with him from the hideout on the Z-trail.

Pelón's shouts and wild brush-wolf laugh hacked into the intense stillness, breaking Mackenna's reverie.

The charred ridgepole had moved six inches and then a full foot under the heaving grunts of the giant Hachita. It seemed to resettle a moment later and, with wild cries, Young Mickey and old Mal-y-pai leaped in under the high end of the big timber and bent their backs to prevent its slipping farther. Francie Stanton, standing with Mackenna, looked at the red-bearded prospector as if to say, "Come on, what's the matter with you?" and then she, too, dived under the fifteen-foot log to risk maiming or crushing, or whatever accident awaited the desperate effort to prevent the heavy spar getting away from Hachita and falling, perhaps to wedge and lock tight, upon the blackened flagstone which their frantic digging had uncovered only minutes before.

"Lift! Lift!" yelled Pelón, who waited with a short,

thick timber to chock the ridgepole the moment its raisers might give the required elevation. "My God, what's keeping you from using your muscles? Are you children? Do you want to leave the gold here, *muchachos?* Ha, ha, ha!"

Mackenna found himself under the sooted ridgepole, straining and grunting and cursing with the rest. His move brought an Apache growl from Hachita, who apparently had not been convinced he should really try his full strength until given this sign of approbation by the white man that his dead friend, Besh, had counseled him to trust. Now, however, he heaved the timber aside as though it were a chunk of firewood, sending it over the waiting Pelón's head, to crash to the ground several feet from the hearth. It was the measure of his companions' absolute distraction that not one of them remarked this casual display of enormous power. Yet it was human power, and that other power which held them entranced was of a magnitude tenfold anything mortal.

"*Madre María!*" muttered Pelón. "Lift the rock, lift the rock . . ."

He seemed helpless to move. He could only stand pointing at the hearthstone, pleading thus with his fellows to remove it so that he might see what lay beneath it. He did not plead in vain. Mackenna, Francie and Young Mickey Tibbs went onto their knees in the ash and hearth char and canyon dross of the thirty-three years, clawing with taloned fingers and pantingly, as so many grotesque dogs, to unearth the golden bone buried there by dead Adams, Davidson, Brewer and their band in that other fated summer of 1864.

The stone was a thin, relatively light flagstone, exactly as Adams had described it. Once their tearing fingers slowed enough to grope with some rational cause, and to find the edges of the irregular rock, it came away easily.

Beneath it yawned the darkness of the treasure pit. To the lip-drawn, glaring-eyed diggers, and to their companions bending motionlessly above them, there came a terrible, growing stillness. The hole below the hearth of the Adams cabin stared back at them. It was as empty as a desecrated grave. The Adams gold was gone.

In the smothering dread which clutched at their hearts, the bandit chief and his fellow searchers crouched there, moving nothing but their facial muscles as the brutal shock of the gaping excavation beneath the fireplace rock registered its sickness on each of their countenances.

Again, it was the yapping laugh of Pelón López which shattered the trance of his comrades.

"Ha, ha, ha, ha!" he cried. "Of course! Of course! Idiots! Fools! Donkeys! We are stupid. We are dumb with eagerness. All but old Pelón. Ha, ha! Do you know what's the matter, *compadres?* The hole isn't empty. It has grown dark while we worked. See? Look! The sun is gone and here we cower like sheep with our heads together and not even looking about us. Hell! There's no trouble with the damned hole under the rock. Make a light, Mal-y-pai! Here, I have the match. Bring me a clutching of twigs and hay!"

The old squaw scuttled to do his bidding. When she had brought him the material, he struck the match to it and held the torch blazing in his hand down to the mouth of the hole beneath the hearthstone. For an instant there was still nothing to be seen. But only for an instant. Then, Mackenna said, "There's an old deerhide down there; it's covering something—as though to keep dirt from falling into it. Here, I can reach it. *My God, my God, my God . . ."*

It was all he could say, and all that any of them could think to say, in that awesome moment.

When his long arm reached down and pulled the old deerhide out of the hole, the light from the wadded grass in Pelón's hand leaped downward to disclose the crude clay *olla* of the legend.

And in the *olla* the raw pile of the Adams gold glowed and shimmered and pulsated as though with an animal life of breath and blood and conscious, menacing will of its own.

The fire in Pelón's hand flared to his whitened knuckles, ate into the stiff black hairs of the clenched fingers, went deeper. The acrid smell of burning human flesh spread over the silence at the hearthstone pit. It went unnoted. Pelón held the torch until it guttered and went out, suffocated in the stink and smoke of the cooking skin of his thumb and forefinger.

37

Thirteen Times the Coffeepot

THE *olla* could not be lifted out of the hole by hand. Not even Hachita could budge it. Ropes were brought in from the ponies and a sling fashioned. Bending their thick shoulders to this harness, Pelón López and the giant Apache brought the clay pot slowly upward and free of the excavation beneath the hearthstone. They lowered it upon the remaining flags of the fireplace footing, grunting like work oxen with its enormous weight.

"My God!" said Pelón, straightening. "There must be a million dollars' worth of it there!"

"Half a million, anyway," guessed Young Mickey Tibbs, having seen more gold weighed and counted than the Sonora outlaw. But neither was close, Mackenna knew.

"Maybe half of a half," he said.

"What?" Pelón was incredulous.

"Watch the bastard!" snarled Young Mickey. "I told you that you couldn't trust him. He's all white; remember that."

Mackenna eyed his suspicious comrades, his blue orbs as calculating as their beady black ones.

"The difference between us," he replied to Young Mickey, "is that I know what I am talking about. It's not a matter of honor but of education."

"Yes, yes," growled Pelón. "What the hell do you think I brought him along for? He is an expert. He hunts this stuff for a living. He went to school and *studied* gold. How do you like that?" He went up to Young Mickey, tapping him on his sunken chest with his stubbed fore-finger. "Be careful," he warned. "I don't like to be made to appear stupid. Besides, Mackenna is our partner. Why would he cheat himself?" He slid over to the red-bearded prospector, a frightening smile whitening his twin knife scars. "Eh? Is it not so, *compadre?* Why should you lie about the total sum, when you are to get one-quarter of it yourself?"

"One-quarter?" Mackenna was puzzled. "There are six of us. You mean one-sixth."

"I mean what I mean. Mal-y-pai and that witless buffalo there"—he nodded to Hachita—"get nothing. They're only Indians."

"But they came with us, Pelón. They took the same chances we did. And, indeed, the treasure is more theirs by rights than ours. No, it's not fair; they shall have a share."

"As you will." The outlaw enlarged the merciless token of his smile. "We won't argue it, old friend. Give them your share. All right?"

Mackenna sensed that it was time to go slowly. More-over, the sight of the gold, now out of its secret repository and gleaming in the light of the additional torches which old Mal-y-pai had fashioned in the Indian manner with grass and pine moss twisted together, glued with pine pitch, had more of a calming than an exciting effect.

It seemed to Mackenna that it was all over now, except

getting the gold out of the canyon and into Grants, New Mexico, for weighing. Or, at worst, fetching it on down to some more "friendly" assayer's office, nearer home in Arizona and farther away from any possibly exercised New Mexican Apaches. In either event, with the Adams gold in hand and with both Pelón and Young Mickey seemingly overwhelmed with the glitter and heft of the yellow metal, the prospects did not seem nearly so severe as they had to the white miner when they were back at the Secret Door, or up on the Z-trail, at Lookout Elbow.

He nodded presently to Pelón and said, "Why, surely, *Jefe.* You are the leader. I will arrange to give the old mother and the dim-witted one a part of my treasure."

"Very fine of you," admitted Mal-y-pai, showing her four yellow tooth stumps in appreciation. "I always liked you, Blue Eyes. You're not much of a *hombre duro*, but for a woman you're the right kind. The tough ones are always getting shot or knifed or hung by the soldiers, anyway. I'll take a good coward for mine. Especially, if he has a red beard."

"*Gracias, Madrecita,*" said Glen Mackenna.

Francie Stanton moved forward. "What will it be worth, Glen?" she asked. "Your share and mine, I mean?"

"I don't know. I could only guess."

"Well, guess then," said Young Mickey in a rasping voice. "I want to know how much I am going to get paid for shooting those two black troopers and riding all this way with you loose-tongued bastards. Honest to God, I never heard men talk like you and Baldy. Jesus!"

"There's the difference again," nodded Mackenna, hating the wall-eyed boy as one hates a poisonous reptile. "You see, it is talk which separates the four-legged from the two-legged brutes. For instance, I have noticed that you don't care for conversation. You might, then, prosper more

in consulting with your pony than with one of your human
friends."

Young Mickey fought his wayward eyes to force
them to center and to bear on Glen Mackenna.

"I'll remember that," he told the white prospector.

"Remember, remember," muttered Hachita. "I wish
that I might remember. I am coming closer to it all the
while, but I don't have it yet."

"Mackenna," said Pelón, "how much gold do we
have?"

"To know that, we would need to weigh it out from
the *olla*," answered Mackenna. "*Madre*, go get the canvas
cover from the packhorse. Bring with it, also, your small
coffeepot; the big one would be too heavy. Now that little
pot holds between three and four cups—a scant quart let
us say. Assuming such a capacity, we can approximate how
heavy it is when filled with the gold, then multiply the
number of pots we fill and measure out upon the canvas
cover."

"*Bueno!*" cried Pelón, well pleased. "You see, you
damned son-of-a-bitch?" he told Young Mickey. "I warned
you this red-bearded one had a brain. And honest? My
God, he's as honest as a gelding in a love affair. I would
trust him with my life, or at least with yours."

Young Mickey said nothing.

The weighing out of the dust and rice gold and acorn
and walnut and turkey-egg nuggets was begun. No one
talked during the affair except to count silently on their
fingers and with their lips the number of coffeepots which
Mackenna filled and leveled from the clay *olla*. When he
had done, there were piled neatly upon the soiled and
greasy tarpaulin thirteen glowing, bright gold heaps of the
pure mineral. At an extremely conservative thirty pounds

to the pot there would be 390 pounds of dust, coarse gold and specimen nuggets taken from the *olla*. Even carefully undervalued as to full weight, it was a literal bonanza. Moreover, it was startlingly close to the worth of the free gold which Adams had estimated that he and his comrades had buried under the cabin hearth. Mackenna looked up from this shimmering treasure now, and nodded soberly to Pelón.

"Taking into account the specific gravity of gold at 19.3, the size of the coffeepot at just less than a quart, the differential in solid and separate particle weights due to air space in the latter, and considering the purity of the recovery, I figure something in the order of $99,000," he said. "Of course," he added, blue eyes twinkling, "that is being deliberately careful, as the occasion demands. I should not be surprised if the true amount were nearer $100,000. Again, that is not yet what we had all hoped it might be, but it is almost precisely what Adams always claimed was beneath the stone. Is this not so?"

"Yes," agreed the outlaw, "it is so. In the story most commonly believed in Sonora, it was $200,000. But when one divides by two, as one always must with Mexican reports, one has your figure. I'll accept it. That's still a nice matter of some $25,000 for each of us." He turned on Young Mickey. "Does that meet with your approval, son of the son-of-a-bitch?"

Young Mickey walled his mismated eyes at him. "You knew my father, didn't you?" he asked.

"Did I know him?" growled Pelón. "You know damned well that I did! He tried for seven years to kill or catch me for General Crook when Old Redbeard was hunting Geronimo. But Old Mickey was always your true father. He was just like you. Just like Mal-y-pai described you. Old Mickey was also full of wind. Well, answer me. Are you satisfied with the division? Will you take your quarter share and be content, sick-brained boy?"

"I'll take my quarter share, you half-breed pig," replied the other. "But I won't be content until I am far gone away from you with it. And when I am gone, I will remember you, along with your little mother and this blue-eyed bastard of a white friend of yours, Pelón, and you remember *that*."

"You make much of Mackenna being white all of a sudden," grinned Pelón. "Can it be that the red spirits of your own Apache ancestors are nudging you a bit down here in this dark hole of old Sno-ta-hay?"

"Go to hell and start making the division of four," snapped Young Mickey. "I want to take my gold and get out of here. That's the best thing for all of us to do; take our part of the gold and split up and make separate trails away from here, and fast. You know that, Baldy."

"No such thing!" cried Pelón. "I won't hear of it. We came here as friends and we will go up out of here as the same thing. In numbers there is strength. We will stay together."

"I don't know, *Jefe*," said Mackenna craftily, "there is much to be said for Young Mickey's idea. As he says, you should be the first to realize that. Four trails are harder to follow than one. I, too, would like to take my gold and get out."

Pelón stared at him.

"You mean with the girl?" he said.

"Yes, with her."

"And her share?"

"Of course."

"Ha, ha, ha, ha, ha! Well, that's nice. You hear me laugh? You see that I am amused? You see that I still ad-

mire your jokes, Mackenna? Sure you do. Ha, ha, ha.
Now, then, everybody to the blankets. In the morning we
will divide the gold and depart. No trouble. Nothing."

He was watching Mackenna and Young Mickey, with
his right hand under his serape. Mackenna nodded cau-
tiously.

"But of course, *Jefe*. Nothing like a good night's sleep
to clear the mind and cleanse the body. It's easy to see why
you're the leader."

Young Mickey again said nothing, but neither did he
offer to push the matter. He just stood there scowling, his
Winchester hanging at his side, his thumb hooked over
its drawn-back hammer.

Mackenna took the blanket which Francie Stanton
brought him. With her, he made a bed on one side of the
canvas tarpaulin. On the opposite side, giant Hachita sat
cross-legged and blanketless. The flanking sides were silently taken by Young Mickey and Pelón. Old Mal-y-pai
built a fire in the abandoned fireplace and put on a pot of
coffee. It was then about ten o'clock, the time having fled
in a manner unaccountable to Glen Mackenna. But he
knew, and he quietly warned his slim companion, that the
next six hours would go in a manner all too unlike the
eager flight of the previous time.

"First light will come a little after four," he whispered
to Francie Stanton. "We dare not close our eyes, meanwhile. Do you understand?"

She squeezed his hand and snuggled to him.

"Yes," she answered, "our friend has already told me."

"Our friend?"

"Mal-y-pai. That's why she's making the coffee. She
said to tell you that. That she was making it for you."

Mackenna looked over toward the withered crone. She
caught his eye and winked broadly at him. He gave her a

quick nod and a return wink, and felt immeasurably the better—and the surer of seeing the morning—for the exchange.

"*Buenas noches, Madre*," he called over to the mother of Pelón López. "*Hasta mañana.*"

"*Hasta mañana*," the old lady grumbled. "Go to hell."

38 ⋛

A Mimbreño's Memory

To MACKENNA'S SURPRISE, Pelón and Young
Mickey, who began by drinking the coffee with him, cup
for cup, were soon nodding. In half an hour both were
asleep. Old Mal-y-pai came over from the fireplace. She
spat on the body of Young Mickey and put her blanket
about the shoulders of Pelón. "He's a good boy," she said
apologetically to Mackenna. "It wasn't that I wanted to put
the dreaming medicine in his coffee, but he left me no
choice. I can't forget that he is one-half Apache."

"We owe you a great deal, Mother; even our lives,
perhaps, if I can think of some way to make good with this
chance you have provided us."

"I can think of a way!" piped Francie Stanton.

Mackenna glanced at her, surprised.

"You understood what I said?" he asked. "Where have
you been hiding your Spanish all the while?"

"I haven't been hiding anything. Working for Mal-y-
pai beats going to school by a mile, that's all."

"Well, I guess!" said Mackenna admiringly.

"No time for guessing," said the girl energetically. "Come on, let's get our things together."

She got up, but Mackenna didn't move.

"Where do you think you're going?" he asked.

"Out of here. We've got our gold. They're asleep. Mal-y-pai says for us to vamoose. So let's go."

"How do you expect to get 'our gold' up that trail?" Mackenna demanded acridly. Our shares will weigh as much as another man—and a big man. Our ponies will be carrying that extra man. Pelón and Young Mickey would catch us before we got to the wagon road. We'd be dead by this time tomorrow."

"That's what we're going to be, anyway, according to Mal-y-pai!"

"Yes, but I'll still think of something else. There's a lot of this night left."

Francie Stanton fixed him with her clear eyes.

"Glen, that's what you said the first night, way back in Surprise Meadow. All you've done since is sit and think."

"That's my trouble," admitted Mackenna.

"Well, it's not mine!"

"A greater truth would be difficult to imagine." He stared at her frowningly. "Francie, the only way we might get up that cliff and escape with our part of the gold is if Mal-y-pai and the packhorse were to go with us to carry the stuff. Yes, and Hachita, too, to guard the rear. Now, if you can arrange that, I'll go with you."

The girl returned his stare. "I've already arranged my half of it," she told him. "Mal-y-pai will go with us. I've promised her she can live with us."

"With 'us'?"

"Well, we are going to have a home, aren't we?"

"Francie, you're crazy."

"Maybe. But I've done my part. Now you do yours."

"You mean Hachita?"

"You're the one that said we had to have him."

Mackenna glanced uneasily across the gold-laden tarpaulin. The Mimbreño descendant of Mangas Coloradas had taken no coffee. He sat watching the white couple.

Mackenna cleared his throat.

"*Amigo*," he smiled, "it is that we have been talking over here of the idea that we might leave this place while Pelón and Young Mickey slumber. We had thought to ask you to go with us."

The big Apache shook his head sadly. "I cannot do it, white friend," he said. "I must remember what my dead friend told me to remember. Until I do that, I cannot leave here."

Mackenna frowned and looked at Francie. The girl was waiting, expecting him to act. He knew, suddenly, that he had better do so, too. Sitting and thinking was not going to get *this* job done. He turned back to Hachita. Quickly he told him that he and the white girl and the old woman would depart with the packhorse and their gold, regretfully leaving him, their faithful Apache friend, with Pelón and Young Mickey. To his dismay, the giant brave slowly wagged his head.

"It cannot be done, white friend," he said.

With the words, he drew his throwing ax from its belt scabbard.

"Until I remember what I am supposed to remember about Sno-ta-hay," he explained, "no one leaves this deep canyon."

"But you may never remember!" cried Mackenna, completely startled by this miserable turn of luck. "We may all sit here until we are as old as Mal-y-pai!"

Hachita nodded gravely. He balanced the ax, turning its haft in his great hand. The firelight ran red as blood along its honed blade. Hachita looked down at it, and then across at Glen Mackenna. "Yes," he said, "we may all do that."

39

Hachita's Ax

IN THE MORNING no hint remained of the previous night's strained camaraderie. If Pelón or Young Mickey realized they had been drugged, neither chose to make an issue of the matter. The bandit leader was particularly sanguine.

"My God, old friend," he greeted Mackenna, "how do you like this for a day? Smell that air. Hear the grass grow. *Ay de mí*, but it is a fine thing to be alive."

"It certainly is," admitted Mackenna.

Francie and Mal-y-pai were putting away the camping things. Birdsong and the sound of the water in the little stream filled the canyon with their happy blending. Looking at the expansive Pelón, Mackenna found it difficult to believe his former and even most recent fears of the Sonora half-breed. When he wished to be, the squat renegade could be a charming host. This day he wished to be.

"Old comrade," he now observed to the white miner, "let us stroll up above a ways and look for the ledge. I think you would like that, as a man educated in such things."

"That's so," agreed Mackenna.

He got up from his place at the breakfast fire. Pelón led the way. Young Mickey moved out to follow them. The outlaw leader stopped. His hand slid beneath the serape.

"Someone should stay with the women," he said.

"But not me," answered Mickey.

There was the least suggestive stir beneath the serape.

"Yes, I think you."

Young Mickey had been caught with his Winchester down. He nodded and turned silently back.

"Let us proceed," smiled Pelón, bowing with a sweep of his long arm. *"Después de Usted, señor."*

Mackenna returned the smile, glad with relief at this turn of the bandit's mercurial temperament, and obeyed the invitation to go ahead.

The waterfall lay as described by Adams. It was about four feet high, and directly beyond it, up-canyon, the bed of the creek bent sharply west to open on the small "upper flat" of the legend. It was here that Nana and his Apaches had camped, and here that the fabled Turkey Egg Ledge should be located. Mackenna's trained eyes sought it out the moment he and Pelón had turned the bend and were out of sight of the lower camp and Adams cabin.

"Alli!" he cried *"Por Dios!* look at it glitter, even from here!"

They went over to the ledge. It was the greatest out-crop Mackenna had ever seen. It was beyond words greater than Camp Condon, Fish Creek, Verde or any of the other Arizona strikes. It was, Mackenna suspected, the biggest deposit of the pure color that a white mining man had seen in all the Southwest since the days of the Conquistadores. He could only stand and marvel.

Pelón seemed singularly unimpressed. The magnitude

of the thing escaped him, and its implications for future return and exploitation were not the occupant of his mind upon that last morning.

"Listen," he said to his companion, looking down-canyon to be sure they had not been followed around the bend, "I didn't come up here to look at this stuff. What I want is down there on that piece of canvas. I am no digger of dust. I am an outlaw, a *bandido;* I steal my gold, I don't sweat it out of the rock or the gravel. The hell with that. I want to talk to you."

The ledge, Mackenna thought, would mine out no less than a million dollars—that much was *visible*—and it might mine two, or five, or ten millions. The water was there in the creek for hydraulic hosing of the canyon wall. It could be another Mother Lode like California's middle Sierra. If it went underground, and stayed pure, it could even be another Comstock or Alder Gulch. There was nothing minerally impossible to that immense splatter and egging of raw gold. It was all that even an engineer's mind could do simply to imagine the scope of the Turkey Egg Ledge of the Lost Adams Diggings.

"Did you hear me?" said Pelón. "I want to talk about Young Mickey. He's plotting to kill us all. You know he's crazy. I wanted to warn you and make a deal. I wanted to tell you that you can count on old Pelón, and that all you need do is leave that boy to me. What do you say? Are you with me?"

"I suppose I am," agreed Mackenna, forcing his mind and eyes away from the ledge. "I'm certainly not with Young Mickey Tibbs."

"Good, then, let's go. I'm eager to show you I honor our old times together. *Cuidado,* now. Leave all the moves to me. I know exactly how it must go."

"Of that," said Mackenna tersely, "I am absolutely sure. Lead the way, *Jefe*."

The camp, when they approached it, appeared normal. The packhorse stood ready, its cross-armed saddle already bearing the few Apache housekeeping items, waiting only the final burden of the gold. Pelón seemed about to give the order to conclude this operation and mount up for the start, when he suffered the first of two singular inspirations. "Wait," he called to the old squaw, who had led the animal into the ruins and up to the tarpaulin. "I have an idea: let us put but half the gold on the packhorse, who could not carry it all, anyway. Then let us divide the other half equally among the four partners. This will give each an incentive to stay with the others. Yet, should we have to flee by separate routes, abandoning the packhorse, we shall each have a tidy fortune of the treasure to reward our hardships and dangers. Does anyone object?"

No one did. It was a hard-headed, practical suggestion, worthy of a bandit chief. The gold was split up.

"Now," announced Pelón, surveying his little cavalcade as it stood ready along the bank of the creek, "I have just had another idea: it is that our friend Mackenna shall take paper from his notebook and draw us a good map of this place—the same map that old Enh drew in the sand for him at Yaqui Spring. This is a reasonable thing. Mackenna has the map in his mind. He is an educated man, very wise in such things by schooling. But the rest of us are poor, ignorant fools, *pobrecitos* with no advantages in learning. What would we do to find our ways back into Sno-ta-hay? What would we even do to find our ways *out* of it, right now? Am I wrong? Do I lie, or deceive?"

Again, the suggestion was logical. No sane human being could have seen the Turkey Egg Ledge above the falls and not demanded to know how to find his way back into

Sno-ta-hay and the Lost Adams Diggings. Without argument, Mackenna procured paper and pencil and drew a
hurried but comprehensive chart of Cañon del Oro, including the Secret Door, the Pumpkin Patch and the military
wagon road leading to old Fort Wingate. When he handed
the map to Pelón, the latter frowned over it for a full
minute before the scarred lips lifted in the wolf smile.

"It is a thing of vast skill, old friend," he remarked
enthusiastically. "With this to follow, a blind man could
return to Sno-ta-hay. *Mil gracias.*"

"Come on!" snarled Young Mickey nervously. "Get
it over with, Pelón."

" 'It'?" said Mackenna, feeling his scalp squeeze small
on his head.

"Oh, yes," waved the outlaw regretfully. "You see, I
forgot to tell you that I also made an arrangement with
Young Mickey; it was to kill you and the girl."

They all saw the long-barreled Colt move beneath the
serape, and Mackenna gasped. "My God, no, Pelón! You
can't do it! Not the girl!"

"I am helpless, *Patrón.* Please to get ready."

He moved his head, black eyes darting to Young
Mickey Tibbs, standing behind and a bit apart from the
others.

"You, too, little son-of-a-bitch," he said.

"Me too what?" scowled the narrow-chested cavalry
scout.

"You too get ready," replied Pelón. "You see, I didn't
tell you the whole arrangement, either; it was to shoot you
also."

Mackenna could see Young Mickey coiling himself
for the counter-strike. He tried to avert it.

"Pelón!" he pleaded, hoping even in that last second
to forestall the gunfire, "*please* let the girl go! Do not per-

mit her to die because of my mistake over you. It's *pun-donor*, Pelón. I claim it in the name of your Spanish father's honor!"

The brute Sonoran was affected. He moved his head unhappily, the pain of the decision twisting his disfigured mouth. Finally he surrendered, but not to charity.

"I am sorry, Mackenna," he admitted, "but my Spanish father will have to understand, and you will have to die wrong about me. I have no soft spot, *amigo*. That was your mistake all the while. I am sad to tarnish your opinion of Pelón, but life is cruel, and full of woe, and fragile as the bones of a baby bird. Good-bye."

"Pelón, my son, don't shoot them."

All had forgotten old Mal-y-pai. Now they saw her. She stood by the packhorse, the big-bored muzzle of Mackenna's Spencer carbine pointed at her murderous child. "Be a good boy," she said. "Bring the pistol out from under the serape, as your mother tells you."

Pelón did not move to obey.

"Mother," he said, "would you shoot me?"

"I don't know."

"Would I shoot you, then?"

"Certainly."

"In that case, be reasonable. Put away Mackenna's gun. And another thing, *Mamacita*, tell that dumb ox of a Mimbreño to quit staring at me and fingering that damn hatchet of his. There's no harm coming to him, and none to you. You're both Apaches."

"But the whites," said the old lady, "they will be killed, eh?"

Pelón at once lost his temper.

"Goddamn it, Mother, listen to me," he shouted. "It is your own people I protect. Apache law says that no man or woman of foreign blood, neither white nor brown nor mixed, shall see the Canyon of Gold and live. Now, that's your own stupid Indian religion, isn't it? Why the hell don't you listen to it, then?"

At this, Hachita, who had been standing by with his customary vacuity, straightened and struck himself a ringing blow on the forehead.

"That's it! That's it!" he bellowed. "It comes back to me when you say it. I remember, now, I remember . . . !"

He danced over to the stunned Mackenna, enfolding him in happy embrace. "Isn't it wonderful that I remembered, dear white friend? It was just as you promised me it would be. Oh, I am so glad. Thank you, thank you."

Mackenna, silently thanking another source for the interruption, nonetheless felt his throat go dry.

"Do you mean," he asked, easing out of the giant's slackening grasp, "that what you remembered is to kill all foreigners to preserve the secret of Sno-ta-hay?"

"Yes, yes, good friend. Isn't that wonderful?"

The bearded prospector could not believe it. He forced a calmness into his voice, hoping desperately to reach some spark of sanity in the huge Indian's mind.

"But the young white girl and myself are foreigners, Hachita," he said quietly. "Surely, you would not kill us?"

"Yes, too bad, but I would. That is why my dead friend and I came to the *rancheria* of old Enh. We were sent to protect the treasure, to preserve it for our people."

"But, Hachita, *think!* We have been your friends!"

The Mimbreño did not appear to hear him.

"Yes, we came to guard the treasure from Pelón and from all others," he said. " 'Kill them all,' my dear friend ordered. 'Do not let a single one with so much as half a tiny drop of white or brown blood get away.' Oh, how happy I am to remember it! Oh, how grateful!"

"My God, you crazy Apache bastard!" yelled Pelón,

suddenly alerted. "I've got brown blood myself. And how about Young Mickey? He has white blood, as well as Indian!"

"Yes, yes; have a good journey to the Dark Place, *Jefe.*"

He moved with the speed of thought, and before Pelón could realize that he meant it. The ax flashed in the sunlight, turned one and one-half times in the arc of its flight, buried itself one-third the depth of its haft in the broad chest of Pelón López. As he died, the bandit staggered one step toward Glen Mackenna, grotesque face ashen gray.

"You see, old friend," he gasped, "you were right, after all; I did have a soft spot, and Hachita hit it."

When he fell, Mackenna thought that he did so with the knife scars lifted upward in a last grin at life. But he was never sure. All that he really remembered was the sudden shove with which old Mal-y-pai pushed him, Mackenna, from behind, into the creek, as Pelón dropped. That, and the slap of the creek water striking him in the face, and the following splash of Francie Stanton's body lighting near his in the long pool below the gravel bar in front of the ruins of the Adams cabin.

Then the old lady was leaning over the cutbank above them and shouting down for them to "Swim like hell; I just shot Young Mickey and then your damned old gun jammed . . . !"

With that, she had leaped in with them and was leading the way across the creek and into its far-side, screening growth of cattails. "Come on, you donkeys!" she sputtered. "Into the reeds! That buffalo will finish off Young Mickey and be looking for you and me! Swim, you fools . . . !"

Mackenna and Francie swam.

They swam and dived and clawed their way into the cattails and up the brushy bank beyond them into the rocks

which footed the zigzag trail. Looking back, Mackenna saw
Hachita bending above Pelón. He saw the flash of the ax
blade as the Mimbreño wrenched it free. He saw the huge
Indian turn and start for Young Mickey Tibbs, who was
on his hands and knees struggling to get up and to escape,
with his left leg shattered at the knee by Mal-y-pai's shot.
He saw the stricken boy take one, two, three tortured,
lurching steps, then turned away as Hachita cocked and
threw the hatchet. He did not see it land. He only heard
it. The sound made him ill.

"God damn!" hissed old Mal-y-pai, from a rock
nearby. "That was a poor throw. It got him just as he was
turning his face around to look back. It took him in the
mouth and stuck in the lower jaw. Look, you can see the
handle bobbing up and down. He's trying to say something
to Hachita. I wonder what it is?"

"My God," said Mackenna, "let's go on."

"I think he's asking him to pull it out."

"Come on, Mother. No more, please!"

"Aha! I was right. There goes Hachita seizing the
handle of the ax. Now he pulls it free."

"Mal-y-pai, we're leaving!"

"It's too late, though. I knew it would be. When the
blade goes in like that, there's no use in pulling it out. Oh,
wait. I am wrong. *Mil perdónes, muchachos.* Hachita
wasn't pulling it out for Young Mickey, he was pulling it
out for us. Here he comes."

Mackenna looked again across the little stream and saw
that it was so; the Mimbreño giant was striding into the
creek, breasting it afoot where they had been obliged to
swim or sink. His eyes were fastened on the reeds and
rocks into which they had disappeared, and his deep voice
was intoning an eerie, minor-keyed chant.

"What prayer is that?" asked Mackenna, low-voiced.

252]

"No prayer," said Mal-y-pai. "It's a song. You should know it, Blue Eyes. Don't you hear the words? He's singing it for you. It goes '*Zas-te, zas-te, zas-te,*' over and over again. It's the death song."

"Mother," groaned Mackenna, glancing helplessly at the crouching, white-faced Francie, "where will we go?"

"I don't know, Blue Eyes. I brought you this far."

"Do you have your knife, Mother?"

"Hell no. I dropped the damned thing back there when I picked up your rifle."

"God! we haven't even got a knife!"

"Bah! Neither did Adams and Davidson."

"Mother, they had guns!"

"All right, Brewer, then. He didn't even have a toothpick when he crawled into that hole up there!"

She hooked a bony thumb over her shoulder, toward the cliff behind them, and Mackenna's eyes narrowed.

"That's it!" he whispered. "That crevice up there at the Lookout Elbow. It saved Brewer. Maybe . . ."

"Don't talk, run," advised the old lady, gathering her skirts to lead the example. "But don't count on having Brewer's luck. It is only this Hachita's mind which is dull. His eyes are as keen as his ax."

"Come on, Francie," said Mackenna. "We're going up the cliff. The old lady's got a hiding place for us."

The girl shivered and clung to him a moment.

"I'm sorry for being so smart," she said. "I'll do the best I can for you, Glen. But I'm scared sick."

"*Climb,*" said Mackenna, "*and pray.*"

The ascent of the Z-trail then began. Mackenna had been climbing up and down such cliffs for eleven years and was a strong, wiry man in the full strength of his middle years. Francie Stanton was of that clean hard-limbed breed of woman which will stay up with many men, and she was vital with the steel and wire of youth. It was the old squaw who could not keep the pace, and who panted farther and farther behind.

Near the Lookout Elbow, Mackenna could see down the trail for several hundred feet. He could see both Mal-y-pai and Hachita. He knew that if he waited for the old lady, there would not be time for getting Francie hidden in the Brewer crevice. He knew, also, that if it came to the choice, the old must die. Happily for him, Hachita spared him the decision.

"Old Mother," called the giant brave, "you don't need to run from me. You are of the pure blood also. I won't hurt you. Wait for me. Stay back. Don't be with those white people when I catch them. Please, now, old Mother."

Mackenna saw the old woman stop. She looked back at the climbing Apache, then up the steep trail toward Glen Mackenna. She waved her arm at the latter.

"Go on, Blue Eyes!" she croaked. "I claim the right of *nah-welh-coht kah-el-kek*. You know that law."

Mackenna knew it. It was the Apache dictum which permitted the hopelessly wounded to remain behind for purposes of delaying the enemy. Under its harsh terms, the claimant of its right was the one to say if his or her companions should go on. Mal-y-pai was not wounded, but her ancient lungs were bursting and her rickety legs shaking with impossible fatigue. Quickly, the bearded prospector waved back. "We hear you, Mother. *Adios* . . ."

He scrambled and stumbled upward. His own lungs were aching, his own calves and thighs throbbing. But Francie was waiting at the Lookout Elbow and she was all right, and the Brewer crevice with its prayed-for safety lay only beyond the next upward turn of the Z-trail.

"The old woman stayed back to argue with Hachita," he explained, panting. "He won't hurt her."

"I won't go on," said the girl. "Not without her."

"She did it for you. You'll go on. Get moving."

"No, I won't!"

Mackenna struck her hard. He very nearly knocked her down. Only her lean strength kept her from falling. She wiped the blood from her mouth, staring at him.

"Go on," he said. "The game is over, miss. Start climbing and, damn you, don't look back, and don't talk back." She still hesitated, from numbness now, but he could afford no distinctions. He spun her about and shoved her up the trail. She staggered and nearly fell again. He was behind her, instantly, with another hard shove. This time she fell, and he was atop her like a cat. He literally threw her up the trail, slashing her with his forearm, and cursingly, across the buttocks. "Move out, damn you!" he cried. "I'm not ready to die to prove how brave you are. You're a brat and a bitch, and you've given me nothing but hand squeezings and headaches since we met. Now you get your hard little man-teasing tail on up that cliff and into that cleft above, or I'll knock it clean off of you!"

She went white as paper and began to cry. But she ran and he drove after her, no wrench of the heart slowing his pace. All he wanted to do now was to live. To live and to get this willful orphan out of this canyon and back to whatever frontier family would be damn fool enough to take her. He knew that the odds were against them. And he knew, as he cursed and fought his way past the elbow turn and into the first tumbled rocks of the Brewer crevice behind the sobbing Stanton girl, what it was that he had to do to beat those odds and to stave off the almost certain death which shadowed so closely and with such ominous silence in their wake.

He had to kill Hachita. And he had to do it a way that was ten centuries times ten centuries old. He had to do it with his bare hands.

40 ≷

Death in the Brewer Crevice

THE CREVICE up which the white couple clawed their way was a peculiar formation riven almost as though by some supernatural lightning bolt in the heart of the towering west wall of Sno-ta-hay canyon. It was neither a wind nor water cut and Mackenna could not place its true nature until he thought of the lava beds outside the Secret Door and surrounding the Apache Post Office. Earth movement, his trained mind recorded, even as he struggled upward. This great wall of the mother rock had been split asunder by some long dead volcanic upheaval. The centuries had filled its V-shaped bottom with detritis, brush and small pine growth, boulders and enough washed-down organic matter to make the poor stony dirt of the tortuous trail they now followed. And, yet, following that narrow roof-steep ascent, Mackenna was struck with still another peculiarity of its origin. Despite its great age and wildly twisted structure, parts of that trail appeared to have been modified by the hand of man. And not in Mackenna's time, nor Chief Nana's, nor even the time of the Spaniard in that land. But long, long before any of them. The discovery gave the bearded prospector's laboring heart a lift of hope. It possibly explained something which had bothered him about the Adams legend from the beginning—how Brewer could have escaped the ambush of his supply party returning from Fort Wingate by such a simple ruse as hiding "in some hole in the rocks such as a rabbit might find." Indeed, the Adams account placed the site of Brewer's escape as "in the rocks right at the door," with Brewer's personal story adding the "rabbit hole" fillip. It was the Apaches' version of the matter, contained in the map of old Enh, which named this route above the Lookout Elbow as the Brewer crevice. This had originally struck Mackenna as a peculiar turn in traditions. Now, fleeing for his own and the girl's life, he saw the evidences of ancient man left in the dust of the trail and he knew—or hoped mightily—that the faint portents did not deceive him. If they did not, and this musty track *had* known the scrapings and shapings of stone-age tools in intelligent hands, then he and Francie Stanton were being led to something better than John Brewer's "hole such as a rabbit might find." It was perhaps four turnings of the cleft from this thought that the trail ended blankly against a crossdam of flow rock.

For a moment Mackenna was stunned. Then he saw them. Faint and filled with the decayed and rocky rubble of the centuries. But unmistakable as the day they had been first cut into the sheer face of the blocking dyke of lava across the cleft's floor.

Steps. Fifteen, maybe twenty of them. A stairway hewn into the crossflow by a race of ancients dead and gone to dust before Christ, before the Pharaohs, before the Mayans and the Incas and the Aztecs.

Francie, who now clung to him, gasping from the climb and sobbing again from the sheer frustration of the apparent cul-de-sac, was roughly shaken from her letdown.

"Don't quit on me now!" Mackenna said harshly, seizing her by the shoulders. "Look over there—you see those cuts in the rock? Those are stair holes. Thousands of years old. But they are *there*. We can use them, and we can pray that they go somewhere better than this damned blind box we're in here. Come on, girl, we're not dead yet!"

"Glen, I can't! I can't move another step. I'd never get up that rock. Not by those little gashes!"

"Those little gashes are a better risk than the big gashes we'll get from that ax of Hachita's. We'll make it up the rock, Francie. It's not as tough as it looks."

"Glen, I'll try; but I don't hear any noise down below now. I haven't heard any since we started up the cleft. Can't we wait and see?"

Mackenna was not going on without her. Yet he knew he could not force her up the rock steps, as he had the rest of the trail. She would have to want to go, and even then they would need luck not to fall off the face of the crossflow. Prehistory man had been agile as the tailed primates. He had not cut this out-leaning ladder of stone for the use of nineteenth-century bipeds. A Zuni or a Pueblo might have tried it for sport, or a big bet, or to impress his sweetheart. But for Glen Mackenna and Francelia Stanton that stone-age staircase held a cold chance of missed hand or foothold, and plunging death.

It was still the lesser chance than Hachita's ax.

"Francie," said the redhaired miner, "did you ever watch a cat playing in the grass where mice may be? The cat has no pretense to being quiet until the mouse makes itself known. Then, on the instant, it makes no sound whatever. It goes from play to hunt in the opening and closing of an eyelid. Down there"—he pointed the narrow throat of the cleft behind them—"Hachita has gone on the hunt."

"But he seemed so simple, so kind, so sad sort of."

"He's an Apache cat and we're white mice."

"He's coming up here after us, then, you think?"

"No, Francie, I don't think; I know. We either go up that stone wall or we wait for him here. And we make our choice right now, child—it's the stairway or the steel."

She shuddered, squaring her thin shoulders. If it wasn't a smile which moved her lips, it was intended to be one, and Mackenna put his arm about her and hugged her proudly close. It was the sort of reward one would give a small brother who had agreed to venture the railway trestle over the hometown river for the first time.

"Come on." He grinned back at her. "Ladies first."

The "steps" in the stone face of the crossflow were three to four feet apart, and zigzagged into the contour of the dyke. There were twenty-two of them covering a vertical distance of some forty feet. Twice Francie slipped and would have fallen, but for the sinewy strength of Glen Mackenna's hands supporting her from below. The bearded prospector was by heredity and by Arizona training a superb "hillman," and he climbed that canyon crossflow as though he had engineered its dizzying path himself. But the ascent took ten tortured minutes, each second of which was divided between the desperate effort to cling to the rock's surface and compulsive glances down-cleft in expectation of Hachita's appearance. Mackenna knew, even as he pushed Francie over the top of the formation and followed to lie panting beside her, that they had lost time they could not afford to lose.

He tried to think, and could not. The morning sun was now boring into the riven prison of the cleft. Its heat was inescapable, like the white-hot eye of a great searchlight. Even this early in the day it stifled the breath, thickened the tongue, made the heart thunder against the heaving ribs. Mackenna knew that he had to get up, had to go on, somehow had to do something.

But a man cannot go on without breath. At this altitude and in the heat, after such a sheer ascent as he and the Stanton girl had just made, human flesh and spirit would not reply to further demand before the life-giving oxygen could be gulped in to regalvanize starved muscles. It was all that Mackenna could do to force his head up off the rock and turn it toward Francie. She did not respond.

Hachita came into view while they lay thus, still exhausted, atop the crossflow. He saw them there. Lungs rasping, he stood a moment looking upward at them, and at the face of the staircase rock. Then he came on. Mackenna, belatedly hearing him, struggled to his knees, seeking desperately to find along the edge some remnant of the "tumbling-down stones" which the ancients ordinarily stored in such places for pushing over into the faces of their climbing enemies. He saw no rock larger than his fist. The top of the lava dyke was flood-washed as free of larger debris as base rock in a swift creek bed. He pulled Francie Stanton up beside him. Together they made it to their feet.

"*Look, Glen,*" the girl cried, pointing on up the cleft, "*a ladder!*" Mackenna knew it could not be, yet instinctively he swung about. It was impossible but true. In place against the sheer ending of the cleft, not a hundred feet across the level clean surface of the crossflow, stood a crude wooden climbing ladder of the type used by the pre-Pueblo people. And more. At its top was a second ledge, and within that ledge—upon it, really—waited the dark entrance to either a natural or a manmade cavern.

"My God," breathed Mackenna, "come on!"

If they could get to that second ledge and pull the ancient ladder up after them, Hachita could not come at them. There was no way in the world that he could do so.

And if they, in the cool shelter of the cavern, could not outlast him, in the burning, waterless throat of the crevice, then Glen Mackenna hadn't learned a thing about survival in the Southwest. And what lent speed to his leaden feet, and gave him the strength literally to carry the sagging girl the remaining distance to the prehistoric ladder, was the glimpse, atop the crown of the second ledge, of dark lichen and pale green feather moss of a variety which grew in one environment only, within that arid land. *There was water up on that ladder ledge.*

He gasped this information to Francie, and it revived her. By the time they had reached the foot of the ladder, she had the strength and the will to climb, once more, and Mackenna, looking back just as the massive face of Hachita loomed above the staircase rock behind them, laughed at the giant brave and shouted an epithet in his own tongue at him. The huge Apache, not understanding that he had lost the game, only grunted and came on, awkward but swift as a galloping grizzly bear, across the bare breast of the lava flow. The sun flashed off the blade of his throwing ax, and off the streams of sweat which spumed from his face and shoulders and ran like swollen rivers through the hairs of his great chest and distended belly. He looked and smelled of death.

"Take your time, Francie," said Mackenna through clenched teeth. "He can't possibly beat us now. One step after the other and don't look down. I'll be right behind you."

The girl nodded and turned. She reached for the first rung with her foot, slim hands seizing the parallels above her head. She climbed three rungs and Mackenna was reaching for his own hold on the parallels when the fourth rung shattered beneath her foot and she came down on top of him, the centuries-unused ladder dissolving as though made of tissue paper and mock glue.

"Dear Christ!" said Mackenna, white-faced. *"Dry rot!"*

He fought the shards of the desiccated wood about him, stumbling to his feet in front of the cowering Francie Stanton. Thirty feet away, Hachita, grandnephew of Mangas Coloradas, greatest white-hater of the Apache people, rumbled a single Apache word, *"Zas-te!"* and charged the slender, red-haired man who waited for him with no weapons but the thin, poor bones of his two knotted fists.

41

The Nephew
of Mangas Coloradas

His eyes, Mackenna thought. Old Mal-y-pai had warned to beware of his keen eyes. Get them then, blind them in some way. Rob him of his sight. Kill his eyes. It was the only chance.

Mackenna stooped to fill his hands with dust. Then he saw the remaining long piece of the stone-age climbing ladder—a section of one of the parallels nearly three feet in length. With this, the giant Apache could be reached with more certainty than the flung dust. Also, the reaching would be from a safer range—from just outside the arc of the swung ax. Mackenna knew the other would not throw the ax. He did not have to throw it, and the risk of shattering it against the all-surrounding rock was too great in case of a miss. So he would retain the blade. The thing then was to frustrate its first whistling swing, and not to think a fraction farther than that.

The white prospector took his grip on the dry-rotted

wood. He went forward three swift steps to place himself away from Francie, to give her the chance to escape.

"*When I hit him,*" he told her, "*you run!*"

"Glen—no, I can't!"

"*You must! Back down the steps!*" He hissed it at her, crouching as Hachita's great bulk loomed before him. "*Get to the old woman . . . down the cliff to the cabin . . . guns there!*"

Hachita was upon him and he swung with the feather-light piece of ladder rail, praying that he had timed his blow to be just inside that of the Apache's whirling ax blade. He had. The powdery wood struck the brave across the bridge of the nose, virtually exploding in his face. The fragments of fiber, dust, and the intact shards of harder outer shell of the rotted club had the effect of a trail branch whipped stingingly and straightaway across the open eyes. Hachita grunted, gasped, aborted his strike with the belt ax in mid-swing. The vicious weapon grazed Mackenna's back, as the latter twisted aside and the giant Mimbreño halted to dig at his eyes and shake his enormous head like some surprised, indignant grizzly stung by an unseen hornet. It was in this moment that Glen Mackenna swept up the two handfuls of rock dust and leaped inward to complete the blinding of the Indian beast. Hachita, sensing his rush, swung about to face it. He had vision enough remaining to see a blurred form, and he saw the white man moving at him. He swung again with the ax, but the aim, confused and distorted by the water and foreign matter in his streaming eyes, was again wide. This time, however, the butt of the haft and the fleshy heel of his great hand struck Mackenna on the shoulder in grazing passage. The shock of the blow was like that of a glancing rifle bullet, and the red-haired miner feared that the collarbone, still tender from Pelón's pistol-whipping at Surprise Grass, had broken.

But the force of contact also jarred Hachita's balance, drawing him too far forward, so that he had to reach instinctively for the ground with his left hand to keep from falling. In this instant of suspended awkwardness, Mackenna came in at him and put the dust into his eyes with the sweep and desperate stabbing intentness of the *banderillero* going in over the horns of the deadly black bull.

And he placed the talcumed "darts" perfectly. The palms of his opening hands smashed into the face of the huge Indian, driving the powdered rock into his eyes. In the same movement, Mackenna dived and rolled over the off-balance giant's back and was free of him.

In the instant it took him to regain his feet, he saw that Francie Stanton had not moved, that she was still crouched against the base of the upper ledge.

"Run, for God's sake . . . !" he pleaded, and could say no more to her. The sound of his voice had brought the blinded Hachita wheeling about, and had fixed Mackenna's location for him. The great brute was atop the prospector almost before the latter got off his warning cry to the girl. As Mackenna lunged desperately aside to escape the tremendous spread of the Indian's groping arms, he knew a cold dread—even without his eyes, Hachita was a deadly foe. He could hear as keenly as a stalking mountain lion. With nothing but the sounds that Mackenna made in moving over the naked rock, he could still follow the white man. He *was*, indeed, *still following* him, even as the new fear seized the latter. And, as he came, he still had in his hand the gleaming ax which had already killed Pelón López and Young Mickey Tibbs. The last thought sang suddenly.

The *ax!* Yes, that was the thing now. The only thing. *He had to get the ax.* He had gotten the eyes but he could not hope to get the ears and so his last chance at life lay in taking the ax.

But how? how? With every evasive leap he made now, the Apache was upon him, the ax blade whirling in the arc of its strike. It missed now by inches, now by feet, and three times it did not miss but cut into Mackenna— breast, thigh and right side—slicing thin cuts which did not wound deeply but bled profusely. And with the blood, Mackenna could feel his strength flowing out.

Sound. The Indian giant was following the sound he made. All right; another sound then. Two sounds—or three —at the same time. With luck, and in the instant of his hesitation, the brute might be brought to stand for the last pass—*el paso muerto*—the step of death.

Mackenna ripped off his shirt, leaping to avoid the slash of the ax which the noise triggered. His belt was next. Then, into the shirt, went his old felt hat scooped half full of rocks. This bundle, lashed hard around by the heavy-buckled belt, made a decoy bait as wispy and tenuous as its maker's remaining life chance. He was ready with it, though. And had to be. Nothing else sheltered him from that razored steel.

Inviting a lunge by Hachita with an extending scrape of his foot to the right, he danced three light steps to the left and in the same motion threw the bundled clothing directly over the Indian's head. The latter, diving at the right-side scrape of the foot, then twisting to reverse himself to follow the footsteps to the left, was pinned in the center of his move by the belted bundle striking the rocks behind him. In the half-breath of his indecision, Glen Mackenna leaped inward toward him and swung his booted foot in a lifting, vicious kick between the spread and crouched thighs. Hachita screamed—the only vocal utterance he made in the battle—and contorted himself into a helpless ball, the immense pain of the smashed genitals destroying even his incredible strength for the time Mackenna needed.

The white prospector had never taken his eyes from the right hand and the ax. That hand was now wrapped about the tortured Indian's knees, the ax still clutched in it. As Hachita writhed on the ground, Mackenna measured the ax hand and slashed it with an upward, ripping cut of his boot heel. The fingers of the hand released the weapon and Mackenna, with reflex speed, kicked it away. It was an unthinking, natural thing to do. He meant only to make sure it went out of Hachita's reach, then retrieve it himself and finish off the downed brave. But the vitality of the giant Apache was a terrible, unimaginable thing. Even as the deadly blade was kicked out of, and then away from, his lacerated right hand, his left hand snaked out and seized the white man's leg above the ankle.

Mackenna was thrown, and thrown so hard that he never saw where the ax stopped. Hachita nearly tore his leg off with the wrenching power by which he brought the bearded miner crashing down. And, as Mackenna struck the rock, back flat, the giant Indian engulfed him with both trunklike arms and began to squeeze the breath of life from him.

Staggering to his feet, Hachita held the struggling white man, belly to belly with himself. The cords of muscle in his neck and shoulders and biceps and forearms rose and knotted into ropes as thick as coiling boas. In another moment Mackenna's spine must separate, his ribs puncture, his heart burst beneath the fearful pressure of Hachita's death hug. He knew that he was dying. His last thought was of Francie Stanton, and the fact that he had failed her, did not even know where she was, or if she had gone over the staircase or still stood paralyzed with terror against the upper ledge.

She had, in fact, done neither thing.

When the honed war ax came skittering and sliding across the bare rock from Mackenna's kick, she seized it up by its leather-wrapped haft, as unthinkingly as the bearded prospector had kicked it away. And with the same deadliness that he had crushed Hachita's manhood and the crazed brave was now cracking his spine, Francelia Stanton ran forward to come up behind the towering Apache and to reach, with her full height and strength, to bury the glittering blade in the brain of the giant Mimbreño.

The grandnephew of Mangas Coloradas died as he had lived; in ignorance of the hand that killed him, and in innocence of the guilt which was his and which guided that hand as inexorably as the lightning of Yosen. He died like an Apache.

4 2

Chiricahua Farewell

THEY FOUND old Mal-y-pai, angry as a wet owl, seated in the trail halfway down the "Z," where Hachita had tied her hand-and-foot with his pony-staking rope. It made no difference to the furious old lady that the slow-witted Mimbreño had done it to "keep her safe" while he attended to the killing of the foreigners up in the Brewer crevice. She only began to be mollified when they succeeded in convincing her that Hachita was dead. Even then, the concession was grudging.

"Well, all right," was the way she put it. "If the girl has split his great stupid head while you held him for her, that makes me even with him for what he did to my daughter, Sally. But I still owe him for staking me out like a damn old horse in this cursed sun. I'll not say the prayer of our people for him."

Wisely, the white couple permitted her to see it her stubborn Apache way. Their own concern was for leaving Sno-ta-hay as swiftly as possible. If that meant Hachita had to find his way to the Dark Place without Mal-y-pai's spiritual intercession, so be it. They were alive and had a

God of their own to thank for the favor. Let their Indian *madre* dishonor her own dead as she would.

Returned to the canyon's bottom, they made the preparations to depart in virtual silence. A peculiar hush had fallen over the place, and the air had grown exceedingly close and oppressive. Since there was no sun yet directly shining in the depths of Sno-ta-hay, the heat of the coming day could not be blamed for the strange "air" which smothered their breathing on the canyon floor.

"Hurry!" urged Mal-y-pai. "Something bad is coming!"

They got the riderless horses roped into a packline, the mounts of Pelón, Young Mickey and Hachita being strung behind those of Mackenna and Francie, Mal-y-pai driving the packhorse free. "Hurry, hurry," said the old lady, "it is coming closer."

Mackenna came up to where Francie stood with the agitated squaw. "We're ready to go," he said to the two women. "What are we going to do about the gold?"

"Do about it?" squawked Mal-y-pai. "What is there to do about it?"

"I don't know whether to take it or not."

"*Ih!* I wish Pelón could hear that!"

"It's true, nevertheless," said Glen Mackenna, and repeated his hesitation, in English, to Francie.

The slim girl looked at him and nodded, unexpectedly. "I feel kind of funny about it, too," she admitted. "I never thought I would, Glen, but I've come to feel more than the gold in this place. Last night I think I would have shot somebody to save my share. This morning it doesn't matter. I don't want it."

"It's an awful sum of money, Francie."

"I know, but I can't help the way I feel."

"Nor I. I don't want it, either."

"What'll we do with it then, Glen? We can't just leave it here for somebody else—some other white people, I mean. That wouldn't be right."

"No, it wouldn't. What I'd like to do is leave it the way it was before Adams found it, Francie. Strew it up and down the stream bed, spread it out from the falls to the far side of the meadow, scatter it and sow it into the water's sand and gravel, put it back where the Apaches had it in the first place. If that sounds crazy, I can't help it. I'm cured of the gold fever, though. When I go out of here, I've made my last prospect."

"If that's what you want, Glen, let's do it."

She left it as simply as that, and he was glad. She went with him, riding the ponies and throwing the dust and rice gold and nuggets up and down the wandering bed of the stream. "One thing," she added, laughing, "this way we can always come back and get it ourselves, if we recover our senses later on." Glen Mackenna laughed with her and said that this was exactly what he had had in his own devious mind all the while, and that he was mortified to be so easily found out. It seemed to both of them in that moment of small embarrassment over their admittedly daft conduct, that they were as close as two people might be, who were fourteen years apart, and when they came back up the stream to where old Mal-y-pai waited with the packstring they were riding knee-and-knee and unabashedly holding hands.

For the old lady's part, she merely greeted them with a headshake of utter disgust, which said it all, and added that they had no time to lose in getting up the cliff.

When, in mounting up to obey her injunction, Mackenna looked up-canyon toward the Turkey Egg Ledge and said, in Spanish, that he regretted not being able to hide that, too, the squaw stared up into the oddly brassy sunlight at canyon's top and told him not to worry. "Leave it to God," she muttered. "He will take care of it."

Mackenna nodded and reached for his horse's reins.

"Mother," he said, pausing for a last look about, "is there anything we have forgotten?"

"I think not, *hijo*," she replied quickly. "You have given my son a decent grave, you have left that dog of a Young Mickey to bleach his bones uncovered, you have filled the clay *olla* of the legend with worthless, barren sand and gravel, that those who come after you will think the gold of Adams has been taken. The white man's fever for that gold will die away and the Apache people will honor your name. They will spare your cattle and your women for a hundred winters and summers. No, my son, there is no more you can do here."

Mackenna took her trembling hand and pressed it.

"Thank you, Mother," he said. "I am remembering what old Enh said to me, and I am glad. He said, 'Are you greedy for gold, Mackenna? Are you the same as all white men I have known? Would you sell your life, or your honor, or the honor of your woman for the yellow metal?' I let him think that I would not, and yet, very nearly, I have done each of these shameful things. That's why I'm glad, Mother. Because my hands bring away no gold, and my heart holds no greed. Old Enh can sleep in peace now."

The old lady pulled her hand away from him. She sniffed, dashed at her eyes and cursed angrily down at him. "Get up on your horse, damn it! We've got to get out of here! God, but you do talk. Pelón was right about you. Come on."

He swung up on his pony and followed her, as she yelled at the old packhorse and started across the stream. The other horses came on, Francie pushing them with her mount. As they reached the foot of the Z-trail, the hush had again crawled into the canyon, more thick and smothering now than before.

"What is it, Mother?" asked Glen Mackenna. "You seem to sense it. Can you tell me what it is?"

The old lady nodded.

"*Terremoto*," she muttered. "*Temblor de tierra.*"

"Earthquake?" said Mackenna. "Good Lord, you may be right. I haven't felt weather like this in eleven years."

"There hasn't been any weather like this in eleven years," she answered. "Come on, you fool girl! Make haste with those damned horses. Here. Wait . . ."

She leaped down from her own mount, ran to the rear of the packstring, whipped out her sheath knife and cut free Hachita's paint gelding. With a wave of her blanket and an Apache oath, she stampeded the nervous animal back across the creek. It came to a stand on the far side, posed in the grass of the meadow.

"Forgive it," said the old lady, climbing back aboard her ancient white mare. "I couldn't leave that poor big fool of a Hachita without a horse to ride. You can't let an Apache walk on that last journey. He doesn't deserve it, but he is an Apache. Come on. I still didn't say any prayers for him. Don't stare at me. You look as stupid as he did. *Arriba!* Skinny Chicken, drive those damned old bonepiles up the cliff. Hurry! Hurry!"

The ascent of the Z-trail was without incident. They were just coming out of the last turn above Lookout Elbow, when the rock below them began to move. The horses bolted the last yards of the narrow track and huddled, bunched in terror, before the Secret Door. It was all that their riders could do, leaping down and anchoring them with short reins and soft words, to hold them. The temblors came one atop the other for a period of two minutes. The roaring of the rock and the falling mountain behind them in Sno-ta-hay was deafening. This artillery barrage continued for another full five minutes after the last rolling shudder of the canyon walls. When there had been no sound, and no movement, for a long following minute, Mackenna took Young Mickey's cavalry fieldglasses and went back to the edge of the solid ground above the Lookout Elbow. The elbow and the entire top half of the Z-trail, including the opening of Brewer crevice, was gone.

Down in the canyon itself the waterfall above Adams' cabin had disappeared and the canyon's passage beyond the meadow and the cabin was no more. It was closed by the total inward collapse of the walls, and the incalculable wealth of the Turkey Egg Ledge lay buried beneath six hundred feet of packed, shattered and shifted baserock. In a thousand years, or ten thousand, it might be seen again. Meanwhile, old Mal-y-pai was right, and the just God of her Apache people had taken care of it.

As for the Adams gold in the stream bed, it lay as Mackenna and Francie had strewn it, the cabin and the meadow and the soft loop of the creek remaining unchanged by the great earth fracture. But with the secret Indian way into the head of the canyon closed—the way by which Nana had come to murder the Adams party thirty-three years ago—and with the upper half of the Z-trail plunged eight hundred feet to the chasm's floor to block still further the lower, naturally blind end of the declivity, the watching prospector knew that the treasure of Sno-ta-hay lay locked forever in the heart of Cañon del Oro.

He returned to the women and told them what he had seen. Both were silent a moment, then Mal-y-pai said resignedly, "Yosen be praised; how long will it take us to reach that fine house of ours which you are going to buy for the Skinny Chicken and your Old Mother?"

Mackenna had to laugh. Francie and the old lady joined him. It was a wonderful relief. When they had it out of their systems they got back on their horses and went through the Secret Door into the freedom of the lava beds. It was still but ten o'clock in the morning and a gorgeous, jewel-bright day coming on. They set out for Pumpkin Patch feeling a common lift of mind and heart. They came to Apache Post Office about 5:00 P.M. Passing it, Mal-y-pai grew very nervous. When Mackenna asked her why, she pointed to the post office and said that the message sticks had been changed. The ones which had been there when they came this way the day before were gone. These were new ones.

Mackenna started to make some light remark to leaven the old lady's superstitious fears, then thought better of it. There did seem to be something tangible hovering about. His glance swept the malpais. Francie was watching him. So was the old lady. Mackenna reined in his mount.

"Mother," he said, "we had better go and see what those new sticks say."

Mal-y-pai was plainly reluctant, but she nodded and turned her pony toward the post office. Mackenna and Francie followed her. Well out from the rock marker, they halted their mounts. Mackenna felt the short hairs rise along the nape of his neck. The sticks *were* new ones and *were* in new combinations. He looked at Mal-y-pai.

The old squaw was feeling the spirits, too. She was clearly agitated, restless, afraid. She wanted to go on, to leave that uneasy place, to ride away from it, far and fast. But she held in her pony, still peering at the message sticks. In the crowding silence, while he waited, Mackenna examined the ground surrounding the pile of rocks. Once more he felt the neck hairs lifting. There were no new

pony tracks. No moccasin prints. No other signs whatso-
ever of earthly visitors around that lone pyramid of
gathered stones. He shifted his glance again to the withered
old Apache woman.

"Well, Mother," he asked softly, "can you read them?"

"Yes," she said, "I can."

"And what do they say?"

In response to his question, she studied him a long
moment. It was as though she were assessing his sincerity
for a last time. In the end, she nodded, satisfied.

"The first sticks say, 'Thank you.'"

"And the others, *Madre?*"

She faced him, withered lips compressed.

"The other sticks, Mackenna," she said, "form the
Sign of the Knife."

He stared at her incredulously.

"*Besh?*" he breathed, "You are saying those sticks say,
'Thank you—from Besh'?"

But the old lady did not answer him. She had turned
her mount away and with Francie Stanton was driving the
packhorses hurriedly toward the darkening head of Pumpkin Patch Canyon. Down there, the ancient ruins of the
irrigated fields and moldering adobe walls waited in the
lower reaches. There was only light enough remaining
to make the journey and be safely past that storied campsite, out of the canyon and finally onto the old Fort Wingate wagon road, before night fell.

Glancing about him, Glenn Mackenna shivered. For
some sudden reason he did not want to be the last one out
of that lava-strewn and lonesome place. He reined his own
horse around and drove him hard after the others. The
sound of the little animal's flinty hoofs echoed clatteringly
in the eerie quiet. The noise frightened the pony. He

snorted and back-jumped, quivering with fear. Mackenna spoke to him, soothing him, steadying him; but he let him run.

Neither did he care to turn in the saddle and look back upon that haunted cairn with its ghostly message sticks and memories.

As such things go, it may have been as well. He never saw the shadowy Indian horseman who sat there, tall and slender on the pale mustang, waving after him the brotherhood and blessing sign of the Chiricahua Apache.

ABOUT THE AUTHOR

WILL HENRY'S novels now total an even dozen, and most of them have been chronicles of the old West. Not too strange when one considers that he was brought up in the Jesse James country of Missouri and has lived and traveled west of the Missouri River most of his life.

His early desire to write of the land he knew best was a long time in fulfillment. After college—Kansas City Polytech—he spent the next twenty years at odd jobs. By the time his first book was published, he had chalked up experience as varied as stablehand, mining-camp cook, newspaper columnist, sports desk cub, motion picture scriptwriter, machine-shop swamper, automobile assembly-lineman, leather worker and ranchhand.

His study of Western legends, history, landscape and folklore, which started as a hobby, has provided the fiber for books about Custer, the James brothers, Wyatt Earp, Chief Joseph of the Nez Percés, and other equally dramatic figures. His last two novels, *Journey to Shiloh* and *San Juan Hill*, dealt with campaigns of the Civil and Spanish-American Wars, respectively.

At present he lives in Southern California.